MW00436211

below the line

j.r. helton

♦

LAST GASP
OF SAN FRANCISCO

Dedicated to Tracy

◆

"Bow down before the one you serve,
you're going to get what you deserve."
Nine Inch Nails

◆

Last Gasp of San Francisco,
777 Florida Street
San Francisco, CA 94110
www.lastgasp.com

Library of Congress Catalog Card Number: 96-84104

ISBN 0-86719-478-2

First Printing, Agarita Press, May 1996
First Last Gasp edition, July 2000

Cover by Robert Crumb
Printed in Hong Kong

Special thanks to Terry Zwigoff and Robert Crumb

INTRODUCTION

After my film *Crumb* was released in 1995, I was spending a lot of time in Los Angeles, trying to get the money to make another movie. Late on a Friday afternoon after a really horrible time-waster of a day spent in such pursuit at several "important" meetings, I found myself once again at LAX a little more beaten-down than even the week before (if that were possible). This film business is tough. Everyone is eager to *talk* about making films; no one, it seems, wants to actually *make* one. It takes courage and that's hard when they don't seem to know what's good and what's bad; they don't even trust their own judgment.

I only had an hour flight home to SF but I couldn't handle it without something to read, and after those meetings I just couldn't stomach the latest issue of "Premiere" and "Entertainment Weekly" I'd brought along for the flight home. I had five minutes to find something else at the newsstand before boarding. I saw a copy of *Below the Line*, opened it to a page at random and read something that seemed truthful about the film business, and because it was so true, seemed incredibly funny to me. If I could get one or two more such laughs out of the rest of the book, I'd be happy, I thought. I bought the book and didn't put it down (except for the cab ride home) until I finished it later that night, countless laughs later. What a great book! This guy Helton could be the next Bukowski! A couple of days later I was on the phone trying to track down two more copies to send to some friends of mine. No luck - no store seemed to carry the title. Finally I wrote the publisher trying to buy a few more - some publisher I'd never heard of in the middle of nowhere, Texas.

Days later I got a call from the author, J.R. Helton. He was thrilled anyone liked the damn thing. He only had four copies left, he'd self-published only 1,000 copies, and somehow they were all gone. He offered to sell all four to me (he was really broke), but I convinced him he should keep one for himself. I sent him money for the other three, and lamented the fact that such a terrific book was out of print. Surely he could get some publisher interested, couldn't he? Nope, he'd been through it too, it seemed. None of the publishers he'd sent it to thought there was enough Movie-Star gossip in it to make it commercial enough. Add some Sex and Drugs and Gossip and they'd be more interested. Either that or make it more "upbeat" somehow! I told J.R. I'd call around and see what I could do.

Meanwhile, Robert Crumb showed up at my house for his annual visit. He found the book on my couch and also couldn't put it down. The next day he offered to paint a new cover for free in hopes *that* would interest some publisher enough to publish it. A month later he sent me the painting he'd slaved over for a week, and I started contacting prospective new publishers. They were all dutifully excited of course. They all loved Robert's work, my films, etc., etc. They all couldn't wait to see the book and the new cover.

One after another they turned Helton down. "It's too negative," "too critical," "too downbeat," too this, too that. Crumb and I even had dinner with a publisher who was an old acquaintance of ours in an attempt to get him to take it on. All through the meal Robert browbeat him into having the courage to publish the book. (This was something most out-of-character for Robert to do, by the way.) Finally, three bottles of wine later, we had a deal. A deal that lasted till the next day when the publisher called and made up some excuse why he couldn't do it. At least this guy could give us a "no." All the others stalled us with, "Well, I loved it, but the other two partners have to read it also," or "I have it on my desk--I'll try and get to it next month." Clearly, none of these pampered cake-eaters would have the foresight to publish William Faulkner if he weren't already famous.

However, Robert took the book to Ron Turner who publishes some of his comics at Last Gasp Publishing here in SF. Ron agreed to publish what you now hold in your hands. To his credit, Ron told J.R. Helton on the phone, "It won't be the first book I've published without reading."

Terry Zwigoff
June 4th, 1999

Publisher's Note: However, Terry, I read this one and was only disappointed when the damn thing ended. I wanted more of Helton's surgical insights and jarring observations. I'm sure you readers will agree.

-Ron Turner

–1–

I was on the final location scout that went through Happy Shahan's Alamo Village in Brackettville, Texas, before filming began on Aaron Spelling's television/video production of James Michener's *Texas*. Mr. Spelling was footing the bill for the history of my state. Mr. Shahan was providing much of the backdrop we would be using.

John Frick, the production designer, the member of the company who is in charge of the art department and therefore responsible for the look of the sets on a film, asked me to come along on the scout, as I was his lead scenic, or set painter, and would be doing a lot of work on Alamo Village to transform it into the several towns it would represent in the various shoots.

There were ten or twelve of us following the director, a tall, obese man I knew only as Rich, like a flock of ducklings. Like most location scouts, it was boring. Rich walked around making wisecracks, looking at all the different buildings Happy had to offer, deciding things like where Jim Bowie would have his Memphis knife fight, how many friars and children would be shot by the banditos when they raided the mission, and where to erect the Austin\Capitol flagpole, consulting with his new designer Frick on the last question.

"So, John, where do you think the flagpole should go?" Rich asked, stopping the group in front of the projected Austin Capitol.

There was a long silence. Frick took off his cowboy hat and rubbed a shaking hand nervously over his sweating bald head. "Well. . . "

More silence. "We could put it up on the roof . . . or down in front here. . . "

My boss said nothing, staring at the building again as Rich waited.

1

After thirty seconds of silence, Rich gave up. "I guess we can decide that later. Let's move on," he said, and we all dutifully followed through the oppressive Texas heat. It didn't strike me as a portentous moment at the time.

Alamo Village was constructed by John Wayne and company back in the late 1950s for the film *The Alamo*. It consists of a replica of the Alamo, including its original surrounding walls, and a town comprised of several streets lined with adobe, stucco, and Old West style buildings. Mr. Shahan later turned the village into a large tourist trap and monument to "The Duke," whose unremarkable likeness can still be seen all over town in the form of cardboard cutouts, statuettes, and framed prints of his giant head hovering ominously over a western landscape. There is even a John Wayne museum tucked away between the town's many curio shops. There's also a Johnny Rodriguez museum. All varieties of European and Asian tourists can be seen wandering and sweating through the hot, dusty streets of Alamo Village, perhaps wondering what brought them to a place that could easily be on the receiving end of a giant magnifying glass held in the sun by a malicious god.

At the hot light's center was Happy Shahan. Happy the legendary cowboy had done it all: making a name for himself as a champion basketball player at Baylor University in the thirties, establishing a large, successful ranching operation, personally convincing John Wayne to shoot his film on Happy's 20,000-acre ranch, and then luring some forty-odd movies since then to Alamo Village. Happy, the man, walked around town in his boots and cowboy hat, a walkie-talkie on his hip like a six-shooter (his handle was Number One), barking harsh orders to his low-paid employees, many of whom are drifters who want to be actors who perform gunfight shows and sing songs in the same cantina where Dean Martin once drank in *Bandelero*, and what seemed to be Happy's main occupation, trying to get every penny he could out of the movie companies: charging them for a broken light bulb here, three lost nails there, a pencil, and the never-ending attempt to get a new roof for the Alamo. Happy shouldn't be accused of being a total cheapskate, however, for movie companies are notorious liars, adept at taking advantage of the locals. Alamo Village is as much a monument to Happy and his business acumen as it is to The Duke.

We began our filming of *Texas* on Bill Moody's 55,000-acre ranch that runs for miles along the Rio Grande near Del Rio. We used the same town that four of us had painted seven years before for the unusually popular CBS mini-series *Lonesome Dove* . Because of budget and time constraints, we changed very little of the town , mainly adding a faux log cabin for Stephen F. Austin. Little attention was paid to historical accuracy by the Spelling production company. In fact, to be very clear with his position on this, the unit production manager, the money watcher for any movie, said to our production designer in a meeting where the sore subject of reality was brought up, "Fuck history." So, as anyone might have seen when it aired, *Texas* was basically a soap opera with made-up characters dominating the script, interrupted by the occasional Alamo battle or a hokey representation of a historical figure.

When I first started working in the film business in Texas seven years ago, there weren't many movies being made here. When I told people I worked as a set painter or scenic artist on films, I was usually asked, "Can you make a living at that?" to which I invariably replied, "Barely." I usually ran into many of my co-workers down at the unemployment office, collecting our checks in the long interim between shows. Things have changed since then with the growing trend of more and more movies being made outside of Los Angeles and New York. There used to be about three crews in Texas: one each in Austin, Dallas, and Houston. Now there are about three crews in Austin alone, which basically means three movies could film there simultaneously using mostly local experienced people and needing to only occasionally bring in a few "keys" or department heads. With the arrival of Ann Richards in the governor's office, and her successful promotion of Texas as a place to make movies, all of us in the film business felt a real economic boom, as did the many small towns where we film and spread money around. The well-paid crews buy things in local retail stores, spend money at local restaurants, use local businesses, craftsmen, and workers extensively in the construction of the sets, hire locals as extras, and distribute a substantial amount of money in the acquisition of locations. And the governor was not lying when she told those folks in Hollywood about how friendly we are down here to movie people. I've worked in small towns and cities all over this state and watched generous Texans, much less jaded in their attitude towards film crews than their California counterparts, let movie crews into their homes, businesses, farms, ranches, and state parks. Unfortunately, as with the discordance between movies and real life, the happy anticipation of a show arriving

3

in town does not always mesh with its departure.

Somehow, people seem to think a movie coming is going to change their heretofore hum drum lives; that something magical or significant is going to happen. Instead, what I've seen is massive disappointment. On most locations, even though my status in the movie hierarchy is quite low, I'm the last "movie person" many of these people will see. The locations department often buys people off with paint jobs, or I'm in these people's homes repairing the damage a movie crew has done. Therefore, I catch a lot of their anger—some of it very serious, verging on physical anger. The fact that I'm from Texas has helped me immensely in dispelling this anger. I usually adopt a "You know how those movie people from California are" stance and it seems to work.

At thousands of dollars a day to operate during filming, the crews move quickly and often carelessly in people's homes with the attitude that "locations or construction will fix it if we break it." So letting a movie crew into your home, especially if you have a nice one, could be one of the worst things you can do. You'll get a little money, but you'll also get scratched floors, stained carpets, furniture broken, holes in your walls, paint ripped off your ceiling, a long caravan of cars, trucks, trailers, and RV's parked down your street, and fifty people running around your house looking at your things while you're shipped off to some hotel. These things usually happen in modern movies where we use existing locations. There are more logistical problems that occur with period pieces, as was the case with Spelling's *Texas* where more set construction occurred.

Like most TV movies, Spelling's *Texas* finished as it began: quickly and chaotically. Stephen F. Austin ended up being played by the incredible talent Patrick Duffy. The entire cast was comprised of B-, C-, or D- list television and feature actors, such as John Schneider, Stacy Keach, and David Keith, playing Davy Crockett, Sam Houston, and Jim Bowie, respectively, if not respectfully. All it takes is working on one film to see the bitter reality of any actor's humanity. Being in the art department, I was able to avoid the shooting crew as much as possible, but I still caught revealing glimpses of John Schneider dancing around like a lunatic, pretending to play the fiddle while David Keith, as a sick (or drunk?) Jim Bowie, waved a rubber rifle and lamely attested to his will to fight, or a view of Patrick Duffy grabbing his crotch and yelling in a falsetto to a woman in wardrobe, "I'm gonna get laid tonight! I'm gonna get laid tonight!"

Though I had plenty of money in my budget for the paint department ($25,000), the incredible lack of both organization and clear thinking (or really any thinking—period), made the *Texas* project very difficult as far as the art department went. This is often the case with television productions. The breakneck pace allows little or no time to prepare the many sets that are expected. So, like most films, there is no glamour, only hard work and ridiculous ironies, like being woken up on an early Sunday morning by Santa Ana's army in full uniform, practicing maneuvers in the Del Rio Motel 6 parking lot, a rude awakening that happened more than once when the "army" was ordered to practice its drills after having marched an entire regiment into a row of mesquite trees while the cameras were rolling.

During my final days in Alamo Village, I ran into Cary White, a production designer from Austin for whom I've worked on several films, and Mike Sullivan, or Sully, his art director. They were in Alamo Village with Tommy Lee Jones, scouting buildings, the same ones I'd just painted, for *The Good Old Boys* , a TNT production. Jones was walking around giving everyone orders, much like his character did on film in *The Fugitive*, only this time he was in his cowboy outfit, replete with spurs, something you don't often see on a person who's been riding around in a car all day. Cary and Sully asked me to stay on and work on their film, helping their lead scenic, an old friend of mine named Ed Vega. I was tired but agreed to sign on. Somehow, it seemed appropriate.

As I said, about seven years ago, I was on the same ranches, the same locations, with all the same people on *Lonesome Dove*. We'd all had a good time back then. There was a group of us, most everyone from Austin. I fell into the business by accident and was quickly wooed by its money and, as it seemed then, excitement. I'd always been a fan of actors like Robert Duvall, and to actually meet him would be a thrill, I thought. I was disillusioned, though. Duvall, like a lot of actors, seemed insecure and self-centered, always wanting all of the attention on himself. On the set, before the camera, he was "lovable ol' Gus" (except when yelling "You don't know what the fuck you're doing" to the director, Simon Wincer). Off the set, without the toupee, he was a small, unassuming man who loved to cha-cha and tango to a ridiculous degree at Memo's in Del Rio, or the Sheraton Dance Room in Santa Fe.

5

He had a personal assistant who served as a peripheral personality, handling interactive things like "Hello" and "I'm sorry Mr.Duvall is still dancing with your wife."

I've worked on many movies since *Lonesome Dove*, a lot of them for television. I work on them for the money now, not to see my favorite actors. Like some movie workers, I'm always trying to get out of the business and into something more steady. This business is much like the carny—only we're better paid and have an attitude. One travels from town to town, an itinerant lifestyle, never knowing when the next job, or "show," will come, living out of hotel rooms, connecting with people intensely for eight to ten weeks and then never seeing them again, all of it becoming so transitory and expendable that real towns become locations and sets, and people become extras, for they certainly aren't the stars.

I wanted some sense of closure on *The Good Old Boys*, maybe a happy ending, like in the movies. But the movie was just hard work, painting building after building made out of fiberglass and Styrofoam to look like limestone and granite or just old wood. There were a few bright moments, such as when my friend Ed Vega and I, having breakfast at the caterer's wagon, spotted the actor Wilford Brimley ordering a breakfast burrito. Brimley, for those who don't know, was in *Cocoon*, playing an old man, and was in a number of other films playing a mustachioed cowboy, and sold oatmeal on TV for seven years, gruffly telling children to "Eat your oatmeal." Ed, a good man about Brimley's age and afraid of nothing, walked up to the actor, put a friendly hand on his shoulder and jokingly asked, "Hey Wilford, are you checking up on everybody and making sure we eat our oatmeal?"

"I don't give a *fuck* what you eat," Mr.Brimley said angrily.

Ed laughed and quickly replied, "Hey, that's not what you tell those kids on TV."

"Listen, they can chew on old used boot heels for all I care," Brimley said, and turned to get his food.

Later, as he passed us in line, he pointed to his burrito and said, "Oatmeal."

As luck would have it, he sat next to me as we ate, and I had to listen to a great deal of "cowboy talk" as he impressed Bill Moody's ranch foreman, John Kincaid, with his knowledge of cattle. There was a lot of cowboy talk on that movie, and a lot of cowboys, or rather, men dressed as cowboys, Jones being the most predominant. His stint at Harvard must have done a number on him; I can't remember the last man I saw who wanted to be a cowboy more, so much so that he's directing himself in a movie as one.

Sam Shepard was in *The Good Old Boys* as well, playing the cowboy Snorts Yarnell. I met Mr.Shepard in Cripple Creek, a popular steak house in Del Rio, while having dinner one night with the art director, Sully, who knew Shepard in his early playwright days in New York. They'd also worked together on Shepard's *Silent Tongue* in New Mexico. He came over to our table to chat and I shook his hand and said hello. By all accounts and impressions, he is as nice and regular as he seems, unlike Jones, who is as abrasive as he seems. I heard several stories of Jones's drunken rudeness off the set, including accounts of his passing out and falling off barstools when the company was in Alpine, Texas. Few said anything about his behavior except behind his back.

This is not surprising, for the hierarchy of power and status is everything on a movie. The stars are at the top as the ultimate royalty. There is really no reason for one of them, other than being nice to a mortal, to acknowledge your existence. They make outrageous amounts of money and get away with murder because of their celebrity. Talking back to an angry star, or just pissing one off in general, could easily cost you your job. I actually found Jones's attitude toward underlings refreshing—at least he wasn't pretending to be a nice guy. That's what he pays his assistant, Jim Burns, to do.

Jim came and sat at our table one night at Cripple Creek toward the end of filming. Several of us who actually work with our hands (something I've heard Tommy Lee Jones admires in people) were sitting there. Jim, whom I'd never seen before, told us all what a great job we'd done in this heat and how grateful he and Tommy were for all our work. He told a few jokes, we laughed heartily, and he left. A carpenter friend of mine from Paris, Texas, Rodney Brown, shook his head in disgust and I asked him what was wrong. "I'm not laughing at that motherfucker's jokes," he said.

One of the producers, Sally Newman, came over and did the same thing, minus the jokes, and promised a great wrap party. Someone then told me they were talking about giving out special awards at the party to people who helped make the film.

"They're gonna give us awards?" I asked.

"Uh no," he said. "I think it's just for the actors."

I sat there at the table and looked at all my co-workers; some of them, such as Rodney Brown, had been on almost every film I'd ever worked on. Back at the Remington Hotel that night, sitting around the pool with everyone, drinking beer, I did the same, and tried to find some meaning in the past seven years, some point to all the movies and all the work. When exactly did it stop being fun? I began to go through some of the films I'd worked on and realized that the fun, as it were, most probably stopped on my second show.

–2–

The movie was initially called *The Von Metz Incident*, a Tri-Star production starring Gene Hackman, Dan Aykroyd, and Dom DeLuise. It was to be filmed primarily at what was then the DEG studios in Wilmington, North Carolina. A young man named Brian Stultz was the lead scenic on the picture. He was the same person who had hired me on *Lonesome Dove*. After working closely with him for three or four months on that show, I came to the conclusion that I didn't particularly like Brian. To be specific, I thought he was a vain, materialistic buffoon who had given his life over to the movies. At the time, I self-righteously assured myself, I would never become like Brian and have my entire identity wrapped up in the fact that I worked on a movie crew. Like him, I didn't want to repeatedly drop the names of movie stars in every other sentence, as though I knew them, as though they were friends, even though as a set painter, albeit a head or lead painter, the only real contact one ever had with a celebrity was either at lunch at the caterer's wagon or maybe bumping into one accidentally on a set. I swore I would never make a fool out of myself, as I felt Brian had done, introducing myself to a star who couldn't really give a shit about who the painter was on the movie.

I remember watching Brian at a swank party in Santa Fe during the filming of *Lonesome Dove*. Many stars were there: Tommy Lee Jones, Robert Duvall, Diane Lane, Christopher Lambert, Anjelica Huston, and others, all of the proceedings being filmed for the peasants by Entertainment Tonight. Duvall was on the dance floor constantly, cha-cha-ing everywhere. He ran up on the bandstand at one point and did a silly imitation of a TV evangelist, something from a project I heard he wanted to do. There was a lot of polite laughter as he finished and ran over to dance with the actress Kelly Lynch. When a young actor, I suppose, her date, had the nerve to cut back in on Duvall and the beautiful Ms. Lynch, he found himself with his arm twisted behind his back being pushed towards a gazebo by Duvall's bodyguard. Somewhere in all of this, my boss, Brian Stultz, managed to pull Duvall aside.

"Mr. Duvall, Mr. Duvall. . . "

Duvall, looking away. "Huh? What?"

Brian stuck out his hand. "Brian Stultz, I'm the head scenic on this picture."

Duvall quickly and perfunctorily shook his hand and said, without looking at him, "Oh yeah, right, right, the scenic. . . "

"I just wanted to introduce myself. My father's a huge fan of yours. I am, too, actually and—-"

As he spoke, Duvall walked away, leaving him standing there talking to no one. Brian turned that chance, we'll call it an encounter, into, "Yeah, I was talking to Duvall in Santa Fe the other day and. . . " Well, you can imagine.

I just didn't want that to happen to me. I certainly didn't want to think my life had become so insignificant that a brush-off from an actor could make it enlightened. Back then, I thought of myself more as a writer than a painter, and it was my little writing secret that kept me, I felt, different and hopefully above Brian. I was just doing this set painting thing for the money. It wasn't what I was or anything. After seven years of set painting, though, that became harder and harder to say.

The DEG studios in Wilmington were comprised of several large sound stages, enough for a few movies to film there simultaneously. Our working conditions were dismal, as were the hours. We worked the standard twelve-hour day, six days a week, in the stifling, humid, and hot North Carolina August. One lonely vent fan at the top of the large, tall buildings was all there was for ventilation. Air conditioning was never turned on for the workers—it was only saved for the shooting crew. The sets we were constructing were fairly elaborate. There was a large health club, run by Dom DeLuise's character and patterned, I was told, after the health club back in England of the production designer, Harry Pottle. I was just one of fifteen painters on the film and so had little contact with Pottle, except for one day when he stood and silently watched me paint for five minutes, finally nodding his head in approval and leaving. I was painting on the obligatory police station set, one of which I've had to paint on almost every movie I'd ever done. After several of them, I had to wonder about the omnipresence of the police in our films, whether it's a reflection on our real lives or the made-up ones. I had only a little experience with the urgency that surrounded the shooting crew during a film. I was the standby painter for one day on the police station set and, numbed by the long hours and hard work, I briefly forgot about that urgency and was quickly reminded. I was doing my job, standing by, when a production assistant with his headset on came running up and asked me and the standby carpenter to make an addition to the set to hide some lights. The surface of the walls had taken a week to prepare—we'd painted them to look like old, weathered plaster—so I slowly and dutifully was trying to mimic their finish as closely and quickly as possible, while Gene Hackman, sitting in a director's chair, and the rest of the crew waited impatiently. After several minutes, a large, overweight man whom I later learned was the director, walked up to me.

"Hey you," he said.

I turned on my ladder, caulk gun in hand. "Yessir?"

He seemed very angry. "What's your name?"

I noticed everyone, including Mr. Hackman, was looking at me, and I had to think.

"Uh, JR."

"O.K., JR.," the director said, pronouncing my name sourly, "you see all these people waiting here?"

"Yessir."

"Good, good. Then you *must* know, the point is to do this *quickly*!"

"I was just trying to make it look right."

I thought he was going to hit me. "I don't give a shit how it looks. I just want you to *finish*! Do you understand me?"

I nodded weakly. "Yessir." I quickly and sloppily finished up and got out of there.

I should have remembered to move fast when on the set. I'd done some standby painting before on *Lonesome Dove* for the friendly, drunken D.P., or director of photography, the person who really shoots the picture. The jobs had been large, whole buildings to paint in minutes, and I'd done well. Whenever my name was called over the walkie-talkie, I first cringed, and then came running. Each time I'd

11

been called, it seemed as though the world had stopped for the first assistant director (A.D.), as he waited on me. The worst incident was at the end of filming near Santa Fe, New Mexico, at the set we called "Clara's house." I was sitting in one of the outbuildings with a set dresser named Jeff Schwinn. We were helping out with the special effects crew by manning a few smokers underneath two chimney pipes in the building. The smokers were little electric machines with a button you pressed to make oil inside them smoke. Every western I've ever been on uses them, pumping so much smoke out of every chimney in town the buildings look like they are on fire. Jeff and I had just smoked a joint and had a walkie-talkie with us to listen to rollings and cuts as our cue to start the smoke. I was very high, concentrating on mastering the button on my smoker, when I heard an urgent call over the radio. "We need the standby painter! Where's JR.? We need JR."

Simon Wincer, the director, Cary White, my production designer, and everybody else around camera were standing out in the middle of a field setting up a long shot on the house. I was so stoned that instead of asking what they wanted over the walkie, I went running out into the field like an idiot, a can of Streaks and Tips and dulling spray in each hand. Streaks and Tips is a colored hair spray used extensively for instant aging and dulling spray is, well, dulling spray used to kill shiny surfaces for the camera lens. I was promptly told to run back to the house and climb up on the slick, metal, two-and-a-half-story roof and spray some dulling spray on a six-inch spot at the very top that was too shiny. Thoroughly un-high by now, I did the job and decided not to get stoned again when I was on standby. This has been difficult to keep up on every movie since, for me, getting high often relieves the tedium of being on set.

Brian Stultz, my leader again on *Von Metz*, had me primarily, as I said, working as a regular painter. Shooting schedules are constantly subject to change, and this resulted in massive overtime for us, sometimes putting in sixteen-hour days for weeks in a row and working through our Sundays. We painted a dockyard, an S&M club, thousands of tiles of faux marble, a torture chamber, slaving over noxious fumes in the steamy buildings. As with my experience with house painting, I quickly became bored with movie painting. Ultimately, after you'd learned most of the basic scenic secrets to faux finishes, it became mechanical, dull, and repetitious. Though many of the people I worked with in the construction department were intelligent and nice, there was a contingent of hillbilly racists who spoke fondly of the KKK and drank and snorted and smoked themselves to oblivion to get through the long days and nights. After hours of working with these guys in often dangerous, accident-prone conditions, I found myself starting to snort and smoke myself to oblivion as well and wondered what I was doing there.

It certainly wasn't to cavort with the stars. A fan of Gene Hackman's acting, I finally saw him up close, along with the other stars one day on the spa set. Hackman walked in with the director. Playing a cop, the actor had a gun on his hip. I was sweeping the faux marble floor so it could be sprayed with toxic lacquer and stopped to stare at Mr. Hackman. I must have been too obvious for both men stopped talking and gave me a get-back-to-work look, which I did. After they left, Dan Aykroyd walked in to look at our set with his pregnant wife, Donna Dixon. He stopped in the middle of the room, looked at all of us moving busily about and pronounced, "I am the baddest motherfucker in this room!" and started laughing, obviously joking amid the Wilmington carpentry community who seemed to have an average height of 6'6". Everyone laughed politely (which, incidentally, is what you always do when a star says something remotely humorous) and they left. To complete the inspection process, Dom DeLuise came bustling into the set, sweating profusely, and almost got stuck in the doorway because of his enormous girth. He proceeded to regale all of us with some genuinely funny, self-deprecating routines, complimented our work, and got out of there.

Young and eager to work on movies for what I felt was big money, I was in Wilmington as a local, which means I was putting myself up. Later, as I gained more experience, I would try to work only on out of town jobs where I would get hotel and per diem. I would try, but rarely got it. Working as a local, as I soon found out, meant most of my money would go out the window on food and lodging and other expenses. I took a room in a house owned by a woman named Gold in the historical district of Wilmington. I was later told this person was slightly insane, but the room was large and three hundred a month and all I could find at the time. The house had been built in 1898 and was a big, two-story Victorian place with columns and gables and a wrap-around porch. Gold had a lot of ornate plaster work on her ceiling that was falling off, which she wanted me to fix, but only if I would work cheap.

I told her that I didn't work cheap and didn't have time, only one of which was a lie.

It was strange living in Gold's house. She and her boyfriend and her son constantly wanted me to have dinner with them, or just spend any time with them. About all I could spare, though, was to smoke a joint with Gold in the evenings out on the balcony, watching horse-drawn carriages carrying tourists past her house. Because I was working on a movie, she felt I had some excitement going on in my life that she and her family could use. Gold even brought over several of her friends to meet me, always introducing me the same way, "He's with the movies," as if this said more about me than anything else. I was asked about the stars often, but could tell them nothing save that I worked in the art department and hung around painters and carpenters all day. I volunteered to tell them about my work, but they didn't want to hear it. Gold's boyfriend was in the construction business and had hopes, he led me to believe, of my helping him land some sort of super-visory construction position at the movie studio. I told him finally, this was highly unlikely as there were many people in line to work at these jobs, most all experienced.

Try as I might, I never could get these otherwise nice people to understand how unglamorous the movie business was. Perhaps to illus-trate the point, I thought of telling Gold's boyfriend and her friends of my one encounter with the construction coordinator of *The Von Metz Incident*, but decided against it. The man, Ray Boyd, walked up to me one day at work. He was officially one of my many bosses. He wore a red, ill-fitting T-shirt, a tweed Englishman's cap, bell-bottom jeans, and was holding a green folder of photographs. I was bent over hundreds of fake-marble tiles, my respirator on. Ray, who'd never said a word to me before, stopped my working, pulled several photos from the folder, and handed them to me.

"I'm gonna blackmail that son-of-a-bitch Bobby Testerman," he said.

Bobby Testerman was a local head scenic and primary competitor of Brian Stultz, who trashed Mr. Testerman often to anyone who would listen. Testerman, like many scenics, was well known for his drug and alcohol abuse, and Brian was in the process, along with another local scenic Paul Oliver (who'd co-led *Lonesome Dove*) , of taking over as the profitable, primary scenics at the DEG studios, both men having first dibs on some of the biggest-budget movies coming to town.

" That cocksucker Testerman," Ray Boyd continued, "put a center-fold layout in my binder when I was making a budget presentation to the production designer and the u.p.m. [unit production manager] and the producers. He made a fool out of me. So, I got him drunk, which ain't hard to do with that fuckin' alcoholic and he was takin' all those little football pills of his, them downers, so I hired this big fat nigger whore to sit her pussy on his face and suck his limp dick!"

I put down my natural sponges and rags and looked at the photos. Yes, a prostitute was performing fellatio on a man.

"See," Ray pointed out, "look at that. He couldn't get it up. I went and got the ugliest nigger I could find."

Another picture of the woman sitting on his face, on top of him, while several men, including Ray stood around and watched. The construction coordinator took back his photos and put them in his folder.

" I'm gonna show 'em to his fuckin' wife!"

My boss walked off then and I got back to work.

Many of my fellow painters were equally scintillating. There was one whom everyone else called the Lizard Man. He worked with me extensively on the torture chamber set, so I got to know him pretty well. The set was in an abandoned cotton-cloth factory, underground. There were signs everywhere: Danger! Warning! Toxic! Do Not Pass This Point! Cavernous green rooms stretched into the darkness. Red and brown stains, like splattered blood, covered the walls, while long-dead cauldrons bubbled over with foul dried fluid. A rectangle of sunlight, two feet wide and forty feet long, slanted down from the ceiling to us each day, reminding us of the outside world. Inside the dusty shaft of light, we could see the air we were breathing, thick with old chemicals and cotton fibers; one deep breath equaled a nice, delayed death. Large, powerful air conditioners and huge fans would be employed when the stars arrived. We made do in the 120 degree heat.

The Lizard Man was pale and short with sharp, pointed teeth and long, fuzzy, red hair that stuck straight up. He looked like one of those troll dolls people used to hang from their rearview mirrors in the seventies. I'd heard he lived on Ding Dongs and Pepsi, worshipped heavy metal, and lived under a rock, all true, save for the last. He had a mother whom he lived with in a trailer near a malfunctioning nuclear power plant. He asked me to meet her one day and offered to sell me a bag of dope in the process. I followed him to the trailer (he drove a purple Gremlin) and we went inside. His mother sat in a ripped recliner. Her yellow carpet was stained, but vacuumed. She had white hair and a flap of skin hanging from her neck, not unlike a lizard. A blue glow from the television set illuminated her head, a miniature set in each of her eyes. The Three Stooges were hitting each other. The Lizard Man introduced me to her and I shook her bony hand. She smiled, a close-mouthed, pleasant smile, and said nothing.

I went to his room, got my bag of dope, and paid him. He told me he was an artist, as well as a set painter, and, with noticeable pride, showed me his paintings. They were very bad drug paintings. He went over each canvas and tried to show me the things he'd hidden in them. One painting, of a carnival, the best one, had a little gremlin with red hair and malformed appendages in a corner. I asked him if it was a self-portrait.

"Yeah," he shrugged. "Sort of. See, he's a magician, man."

I told him I had to leave and he offered me a glass of water. We went into the kitchen. I saw his mother staring at the TV set, silent and still. He filled a glass and handed it to me. Odd, misshapen daisies were painted all over its surface. He frowned. "I painted these glasses for my mom on her birthday," he said.

"They're very nice."

"No big deal."

I drank the water down, said good-bye to him and his mother, and left the trailer. As I was getting into my truck, the Lizard Man yelled out to me from behind his screen door, a strange thing that has obviously stuck with me.

"Watch out for those movies, man! Watch out!"

I was usually so tired after work all I could do was eat a quick dinner somewhere and fall into bed. I rarely went out, although my immediate boss, on two movies now, Brian Stultz, was constantly calling me or coming by trying to get me to join him and his fiancee Kelly on a tour of the Wilmington night life. I had mistakenly consented a few times and was thoroughly embarrassed by Brian's obnoxious behavior. His favorite restaurant was the only sushi bar in the small town and he acted as though he were a ravenous big shot the whole evening, ordering hundreds of dollars worth of food, getting very drunk, offending everyone around him, including the nice people who ran the restaurant, and talking in an incredibly loud I'm-an-important-person-who-works-on-movies-and-these-are-some-of-the-stars-I-know voice at a volume that wrongly assumed people in South Carolina wanted to hear what he did for a living. After several of those nights, I took to actually hiding in my room upstairs at Gold's, looking cowardly out the curtains at Brian and Kelly on the sidewalk standing, obviously confused, in front of my parked truck.

I'd always thought I was tough, at least a tough worker, if not a person, but *The Von Metz Incident*, coupled with my boss's social demands, wore me out. You have to understand the delicate situation I was in. To work on a movie is to work for a myriad of personalities. It's still a wonder to me how all these clashing personas can even get a movie off the ground, much less finished and in a theater. People are often hired solely for their personality, or really, their good attitude: "I'll do anything you say." Experience doesn't always matter if you are a hard worker and have that eager attitude—which often leads to naive youngsters getting used, their asses worked off for nothing. It's one of the reasons why there are so many young people on movie crews. Most importantly though, in the attitude category, is the definitive amount of ass-kissing, even at my level. Ass-kissing permeates the entire movie business (to the point, I'm sure, of literal ass-kissing) but if done properly, and I feel I'm a master, there can be a minimal amount of loss to your dignity and soul. The extent to which I kissed Brian's ass was that I pretended he had half a brain outside of work and would listen to him talk, something he did often. Brian, I found out, had written a screenplay. When we were working on *Lonesome Dove* and I told him I was a writer, it cemented our bond, and he would talk to me about writing and writers every other day.

So I listened to him talk and did what he said on the job. It soon became obvious to me, though, that Brian was a head scenic who talked about writing rather than actually doing it. Call me a wimp, and others have, but I couldn't take one more day of his writerly blathering. I could not listen to one more of his derivative movie ideas and nod my head and say, "Hey, that sounds really good. You should write that down. It's a hit" and still look at myself in the mirror. And the hours, the overtime, it was all too grueling. I felt like I was working in a grim factory. Finally, after two months, we parted amicably—I mean, I quit.

I tried to stress the "amicably" part, for it is not wise to burn a bridge in the small community of the movie business. I kept my lips puckered as I told him I was leaving and tried to maintain that eager attitude, or maybe you could call it just being positive: the ability to pretend that whatever you were working on, no matter how ridiculous, was important. At least I'm working on a movie, I thought at the time. I'm not like those people in the real world, going to the same set every day. I kept that attitude all the way out of town, saying good-bye to a disappointed Gold (her life had not changed), all the way back to Texas. *The Von Metz Incident* would finish surprisingly, without me. It went on to be called *Loose Cannons* upon its release and thoroughly bombed. Still caring about seeing my work on screen, I went to see the movie and, like probably the rest of the audience, fell into a deep sleep.

−3−

I was living in Austin then. Already out of money and on unemployment, I frantically called friends and the Texas Film Commission looking for work. I heard about a movie filming in Brenham, Texas, a CBS Movie of the Week called *The Fulfillment of Mary Gray* . The construction coordinator from *Lonesome Dove*, Pat Welsome, was doing this movie, and through him I found out the head scenic was a man from L.A. named Jerry Palermo. I called Jerry in L.A., told him of my brief experience, and mentioned that I knew all of the carpenters and the construction coordinator. Jerry just wanted to know if I had a truck, which I did, and he hired me over the phone. When he reached Brenham, he called me in, and I definitely had the job.

The whole crew, the stars included, were holed up in the Coach Light Inn in Brenham, which meant that we would all see each other not only all day but all night as well. I had my first real experience with negotiating my "deal" or signing my deal memo, something you have to go through on any film. Basically, you meet with the unit production manager, the person who hires and fires and says no to everybody, and tell him or her how much money you want. Then he or she says no and you settle for whatever you get. That's what usually happened to me, at least, and it did again with Greg, the u.p.m., on *Mary Gray*. Greg was a young guy who spent all his time in the office, rarely visiting the set, unlike some u.p.m.s who spend a lot of time there. I made it a practice to avoid u.p.m.s whenever I saw them. Their power always scared me and whenever one looked at me, I always felt nervous, like I'd been caught at something.

The production designer was a man named Jim Hulce, who had

won several Emmys for his TV work. He wouldn't be getting one for *The Fulfillment of Mary Gray*. The star of the show, playing the courageous pioneer woman who wanted to have a baby by her husband's little brother or somebody, was Cheryl Ladd. I'd never seen Ms. Ladd in anything I could think of, so when I finally saw her on the set, I was surprised at how attractive and nice she was. She still had that I'm-a-movie-star look in her eyes, but acted pretty normal. Her husband was producing the film and looked, to me, like a young Porter Wagoner. The other two actors were relatively unknown. The cute little brother was played by some smiling guy I'd seen in some low-budget bombs. The husband was a good actor named Ted Levine, who would later play the psycho in *Silence of the Lambs*. Far from a psycho in real life, he mistakenly asked me if he could buy the curtains off one of the sets—his wife would love them. I referred him to the set dressers, the people who are responsible for all the tables, chairs, curtains, dishes, and what not on a set. They're basically furniture movers who make, oh, I'd say, $900 a week more than real furniture movers.

When I met up with Jerry Palermo that first week, I knew I would like him. In keeping with the stereotype of most house painters and scenic artists, Jerry was an alcoholic, but a kind one, and a very good scenic artist who knew all the tricks. After watching me work, he told me he thought I had a knack for it and should try to become a full-fledged lead scenic, and he offered to teach me everything he knew.

My first job every morning was to take some of Jerry's petty cash and buy and ice down a case of beer, which would, without my help, be gone by six o'clock that evening. Jerry started popping beer tabs at six-thirty in the morning and didn't let up, working and drinking all day. At night, he started in on the vodka and passed out by eleven or so. There was many a night, Jerry called me, blubbering from the bar, begging me to join him for a drink. Not a drinker then, I usually refused. Since I was functioning as his horse during the day, climbing up on roofs and barns, doing most of the heavy, physical labor, I needed my strength.

I asked Jerry once if he drank like this at the studios in L.A., when he wasn't on location. He said he did and he and his buddies had all sorts of methods of hiding booze, including false bottoms in paint buckets, hidden caches on the shooting set, and even empty, faux spray cans housing cold beers. I liked Jerry despite his drunkenness, but got a little embarrassed by him at the end of the long day. He was stumbling by then, a panty hose or lamp shade, usually something, on his head. He always got the sets ready, the work done, though, the bottom line on any movie crew. People would put up with a lot if you were good.

Our construction coordinator, Pat Welsome, famous for his hardass-ness, didn't know what to do with Jerry. Pat was from the real-world, general-contractor, "I wanna see assholes and elbows" school of army management. He'd been a major prick on *Lonesome Dove* , alienating everyone in the art department. He and Sully, the set decorator on *Lonesome Dove*, had had screaming fights every day to the point that Pat took to bringing out his gun and taking a little target practice whenever Sully came to the set. Sully isn't known for his quiet demeanor, either: he choked one locations woman on a set one day, put his lead man set dresser in regular, fistfighting headlocks, quit on a weekly basis, almost hit me once with a plaster tombstone, yelled at everyone when angry, made his set dresser Barbara Haberecht cry much too often, and often took a destructive hammer to things he shouldn't have taken a hammer to. Pat had been an alcoholic once, his right hand man, Dave Wilt, told me, but was now off everything (including, I presumed, his lithium). Pat enjoyed screaming at people, too. He and my boss on *Lonesome Dove*, Brian Stultz, had many screaming arguments. Pat would come tearing up to the set on Moody's ranch every morning in his giant truck and skid to a stop just in front of a building we had been working on all week, and jump out of his truck shouting a new command.

"Don't anybody ever go to the Chevron on 277 ever again! Nobody! That place sucks! They're slow as shit! Nobody gets gas at the Chevron!" or "Don't anybody ever go to Memo's for breakfast again! That goddamn fat-ass bitch made me wait ten minutes for some motherfucking scrambled eggs!" Then he'd run around the set yelling at everyone for being two minutes late to work the week before, shrieking, "I got a well-oiled machine here and you're fucking it up!" He knew little about the movie or TV business, exclaiming one day at what he felt was some bad casting, "There goes our fuckin' Enema!" meaning, I hope, Emmy. He treated his carpenters like children, telling them when to go to bed, when to play a radio, where to eat. He made sure they knew, every day, that he was the reason they had this job and they better fucking appreciate it. I'd seen a dozen general contractors just like him in the real world as a painter, so he didn't really bother me. I just did my job and stayed out of his way. He didn't bother Jerry Palermo, either. Jerry had been on a·few, not-so-fun tours of Vietnam as a marine and despite his small size (friends called him the Penguin) had no fear of a blowhard like Pat.

Mary Gray, for the art department, was just a few sets: a couple of farmhouses, the obligatory graveyard, and several real, gigantic green oak trees I had to paint to look like colorful maples in the fall. Jerry and I painted thirty or forty Styrofoam tombstones for the movie, many of which I would see circulating on different films for the next six years. After about a week of work, Jerry said he had the money in his budget to hire a helper and that he wanted to employ a girl with large breasts who would maybe have sex with him. It didn't matter whether she could paint. Amazingly, I'd seen this employee description for several departments on only three films. Jerry found the girl, a local Brenhamite, and did his damnedest for the rest of the shoot, but never got any further than flirting. And she turned out to be a good painter, so it was a wash on his plans. The three of us worked hard for the rest of the show.

I made a point, at the end of shooting, to shake hands with Pat's foreman, Dave Wilt, since the word was going around that Pat was out and Dave would probably take his place as the primary local coordinator for Cary White, the designer on *Lonesome Dove*. Cary was our unofficial movie leader in Texas and many wanted to hitch their wagon to his to get movie jobs. Cary was, and is, something one rarely sees in the movie business, a nice guy. Pat Welsome didn't fit in with Cary's laid-back way of operating an art department. I knew, as did everyone except Pat, that Dave Wilt would fit in and would someday be yet another boss for me. It doesn't take long to get out of the movie pipeline. Someone is always there to replace you. After *Mary Gray* I never saw or worked for Pat Welsome again.

At the end of the show, there was a little controversy with the special effects department: that is, they were running a scam with the fake snow. They bought hundreds of extra bags and then told the young u.p.m. they were almost out of snow between a couple of big scenes where it was required. More fake snow was ordered and they squirreled the bags away at the art department warehouse. A curious production office coordinator happened to come by the warehouse taking inventory and caught effects loading a semi with fake snow which they would probably sell to another movie. Special effects departments always seem to be a little shady and sleazy, so it wasn't surprising.

I went to the wrap party, which was held in a bowling alley with an open bar. There was a lot of drinking and drugging and carrying on and I had a good time. For some reason, the u.p.m., Greg, decided we were buddies that night and got me on his bowling team where he kept giving me embarrassing high-five's. Maybe he just wanted to be one of the guys. Or maybe he thought I had some cocaine, a lot of which was floating like fake snow around the set. I didn't, though, and even if I had, I wouldn't have given management any. Jerry Palermo and I said our good-byes. His last words to me were, "Stick with this shit, JR. You're pretty fucking good at it." Not very poetic, but I believed him.

—4—

There was nothing going on movie-wise after that, except for a low-budget West German detective series for German television filming in Houston. A friend of mine from *Lonesome Dove*, Barbara Haberecht, was the set decorator on it. John Frick, the art director from *Lonesome Dove*, was taking his first shot as a production designer. Barbara was constantly calling and complaining of John Frick's indecisiveness and saying she could never find him. I told her she was overreacting. I asked Barbara for some work and she said she could use me as a set dresser for a few weeks converting a mansion in Houston's Memorial neighborhood into a Colombian drug dealer's palatial estate. It was to be the set for a big scene in which two young female cops, one American, one German (it was called *Miller and Mueller*) catch the drug dealer by discovering his cocaine stash in a floating duck in a pond in his living room.

I went to Houston, staying with Barbara in Montrose, and did things like go with Jim Kanan to get lily pads for the pond and antiques and plants for the house, weed-eat the yard, find artwork for the walls, and did a lot of drinking with Barbara and her then boyfriend, a severe alcoholic and genius (in that order), Frank Pierce. We hit the nicest restaurants in town and were promptly moved to the back of them when Frank started his drunken routine which, to give you an idea, included an imitation of Toulouse-Lautrec.

Miller and Mueller turned out to be almost enjoyable actually. Small productions like that often are. Everyone has to pitch in and help everyone else do his or her job. On any given night, you're helping props, or extras casting, or the set dressers, or giving the grips a hand.

I found myself chatting with the attractive female producer from Germany about her script, or I had the chance to talk with the wacky German D.P.(director of photography) about Colombian drug lords and what they were really like. Randy Moore was the special effects department on the film, the man responsible for the exploding, coke-filled duck. He did a good job and the duck blew up, sending talcum powder everywhere. After shooting all night, the scenes in the mansion were finished. Not being a German TV viewer, I never saw *Miller and Mueller* but heard it was very successful over in Germany. Of course, there's that David Hasselhoff thing there, so. . .

The Fulfillment of Mary Gray did come on my TV, though. I tried to watch it, but it was so horrible I couldn't. I couldn't watch *Loose Cannons* and, although this is sacrilege to its many fans, I couldn't sit through all of *Lonesome Dove,* either. Maybe I'd seen too much of the filming and it seemed repetitive. The best thing about it was Robert Duvall. When he wasn't on-screen, the show seemed to deflate and I lost interest. That was three movies now I couldn't watch and I watched everything back then. The fourth, not surprisingly, turned out the same way. I'd been on unemployment for a few months when ABC and Universal Pictures television came into town with an episode of a new Lou Gosset series entitled *Gideon Oliver.* Our episode was to be "The Kennonites" which finds our hero Lou in an Amish-type community looking for a murderer (I don't know what's up with those Amish guys, this has happened a few times now). Cary White was the production designer, John Frick his art director, Sully was the set decorator, Barbara Haberecht the lead person, and Jeff Schwann her main set dresser. Dave Wilt was the new construction coordinator, and I was, for the first time, the lead scenic artist. Not knowing what I was doing, I hired a lot of inexperienced people like myself and we worked our asses off.

I painted quite a few buildings and barns, water towers, false fronts, Styrofoam bricks, and yes, tombstones, for Cary and company. Eager to please, I followed Cary around whenever I saw him, showing him what I was doing and asking too many questions. I figured it was his fault I was there, anyway. He was the one on *Lonesome Dove* who'd encouraged me to become a scenic, who told me I could do it when I constantly said I couldn't, so I tried hard to please him with my work.

His art director, John Frick, was never around except to shave his beard like an Amish man and work as an extra, mostly staying in the art department doing what he was good at—drawing plans. Sully was just Sully, quitting the show several times after screaming matches with the u.p.m., Kevin Donnely, and making Barbara cry a few times.

The first director of *Gideon Oliver* was fired after a few days. I'd heard he was a screenwriter and this was presumably his big chance to be a director (quite a leap). I don't know if Lou didn't like him or what, but the man was soon gone and replaced by the actor/director Bill Duke, the man you might remember as the pimp to whom Richard Gere proclaims "I don't do fag stuff" in *American Gigolo.* Mr. Gosset and Mr. Duke were friendly, nice people who treated everyone with respect and kindness. Little did they know, or maybe they did, that they were in the middle of redneck Texas where, many a time, after they passed a group of carpenters, nodding and smiling hello, the carpenters remarked that "two niggers were running the show."

We were filming at Camp Friday Mountain in the picturesque Hill Country near Dripping Springs. Occasionally, I would go down to the mill set we had by a creek and do a little work while smoking a joint with my enlightened, wood-butchering comrades. There was a stunt scene that played there one day that almost resulted in tragedy. A young man and woman were supposed to drop from a long rope with a tire at its end into the creek below a cliff. The shot was from a plane flying above. The stuntman was young and inexperienced. The stuntwoman was young and quite good. When the time came and action was called, they both let go of the rope and dropped from the cliff. The woman, planning her fall perfectly, hit the water. The man, dropping sixty feet, his legs spread wide, landed squarely on the tire before he sank, painfully, like a rock into the creek. The stuntwoman, Casey Justice, swam to shore (she would, not long after this, become a producer along with her friend and partner, Debra Simon, a second a.d. on the picture, and I would work for both of them on two movies.) The stuntman continued to sink like a rock. The stunt coordinator that day, an overweight man in sweats, finally realized his boy wasn't coming up and dove, or rather fell, into the river and pulled the wincing stuntman from the water.

The female star of this *Gideon Oliver* episode, playing an ambitious, progressive, modern Kennonite woman—qualities I thought were mutually exclusive in the Amish world—was Melissa Leo. We talked and she seemed nice. I may have had a little crush on her even until I saw she had a boyfriend, who drove up to the set one day while we were shooting. I was busy freaking out, screaming at an old Teamster because the man wouldn't move his semi and trailer, which was parked next to a pole barn I had two hours to paint. Cecil, the Teamster captain, a reasonable professional who has seen it all, pulled me aside, calmed me down, and got the guy to move. As I got my Hudson sprayers, full of raw umber, wash ready, Melissa's boyfriend, the actor John Heard, stepped out of his car, parked next to my barn, a big grin on his face, and gave me an exaggerated "Howdy, pardner!" I set down my sprayers, thought of smacking him, but instead, said hello, showing him with my eyes, like an oriental bow, that I knew who he was. He wandered off and, after convincing his driver to move his car away from the barn, I began to paint the beams above my head, covering myself, quite completely, with paint.

At the wrap party for *Gideon Oliver* everyone got drunk, including my construction coordinator, Dave Wilt, who was practically falling down trying to play horseshoes and starting fights with one of his carpenters, Tim Lobdell. Some of the grips and electricians hired a limo to take them and their buddies to the party. This particular group had several guys dressed like rock and roll stars with their hair moussed up in all directions. The grips are sometimes the worst for adopting that bigshot, movie-guy persona. Because they are closer to the almighty camera, they can have more of an attitude and subsequently make some of the more serious fashion errors on the set. All in all, the party was a mess and petered out quickly.

Not long afterwards (it doesn't take but a few months to air TV) I watched "The Kennonite Episode" of *Gideon Oliver* at a party at Sully's house and we had a good time. I don't think any of us actually watched the show and those of us who did, couldn't understand it. It was a sad commentary, I thought. We'd all read the script and worked on it and still couldn't fathom it. What was TV America thinking? Most probably, nothing.

–5–

After *Gideon Oliver* I was on the dole for months trying to find movie work. That was four shows now that I thought were unwatchable. I began to wonder if I really wanted to be a lead scenic on movies for the rest of my life, making lots of money, drinking lots of alcohol, smoking lots of dope, working lots of hours, in lots of different towns, with lots of different people, meeting, I hoped, lots of different women, and, most importantly, forgetting about that little thing of looking in the mirror in the morning when I shaved. I thought, maybe it's not the quality of the projects, it's what I'm doing, all this painting. I'd never wanted to be a painter. I could draw, had something of an eye for what looked right, and had skills as a house painter. These things, coupled with chance, had brought me to the position, and money was keeping me there, the need for it. Was painting fake buildings what I really wanted to do?

Maybe it was just what I did in the movies. Maybe I could be a first a.d. No, then I would have to start all over again at the very bottom as a low-paid p.a., or production assistant, people who were coffee getters, gophers, and anyone's slave. Besides, as an a.d., one had to be completely plugged in to the goings-on of the set, knowing where the actors where and how long they'd been there, the extras, the shooting schedule, everyone's overtime, the script page by page and line by line, the weather—everything. You not only had to give a shit about whatever stupid project you were on, you had to live and breathe it. I didn't want that. I thought of the locations department, but nixed that, not wanting to be in the business of screwing all the people I lived with in Texas or elsewhere, having to really deal with their expectations and disappointments, contracts, and, worst of all, where the Teamsters are going to park all of their vehicles. Makeup, hair, wardrobe, all that crap was out since I had no desire dress up actors and make them pretty. The grips, well, I wasn't cool enough to hang out with them. And production, I hated production. It was all office work, worrying about the money, the insurance, the overtime, plane reservations for actors, rental cars, hotel reservations, phone bills, cutting checks, signing checks, canceling checks, making sure the film gets delivered and developed, on and on, one money concern after the next. And again, you had to outwardly care about Project X. How else could you order a hundred dollars worth of roses for a disgruntled actress who's unsatisfied with the cotton count on her sheets?

No, if I was anything, I was an art department person. The art department was where you could hide out, away from the celebrities, the shooting crew, production, everyone. It was where I could do a good job, get my check, and pretend I really was doing something important in my own little dream world. Away from those people of such great importance in the movie hierarchy, it was almost like I was a real person too, and had an opinion or a life, things like that. The art department was always there before everyone else got there and after they left. Many a location, or set, was ruined, I felt, once production arrived (literally, since the grips usually disassembled everything we'd built during shooting). I'll never forget, on *Lonesome Dove*, the town finished, our work done, standing on a cliff overlooking a spectacular bend in the Rio Grande, with horses and cattle from Mexico wading into the water, the children of ranch hands playing in the shallows, idyllic and peaceful, only to be interrupted by the whole monstrosity that is the shooting crew, producers, actors, extras, u.p.m.'s, d.p.'s, a.d.'s, p.a.'s, grips, electric, makeup, hair, wardrobe, Teamsters, a giant walkie-talkied crowd, moving amorphously toward my peaceful set. Many times—well, let's face it—every time, even though they were the reason I was there, I felt they were ruining it.

I stayed in the art department and thought of maybe trying to be a lead man for the set dressers. Young and inexperienced, I thought I should get a feel for all aspects of the art department. Maybe I could be a production designer some day like Cary White although, that prospect wasn't very heartening, either. Cary, unlike me, had to peruse the script thoroughly, breaking it down into sets, caring about the show to a far greater extent than me. And, as part of the big seven on a film, the designer had to pretty much let each show take over his life. Many a time, I'd seen Cary out there on the set at midnight with the rest of us, hanging up a curtain, helping with the painting or carpentry, placing a last minute tombstone, trying to give the set that last little touch of reality . Ultimately, as the head of the department, it was his butt on the line. A good designer had to know every aspect of his department. If I ever wanted to be one, I'd have to learn about set decorating.

The job then, my mission, would be working as lead man for the swing gang (set dressers) on *The Challenger Movie: The Story of Flight 51-L*, a three hour movie for ABC television, produced by King Phoenix Productions. I drove down to the Sheraton Kings Inn in Clear Lake City, near Houston, where King Phoenix had set up shop. I interviewed with Bob Checci, the production designer, for the job. Bob was around sixty years old. He had white, closely cropped hair, chain-smoked Vantages, and inhaled a lot of black coffee. He was also hard of hearing, a former landscape designer, and a navy man. He had worked with the director, Glenn Jordan, on twelve shows and the two had garnered several Emmys.

Bob's hands shook too much, so he had a set designer who did all his drawings for the sets. The assistant's name was Richard Wright. I wasn't sure what Richard was supposed to do when he finished all of Bob's drawings, but that little mystery was soon solved.

I was very nervous at the interview. I'd rehearsed a little speech I immediately forgot with Richard watching and Bob giving me his stare-for-a-thousand-faces. After I mumbled for a few minutes, Bob cut me off and said curtly, "You seem like a quiet, soft-spoken guy. You're going to probably have to fire people to keep the swing gang in line, keep them from stopping off and having breakfasts and long lunches when they go out for pick-ups in the five-ton, keep them busy at all times. Are you sure you have the balls for this job?"

I was taken aback. Nobody had really asked me about my balls before. I took out a Lucky Strike in order to appear tougher and assured him I could be a jerk when I had to be. That seemed to satisfy him. He made a call to the first of three production managers we'd have, Art Levinson, and said I was coming over to talk about money. Then he hung up the phone, reached across with a light for my cigarette, and let his lighter hand rest just a little too long on my hand. I got a queasy feeling, like I'd just sold a little part of my cheap soul, and thanked him for the job.

I walked over to the production office at the back of the hotel to meet with Art. He'd just finished as the u.p.m. on *Great Balls of Fire* and seemed like a busy person who knew his business. Art was very cordial, polite, and told me I had one minute. He was sorry but he was already late for a meeting with the producers, Debbie Robbins, George Englund, Sr., and young George, Jr. I told Art how much money I wanted and he said no, I can only give you this and wrote the small figure on a piece of paper and handed it to me. Being a tough negotiator, I immediately said yes, shook his hand, and thanked him. "We'll talk later," he said, and was gone. I said good-bye to the production office coordinator, Francine, and went back over to the art department.

Richard Wright, the set designer, stopped me there, introduced me to Tom Kirkpatrick, a young intern who was to be on the swing gang, and then asked me to turn around so he could check my asshole.

"I beg your pardon?" I asked.

"How bad are you bleeding?" Richard asked. "Did Art fuck you in the ass like he fucked everyone else?"

The art department was starting to sound a little crass. Richard then started to do some sort of strange pantomime that, I guess, was supposed to be Art fucking people. I said no, I hadn't been financially sodomized, Art had been reasonable and seemed like an O.K. guy for the two minutes I'd met him. Richard looked at me as though I were a traitor, telling me that art departments were supposed to hate production managers. I told him to tell Bob I was on and I'd see them in a few days. Out in my truck, I wondered if I was stepping into a den of slightly inept, sexually frustrated, insecure, weird people. But then again, that described the whole movie business.

Clear Lake happened to be one of the few areas in Houston that was booming in an otherwise depressed real estate market. I talked with Jan, an original Clear Lake girl, at the Apartment Connection, and the only places she could find for me on a monthly basis were corporate lodgings that provided everything and cost between $800 and a $1,000 a month. I said I needed something lower. This disappointed her, but she persevered and found me an efficiency in the Surf Court, a place she called a hole-in-the-wall next to NASA. We drove over and I met with Helene, the apartment manager/artist from France. She showed me the

31

apartment, which was grim, furnished with a bed I should have tested and a battered chest of drawers. As I gave her three hundred and fifty dollars, Helene casually mentioned that the man who lived in the room on my left was completely insane, "but harmless if you don't talk to him." I promised her I wouldn't and moved in.

I started a week after my interview. A large tropical storm had parked itself over Houston by then and everything was flooded. I went over to production that morning to sign my start papers and get start papers for the crew and found out Art had been let go by the producers and Francine had subsequently quit. The office was far from bustling with activity. A few people walked around lost, in a daze. I signed my papers with Susan, the new temporary u.p.m., and tried to decipher the mystery of the copy machine. Stacy, assistant to the director, mercifully showed me which way the paper went. I left the office depressed. How could I be the lead man and keep track of all the time cards and rental receipts, the set-decorating budget, and the check requests, if I couldn't even run the copy machine?

There wasn't much to do yet in the art department. Well, there was a lot to do, but nobody knew where to start. We all just eyed each other suspiciously. Bob told me where to buy picture frames (at Michaels), how to put them together, then had me buy more picture wire, not exactly daunting. I had all this energy but nothing to do. I paced back and forth that first day. At one point, I glued Bob's broken glasses together and felt like a suck-up. Richard, anxious to win points, seemed to resent me. He watched me like a dull-brained hawk whenever I talked with Bob. Then, that evening, to my surprise, Richard and Tom asked me if they could bunk with me, as it were, at my apartment.

"We have this other set dresser coming in and he needs a place to stay, too. We can all sleep on bedrolls on your floor," Richard said.

He seemed to fully expect me to say yes. Instead, I declined, saying I liked my privacy, which was true, and that there were a lot of roaches on my floor, again, true.

"Oh, I see," Richard said, "You'll work with us twelve hours a day but you won't let us stay with you."

" Exactly."

More looks of resentment. I wasn't becoming one of the guys.

The next few days were better and work became more work-like. At Bob's insistence I had to fire one of my guys (who had more experience than me) first thing for some trumped-up reason. I ordered the five-ton from the transportation coordinator, Ron Kearn, and met with the art department driver, Ray Bellamy, a veteran of the Korean war who carried a .45 with him (if a movie is ever attacked the Teamsters could defend it) and was fond of humming "The Star-Spangled Banner." I went with Bob over to our rented office buildings at 1840 NASA Road One and met the director, Glenn. He was from San Antonio and seemed like a nice person. He had Bob hopping around the empty offices and I took notes of everything they said. Bob kept looking at me—in desperation like, "Are you getting all this down? Because I'm not gonna remember a thing." I got it all down and he and I left to rent furniture.

I think Bob alienated at least half of the city. He made women cry in fabric stores, pissed off salesmen at furniture stores, complained about Houston, saying how in L.A. people want to do business, "They know what found money is, for Christ's sake!", called the new locations manager a cunt (" I'm gonna walk all over that cunt and then I'm gonna lay her down and *kick* her in the cunt!"), drove erratically and dangerously across the freeways, and all the while smoked like an indignant chimney. He had a terrible cough that would go on for minutes until one of his lungs came up. He'd sit there for minutes with his eyes closed, recovering. Several times there, I'd thought he'd died at the wheel.

Riding around with him all day got to be too much. I guess he wanted me to think he was a genius or like him or something. But everybody wants that, right? I was just having a problem faking it. It's essential, though, in the movie business to feign fondness. He kept telling me about his house in Greece and how he was trying to sell it, about getting a place in Switzerland, his lawyer suing someone, his artist friends, his good buddy Martin Sheen, whom he worked with on *Blind Ambition*, being a landscape designer, going to U.T., firing this guy, firing that guy, his special vodka martinis, and something about Turkish prisons I pretended not to hear. And he kept going to the bathroom at every store we hit, always mentioning the bathroom, what condition it was in, what it smelled like, this one's clean, this one wasn't. He was a bathroom connoisseur.

His mind didn't seem to be on the job. At Michael's, when we should have been buying frames for the hundreds of pictures we had for our eighty-four sets, he would stand at the poster rack gazing at shirtless men in cowboy hats. At Tramat and Scott furniture, I'd follow him around in circles for five, six, seven hours, as he examined each chair and desk as though he were trying to read its mind, managing to lose his set book in the process. Just when I thought we weren't going to rent anything, with the store closing, he picked out fifty pieces in thirty seconds. I was confused. Was he pretending that these were incredibly difficult artistic decisions he was making? Or was he old and tired and just wanted to get back to the Kings Inn and have a martini in the director's office?

The few times I tried to help by picking something out, or sending one of the guys out to find something, I was slapped down immediately. Bob would become insecure and adamantly tell me that wasn't my job and that everything, *everything* , would go through him. I wasn't to hang a picture, move a desk, or clean a window without his say-so. Fine. I meant it, fine, just give us something to do.

The work came in slowly, though, and the swing gang became the Sit-around-and-wait-on-Bob gang. I was fucking up somehow and B. was letting me know it. The prop people, David Harshbarger and his assistant, came in from L.A. and that provided a little relief to the tension. David was an overweight, bald, affably sleazy guy who, for the first week interviewed a series of attractive young women for an assistant props position, finally settling on one with a sort of vulnerable, don't-get-me-drunk demeanor.

Shooting started over in the Launch Control Room at NASA. The production company was paying NASA $85,000 to shoot in their facilities for a week and NASA, in addition, would get some good P.R. on network television for blowing up the shuttle. Before the director and the d.p. pulled off their first shot, Glenn called the crew together around him, introduced himself, said we were working on a good project and he hoped we could all get to know each other's names if not each other. Bob was nervous as hell on set, freaking out, running around yelling at Richard and me, all of it unwarranted since this was actually an easy shoot for the art department, mainly a bunch of offices and NASA.

We were working from seven a.m. to eight p.m., so late in the evening I was officially out of Bob's control. I'd go over to the set, where they were having late calls and shooting all night in Building 9A, a special spot where some NASA employees couldn't go. They had two full-size segments of the shuttle, a payload bay, a mock-up of the cabin, and lots of other weird technical astronaut-type things. I talked with one of the technical advisers, Tom, who answered my questions about astronauts puking in space. All interesting stuff, but what I was really doing was trying to get a look at Karen Allen, Indy's girlfriend. I had a little fantasy, make that a big fantasy, that Karen and I would see each other from across the control room and despite our age and earning differences, would fall in love, have a child, and move to Connecticut. This never happened though, since I never even saw her. I kept seeing the nerd Brad from *The Rocky Horror Picture Show*, Barry Bostwick. The man was everywhere. For some reason, all I could think of was his portrayal of George Washington years ago on TV. David Harshbarger, the sweating propmaster told me heartlessly that I wasn't missing much. That Ms. Allen looked like the girl next door and was much older than he thought she'd be.

"She also has freckles all over her face," he said.

"I like freckles."

"Yeah? Well, she's short too. About yea-high." He held his hand at the bottom of his large stomach. "Perfect height for blow-jobs."

Perhaps it was the realization that I didn't want to be a set dresser, or not getting to see Karen Allen, but my will to work left me after the first week of shooting. The majority of our sets were done, and I was getting tired of riding around shopping with Bob. I didn't like shopping, with him or without him, and I was doing a lot of it. A woman at K-Mart asked me if we were going to show the Challenger astronauts screaming and flying down into the ocean. I told her no, it was being done tastefully, there'd be no explosion. I had pictures I'd framed of all the astronauts, and looking at them, wondered what difference it would make. The people in the pictures were real and we all knew how they'd died. Instead of an explosion and death, the TV Christa McAuliffe would recite a poem at the end, Karen Allen's face, like an angel on the screen.

I finally moved out of the Surf Court. My insane hermit neighbor, from whose room I'd heard noises I can't describe, had taken to leaving his large, silently menacing pit bull chained outside his door to the balcony railing, forcing me to walk past the dog twice a day. I told Helene, my Impressionist apartment manager, I wanted to meet her and get my money back. She kept putting me off with guilt-tripping excuses like, "I'm sorry, I have to drive my husband to his chemotherapy treatments."

I finally wrestled part of the amount back from her, called Jan again, and ended up renting a one-bedroom, furnished corporate apartment for eight hundred a month. All I'd been doing for three weeks was renting apartments, eating out every night, and drinking heavily. Then I got fired.

Bob was always snapping at everybody. I don't like people who snap at me. I tend to snap back. You don't do that on a movie. You obey the hierarchy, or you're simply gone. If your boss is an unreasonable crank, that's just part of the job and you better be able to deal with it.

It was something little. Bob came in and asked me angrily why we'd only carried five tables down to the Morton Thiokol Conference Room. He'd been giving me shit all morning on tiny things like this. The Morton Thiokol Conference Room didn't shoot for a week.

"Look Bob," I said, clearly irritated, "I guess it's because you told me only yesterday to bring down *five* tables."

He gave me the Look of Death and stormed out of the room, Richard close on his heels. I told the swing gang I had a feeling I wouldn't be with them much longer. That afternoon at the art department's office, Bob called me over to his desk and told me he felt things weren't working out, and this was hard for him to do, but he had to let me go. I should have just shaken his hand and left. Instead, I threw a little fit and gave a speech I didn't mean about how much I cared for this job, how I'd never been fired from anything, that he had no real reason to let me go and, finishing with a flourish, that I thought he was an asshole.

"That's O.K.," he croaked, "the director called me an asshole last night."

"Well, he was right."

"Look, you can call it a personality conflict if it makes you feel better, but Richard's going to take over from here."

"Good thing all the sets are ready."

Bob shrugged and I felt silly about my tirade. I wasn't going to faze him. Truth be told, I wasn't even mad. Though he was positively a jerk, I kind of liked the goofy old guy. "Anyway," Bob said, "you can finish out this week and——"

"Finish? What? You think I'm gonna stick around here?"

Bob looked very worried. He'd been too eager to fire me and consequently overplayed his hand. "You have to. You've got all the rental return information. All the receipts . Nobody knows where anything goes. You've got to at least stay one more day."

"Bob?"

"What?"

"Figure it out."

I exited the room dramatically, jumped in my truck, and got caught in a huge traffic jam on NASA Road One, directly in front of the art department. I could still see Bob thirty yards away, yelling at someone on the phone, smoking a Vantage. There was nothing to do but sit there. Movie job anxiety began to creep into my mind as my truck overheated.

–6–

Because the movie business is so transitory, you never know when you are out of a job for good. Maybe it's inherent in an industry where your job is always ending, but most people I know in this business, no matter how experienced and secure, get a little worried when a particular movie they're working on ends. It's that unknown factor, when and where the next job will come, that's unsettling. The work always seemed to find me, though. Back in Austin, I heard that Cary White was putting together an art department for a new film called *The Hot Spot* to be directed by Dennis Hopper and starring Don Johnson, Virginia Madsen, and Jennifer Connelly. They had already set up an art department in Taylor, Texas, a small, cotton and maize farming community thirty miles north of Austin. Cary had hired Ed Vega as his lead scenic. Needing a second to help Ed, they hired me.

The Hot Spot was appropriately named; we were doing the prep work in August in Texas. I was basically Ed's horse and did much of the straight painting while he concentrated on the signs and fiberglass limestone in the 110-degree heat, twelve hours a day, six days a week. I was working and sweating one of those hot days inside the main set, the Harshaw Used Car Lot, when one of the early scouts came through with Hopper the director, Don Johnson, Jennifer Connelly, and several others. Johnson was smoking Lucky Strikes and busy looking cool and bored. Hopper was hopping around, talking very fast, and trying to give Johnson and Connelly a mental picture of an upcoming scene. He also seemed to be trying to get at least some reaction from the two actors who looked like they had the emotional range of plywood.

"See man, this is what we're trying to do. Go out this window of your office here. See, you catch the murals there, we can see 'em. It's sort of a fishbowl effect, you know what I mean? An' see, look, we can see," he pointed to where the starlet Connelly would be sitting across the lot, "we can shoot right up her dress from here. That's where her desk is."

Everyone laughed lightly, except for Johnson.

"So," Hopper said to his big-money star, "Whadda ya think, man? Whadda ya think?"

Johnson nodded his head, obviously unimpressed, and gave a wooden reply. "Oh yeah. Great."

Hopper seemed irritated but tolerant. As the director, he would have to carry the show. The director on any movie is really the bottom-line guy. It's often up to this person to have the energy to see a project through, to give a damn when no one else does and set the tone for a production. If a director is dedicated, talented, worthy of respect, and lucky enough to have a good script and good actors, you can have a good movie. If the director acts like a schmuck, like say, Anson Webber did, whom we know as Potsy from *Happy Days,* on his forgettable TV movie *Home by Midnight,* filmed in Austin, then your movie's going to suck. Dennis Hopper is no schmuck, but his stars were and his script sucked. Therefore, well, go rent the movie for 49 cents at your local video store and you'll see.

Hopper kept moving around the set, excitedly, explaining scenes. "Great, great, O.K. Don, let's go over here to the other office. I want you to check this out."

Johnson, talking to Connelly, ignored Hopper.

"Don? Don?" Hopper asked, leaving the set, trying to get his attention.

"Huh?" Johnson said, not listening.

"If uh . . . if you could just follow me over to this other set. . . "

I almost felt sorry for Hopper, having to deal with Johnson for the next three months, but who knows? I'm sure Dennis Hopper the actor has done his share of aggravating directors over the years. Maybe it was justice. Still, Johnson was making several million off the project. His director probably expected a little enthusiasm for that, if nothing else.

As they left, I continued to paint the trim inside the set. A working technician, I'd been ignored and walked around during the tour.

Sometimes I was told to leave when a big scout came through a set, or I left on my own, not wanting to get in the way. This time, having a lot to do, I'd stayed. Beaten down by the August heat, my insignificant station in life, paint fumes, and sweating profusely, I heard a noise behind me and turned. The young star, Connelly, was standing there in the doorway of the set, looking at me. The sunlight was coming through her long hair and short skirt. Her perfect face expressed no emotion. I'd heard she was a model making thousands an hour before this job in Japan. She stared at me for several seconds, until it became awkward. I broke down and said, "Hello." As if on cue, she turned, left the set, and joined the others in their well-paid group. I went back to painting.

I say I almost felt sorry for Hopper, stressing the *almost*. The man was an American icon, a successful actor and director, making very good money. His new, young wife was the true object of my envy for him. Twenty-three-year-old Katherine La Nasa was a former ballerina who was working in our art department as a set dresser. Most of the men on the crew watched her movements with no small amount of lust. I particularly fell for her and let her know in subtle, non-existent, imaginary ways, I was available if she wanted to leave her extremely successful clean and sober and rich husband for a burgeoning alcoholic, drug-addicted painter. Surprisingly, she didn't take me up on it. Katherine, however, was a big flirt, prone to doing stretching exercises in front of me in short shorts at the drop of a hat, and more than once, she had some fun at my frustrated expense. The worst time was when we were upstairs together in the large house that would belong to Virginia Madsen and her wealthy husband in the script. We were in Madsen's character's bedroom and the idea was to make it a sex den, since her character fucks her husband to death in one ridiculous scene. I was trying my hardest to be entertaining and somehow cool with Katherine as I painted two columns phallic pink next to a large sunken tub we'd installed. Katherine was dressing the bed with stuffed animals, talking to me about, well, sex, rolling languidly on the bed as she spoke, turning on her stomach and then on her back. As she got up from the bed, she straddled a very large Teddy bear and stopped there with both legs wrapped around his back. She looked at me for what I felt was a definitive moment, smiled leeringly, and began to hump on the bear as though she were having sex. All coolness gone, I dropped my paint brush. She got off the bear laughing and left the room. I had fantasies for days on that one, until Ed and I accidentally locked her inside the bank set one day where she was stranded for hours. She came out fuming, complaining to a set dresser friend of mine, Joe Self, "That fucking drug addict painter locked me in there," and my imaginary romance was over.

The town of Taylor was just as smitten with Don Johnson as I was with Katherine La Nasa. The poor saps, *Miami Vice* fans, I guess, lined the streets in the hopes of seeing this actor. They had their autograph books ready (to no avail) in hopes of seeing a star. And Johnson kept up with his big star image, bodyguards flanking him, flying to the set every day in his own helicopter, being chauffeured everywhere. A brand new black BMW waited on set every day for Johnson, a Teamster driver inside, the car's engine and air-conditioning running, lest the man should break out in a sweat on his way from the trailer to the set. Of course, none of the Taylorites ever got near Johnson, which compounded their disappointment when the movie left town.

But Johnson did give us on the crew a few glimpses of himself, when he had his bodyguards yank the cameras off the wrinkled necks of friendly old tourists who'd somehow reached the set. I watched as a co-worker, an overly friendly location manager who had the sheer audacity to touch Johnson's arm when saying "Good morning," got picked up and slammed down by *his* neck by another bodyguard. And there was the afternoon Ed Vega and I watched this pillar of the community Johnson making out heatedly with his young co-star Connelly between takes, while his wife, the actress Melanie Griffith, was delivering their baby, Dakota, in an Austin hospital.

While Johnson smooched with Connelly and did that thing in front of the camera, uh, acting, I was cleaning out brushes in the old grease pit that was behind our art department. Movies are notoriously cheap when it comes to renting an art department warehouse and this one was no different. Ed Vega and I were sequestered in the back of the old, dilapidated warehouse. We shared a space with the special effects crew, run by Dennis Dean and his relatives out of L.A. In keeping with the Special effects sleaze factor, Dennis seemed to be more concerned with snorting cocaine next to our paint shop and procuring large-breasted strippers from Austin's topless bars than with special effects. Dennis was constantly running around at a frantic, but friendly, pace, and those of us in the art department were wondering when disaster would strike.

The primary reason for Dennis being there was the big fire scene where he would attempt to make a building look like it was burning down without, hopefully, burning it down. This would involve lots of propane, butane, gasoline, hundreds of feet of pipe, gasoline jelly, gigantic flames, and falling timbers. We were naturally worried since open flames and coke don't mix, unless you're freebasing, and even then it's not a good idea.

The scene called for Johnson setting the fire so he could cause a distraction and rob the local-yokel town bank. When the big fire day came, a small disaster did strike. Dennis Dean had hired a few local people to help man the gas flames including a local movie worker named John Huke, who was on the fringe of the Austin film community and billed himself as an artist. Coupled with another movie worker, Rob Janecka, they were known as the local Styrofoam and sculpture guys. Though Huke had left me hanging several times with crappy work, I didn't think he should be burned up. Huke was hired by Dennis Dean as a day player, to work when he needed him. The set dresser, Joe Self, who was helping with special effects, had recommended him, an important detail when the lawsuits started flying. Unfortunately for Huke, Dennis Dean needed him on the day of the big fire scene where, after the first rolling, he was promptly set on fire by an invisible igniting cloud of gas seeping from a poorly connected pipeline. Huke went running down the stairs where he was put out and then told to wait a moment since, well, they were still rolling and he'd be in the shot. The show must go on, I suppose, no matter what, even if you set people on fire or cut off their heads with errant helicopters like John Landis did to Vic Morrow and those two children in *The Twilight Zone*. Having seen a number of movie accidents, many involving electrocution and burns, one wonders whether there shouldn't be tighter controls, at least somebody monitoring the filming conditions and the special effects departments, whose fires and explosions can easily get out of control. Of course, if they do kill you while making a movie, and you're half-assed important, you might get a small dedication at the end of the picture.

On *The Hot Spot* I got an interesting look at a day in the life of a stunt coordinator, a man named Eddy Dono, whom I heard others call Eddy Don't Know. Mr. Dono came out to a set we were building one day near Smithville, Texas. The scene was to be a steamy one where Virginia Madsen, after screwing Don, tells him she's pregnant and jumps, completely naked, off a giant tower into a mountain of sawdust below, climbing back up the sawdust so vigorously she aborts her baby. I'm not sure who thought up this stupid scene, but Virginia Madsen wasn't going to make the jump herself. We were out on the location, an abandoned lumber mill, finishing up the wooden tower. I took a break to smoke a joint and practice my shooting using guns I borrowed from the construction coordinator, Dave Wilt. Eddy Dono came up with a young woman and asked where the outhouse was. He escorted the woman to a port-a-can and, after watching her take her clothes off (jeans and a T-shirt) to change into, uh, jeans and a T-shirt, escorted her to the top of the wooden tower. He had her jump off about a ten-foot drop to the sawdust a few times. He escorted her back to the port-a-can where he watched her disrobe again, and they both left, another hard day's work done.

Having slaved like a mule for several months on *The Hot Spot* , I was thoroughly sick and tired of the movie business. Ed left town a little early for personal reasons. I finished up the show and foolishly agreed to do another one that was starting immediately. Cary White, the show's designer, asked me to be the painter.

The movie was a hopeful television pilot called *A Pair of Aces* starring Willie Nelson and Kris Kristofferson. This show found our favorite, renegade country stars as, what else, a couple of reluctant detectives, one a lawman, one a bandit, forced to solve the case together. I don't know. I think there's something wrong with the world when Willie and Kris have to be detectives.

As usual, even though I didn't consider myself really a painter, I took to the job dutifully and compulsively, trying to do my best, operating on the Zen premise that if you don't at least do your shit job right, you'll never do anything right. I hired a competent scenic named Karen Luzius to help me out for a few weeks and bored her with my frustrations with the movie business as we worked. At the end of shooting, I went so far as to give Karen many of my scenic tools, Hudsons, a ladder, and tint racks, with the announcement that I was leaving the movie business. Karen, older and wiser than me, said she'd hang on to them until I came back. Many people talk about leaving the business but, once you're in it, unless you're forced out, you usually stay. I told Cary White the same thing on my last day. He stopped me outside of the art department and mentioned a TV movie in Montana called *Son of*

Morning Star and asked if I'd like to be his lead scenic on it. I told him no, that I was going back to school to finish my degree, that I was through with the movie business. Like Karen, I could tell he met this statement with skepticism. Even though working on a movie could be trying, it was still better than a lot of other jobs out there.

−7−

As soon as I finished *A Pair of Aces* I realized that I'd been doing too much cocaine on that movie and really every other movie I'd worked on. There were always a few people around the crew doing it then, in the eighties, and even though it wasn't fun anymore and I'd been hospitalized for it twice, I still couldn't seem to turn it down. Coming to the conclusion, finally, that I was addicted to the stuff, I decided to take some time off before the semester started and dry out. The last time I'd tried to dry out, I'd sold everything I owned and moved to a small town in England for several months. This time, I figured I'd take the cheap route and just go to West Texas, specifically to a little-known spot on the border below Marfa called Kingston Hot Springs.

I unplugged my answering machine, filled the truck up, took some money out of savings, packed up my typewriter and some supplies and left Austin, heading west for I-10. Ten hours later, at Fort Stockton, I turned off on US 67 and headed toward Alpine, and on to Marfa, pushing my truck to the limit. I was hurrying. Speeding. Rushing toward something. I turned off on RR 2810 and was deep in the desert. The radio was now dead. No one passed me on the highway. Tumbleweeds blew across the road. I saw one truck, an old man in a cowboy hat driving thirty miles an hour. I sped around him at seventy.

My instructions from Dot and Bill, the people I'd spoken to at Kingston, were that the road would become unpaved after thirty-two miles. Even though I kept track of the mileage, it still caught me by surprise when the road changed to bumpy gravel. I skidded all over the place and slowed to thirty miles an hour. The land was flat around me, covered with orange and red weeds with white tufts at the ends of their stalks, which gave the land a deceivingly soft appearance. I saw brown and green and purple mountains in the distance and drove toward them.

After several miles, I entered Mustang Canyon. I had to really slow down then. The road became steep and filled with sharp curves, deep drop-offs. I stopped at one point, got out of the truck, and admired the beautiful canyon around me. After a few minutes of admiration, I got back in the truck and sped on, reminding myself: slow down, no need to go off a cliff now. I saw an old abandoned mining operation, drove through its grounds, and kept on. A friend of mine, Barbara Haberecht, had told me, it seems like you're never going to get there, but then you do. Searching, I saw a sign that told me I had seven miles to go. I made a wrong turn and got a little lost. I was down in an immense valley. Whenever I reached a hilltop, I saw a few dirt roads heading off into different directions. I luckily got back on track and saw a sign: Hot Springs, three miles. I saw a rattlesnake on the road. As I drove past it I saw it was dead, run over. A hundred yards later, I slowed for a tarantula crossing the road, moving its legs slowly. I came to a large sign made from limestone rocks painted white and laid on the ground in six-foot letters to read: Hot Springs. There was a little arrow pointing the way. I followed the arrow around a hill, saw a few white boxes, bee hives, and drove down into a small valley.

There were seven cabins painted light brown with dark roofs. I saw an old woman leaning up against a cabin, sitting on the ground. From her posture and strange mannerisms, she appeared to be insane. A small fox terrier ran around her and barked and she spoke to the dog conversationally in a loud voice. Well, I figured, I'm here. I had a thought that maybe everyone there was insane. That this was a place for people who'd lost their minds. I remembered that Barbara tended to be a little unstable herself.

I stopped at the first cabin. It had a sign that read "Office" and a satellite dish out front. About thirty cats, a huge array, ran around in the small rock yard. An ancient man opened the screen door and peeked out. He wore old blue jeans and a white T-shirt with holes in it, stretched ridiculously by his enormous gut. He had a few scraggly strands of white hair on his head, some faded, misshapen blue tattoos on his arms. I got out of my truck, stretched, and told him my name was JR. He said hello, and told me to follow him inside the house, to the kitchen.

"Have a seat," he said.

I sat at his table. I noticed a can of Skoal, a pack of Carltons. He returned with a card for me to fill out and told me I was in cabin 4. I saw pictures of daughters and sons on the walls. His name was Bill and he had at least half a can of snuff in his mouth. He pulled up a green plastic trash can filled with dirty napkins, and spit, or rather, opened his mouth, and let loose a pint of tobacco and saliva into the can. He also carried with him a quart jar full of slightly brown half-and-half he sipped on, he said, all day for his heartburn. His skin was pink and nicotine yellow, filled with wrinkles and pockets of wrinkles and wrinkles inside the wrinkles. Long white hairs hung out of his nose and ears. He said I could switch to a single cabin in a few days. They were all reserved right now. He said there was a little store over there across from his house. I looked out the door and saw it: Dee's Place. I signed some papers. Bill said his wife, Dot, was in O.J. over in Mexico. He hoped she got back soon.

"She shoppin' or somethin'."

He walked, or shuffled, out of the house and led me to my room. He turned on the lights, showed me the electrical outlets, opened the icebox.

"This here's a jug of water. You want some more you cun get it from the tap outside over yonder."

"Great, thanks."

"Here's a table. Four chairs. This is a double, we'll get you a single when one opens up. We got people comin' in, I think. Let's go outside."

I followed him out. He pointed to a small brown shack with a red roof. "Those're ya bathrooms. Down there's the hot baths. Let's go look at them."

He walked down the wide steps slowly, so I followed him slowly. We stopped at a three-inch pipe: water ran from it into a little clear pool. From the pool, the excess water flowed through a small ditch down toward a small creek. High pink and white cliffs rose above the other side of the creek. Large cottonwoods lined its banks. Bill showed me one of the baths. He pulled a bath mat off the bench and threw it on the floor.

"I'll just put this here. See, ya got a light here on the inside. In the uh, in the other. . . bath. It's outside. We had this one tiled a while back."

I looked at the pink and cream tile. "Yep."

He turned on a large rusty spigot that hung over the tub and water came gushing out. "This water's a hunnerd an eighteen degrees."

"That's pretty hot."

"Uh-huh."

We stood there. "That's it," he said.

"O.K."

"Uh-huh." He walked out, turning off the light and I followed him back up the steps.

"You need anythin', you just holler," he said. "I'll be right up here."

"Thanks, Bill."

I quickly unpacked all the things in my truck. Two suitcases, hanging clothes, CD player, my CDs, my typewriter, typing paper. I stood there, outside the cabin. A dull roar filled my ears. I didn't have any cigarettes. My noble plan was to come out there with no tobacco and quit. I almost ran up to Dee's place. A sign said they had a few groceries and to go around back if no one was there. At the bottom it said: Have a Happy Day.

I went around back and knocked on an aluminum screen door of a small house attached to the store. I saw an old man stand up and put on his cowboy hat and glasses inside the house. He slowly walked out. He was about five nine and wore a black vest, jeans, and boots. His head was real big. His eyes were blue and glazed and he looked at me with a tilt to his head like he was confused or couldn't hear me.

"Howdy."

"Hello," he nodded.

"I was wondering if I could buy something from your store here. Actually, I was wondering if you had some cigarettes."

"No, don't have any cigarettes. They're too expensive now."

"Damn. Do you sell any tobacco ? Skoal? Plug? Anything."

"I'm afraid not. I've got some here that I smoke. Got 'em from the commissary in Presidio. I can let you have a pack of those, I guess."

"That would be great. I'll pay you for them."

"Just a second."

He went back into the house, slowly, and came back with a pack and handed them to me. We walked toward the store.

"Those're generic," he said. "They're O.K. They don't have filters. I think they're Chesterfields." He stopped from unlocking the door and turned to me. "I'm Jack."

I shook his hand. "Oh, my name's JR."

"Oh yeah?" He gave me a funny look.

Inside the store, I bought a few cans of ravioli, some beans, and Rolaids. He had a very little bit of everything in there—from Summer's Eve disposable douches to canned Spam. He told me the difference in the price of cigarettes at the commissary and in regular stores in Presidio. I thanked him profusely for the pack he'd given me (he wouldn't take money for it) and went back to my cabin.

I met with Dot outside my cabin and we talked about the purple mountains in the distance. She said they were in Mexico. She was very nice and sweet and offered to do my laundry, to which I said yes. I watched Bill feed his cats five pounds of canned dog food. I think I typed some. A loud couple, with children, moved in next door. I heard them sniff a few times, blow their noses, and cough. I thought they might be doing coke, which was a stupid thought, but one that showed where my mind had been for the past few years. I'd brought a small amount of marijuana with me for an emergency, but didn't smoke any of it. I listened to my CD player, my salvation. I told myself again and again how glad I was I'd brought it. To break the silence.

I went out for a walk down the creek and up a hill. I looked at the mountains around me, the mesquite, the boulders, the dirt. I felt a profound sense of loss and self-pity. I was truly alone now and felt I didn't exist. I wondered how Cary White, Dave Wilt, and the others were doing on their movie up in Montana. I'd heard Cary had tapped Ed Vega for the lead scenic position. I went back to my cabin depressed. I drank several beers I'd bought in Marfa. I typed some, read some, smoked too many cigarettes, and went to sleep.

The next day, I woke up at I don't know what time. I typed in my room. I saw Jack sitting out at a picnic table, looking dignified in his black vest and cowboy hat. He was smoking his generic Chesterfields. I remembered the day before when he told me he'd smoked Camels since he was seventeen. Putting him at over seventy, he'd been at it a while. The fingernails on his left hand, his smoking hand, were yellow, nicotine-stained, and crumbling off. The nails on his right hand were still smooth. He had to take a deep breath after every four or five words.

I watched him speaking with the nice family, who were now leaving, and I typed away.

I moved to a single cabin with a private bath down by the creek. One afternoon, that first week, I walked over to where Jack sat under an overhang in front of the store at a table. We started talking. He told me that he had two sections of land, that he'd married into the land. We watched his dogs, Duke, Suzy, and Sweet Pea. He said he was partial to dogs. That Bill over there was a cat man. That Bill dipped three cans of snuff a day and "was messy with it." Spat all over the place. That Dot chewed tobacco, too. He said Bill was trying to lose weight with a new thing called Slim-Fast. That Bill drank a quart of half-and-half a day. That he, Jack, liked to sic his dogs on Bill's cats but that they were just playing with them. That Bill was his brother-in-law.

He asked me what I did. I told him I was a painter. I said I painted the sets on movies. We talked about *The Alamo* being made in Bracketville. He told me his daughter had been in it as an extra. "She fed chickens all day on the street with a Mexican woman." That the little girl was now a geologist.

"She got to meet Happy Shahan," he said.

"Yeah, I've met Happy."

"He was a friend of John Wayne's," Jack said, as though the actor were akin to God.

"Happy is John Wayne," I said.

"Huh?"

"Nothing."

Jack went on, telling me he'd been a welder for years, and a bus driver, and had retired from a concrete plant in San Antonio. His wife was in San Antonio now, but she'd left him some homemade frozen dinners. We talked a little politics. He asked about my set painting and, I told him how I'd accidentally fallen into movie work but that I was sick of it now. I said I felt like I was wasting my life working on movies.

"Well," he said, "my momma used to say to me, each day is like a life. An' you're born in the mornin', grow old during the day, an' ya die at night. So every once in a while, you better pay attention to what you're doin'."

"Yeah, I guess so," I said. "It's just that the money is good and it seems like you're doing something important but. . . I don't know. I feel like I might be missing something if I leave it."

Jack lit a cigarette and stood up from the table. "Yeah?" he said, uninterested, "Have you had supper yet?"

I said no. He walked inside the store and returned with two beef pot pies.

"What do you think about these? I never ate 'em before."

I said they looked fine and he went inside to put them in the oven. I petted the dogs. Soon, the pies were ready and we ate them. Still hungry, I asked if he had any ice cream and root beer. Sure enough, the man got up and went into the store and got me some. He also fixed himself a drink (it's Happy Hour, he said) and handed me a plastic U.T. cup and spoon. I made a float, two floats, and ate them. He sipped his drink. A bee landed in his whiskey glass and he took the bee out and set it on the table. We thought it was dead from the alcohol and started talking about toxins in paints, wearing respirators and welding. We watched the dogs fight over a bone. We talked about the hot springs. How mountain lions, coyotes, and wild boars were all over but the dogs usually ran them off. He guessed my age at thirty-three and I told him I was twenty-six.

"Whoa, sorry, I missed that one by a long shot," he said.

"I look a lot older than I am," I explained.

He said he was nosy and asked how much I made on those movies and I told him in detail. I started complaining again, telling him I wasn't going to work on them anymore, that I was going back to school, that I——

"Lookie here." He pointed to the bee which was now moving. "I thought he was dead. I guess he's just drunk. He might make it after all." He watched the bee struggle to get its legs dry, to stand on its feet. Jack pointed out all the different kinds of birds around me. He told me Bill was sleeping his life away. That himself, he didn't like beer. It made him mean. That milk gave him gas. A joke about a golfer, a genie, and a parish priest. I looked at the sign above his head: Have a Happy Day. He spoke of "the Mexican who kind-of screwed up my tile job in the baths" and about his old dog Spot, who was dead now. "His grave's up on the hill, by the hot springs sign. Sometimes he says things to me when I visit him. Go on up an' see it tomorrow."

I got up to leave and he asked me what I was typing.

I said I was writing a story.

"What's it about?"

"My favorite subject."

"What's that?"

"Me."

"Well, that's O.K. Maybe you can work Kingston Hot Springs into it. It can be the Kingston Hot Springs book."

I said maybe so, and walked back to my cabin.

That night, I went down to the creek and lay on a picnic table under a cottonwood tree. There was a giant white ring around the moon. I'd been dreaming about doing cocaine, and smoked a little dope to calm down. I hadn't smoked in days and it only made me paranoid. I heard a noise and jumped. I was far from peaceful. All I could think of was: MOUNTAIN LION. Duke was barking at me on the hill. He just wanted to check me out but, for an instant, I thought he might want to come bite me. I heard a rustle in the bushes and imagined a giant javelina with sharp tusks. Duke was suddenly there and I petted him. He smelled my hand and left. I did hear then the distinctive, unmistakable, but distant, growl of a mountain lion and practically ran back to my room. Wilderness Man. I got under the covers. I tried to read but my brain wouldn't work. All I could think of was cocaine and cigarettes and the movies. I got up and had another root beer float. I went to bed, turned out the lights, and lay there jumping at the noises of coyotes being chased by friendly dogs and cats playing on my roof.

In the morning, I ran a few miles, still jittery, mindful of tarantulas and rattlesnakes waiting to jump out and bite me in the neck. The high altitude made me even more short of breath than usual. I came back and took a hot bath in the springs. I changed clothes and went for a walk. On my way out, I said good morning to Jack and he asked me again to stop off on my way and take a look at Spot's grave up on the hill. So I did. I walked up that hill, past the bee hives, past the sign, and stopped at the top next to a small white cross. On the cross I read: A Faithful Companion, Our Dog Spot, 2-14-79 to 11-7-88. Under the cross, embedded in concrete, was a small rock with writing on it. It said: "Spot's rock." The grave itself was a large pile of big stones that were cemented together. Spot wasn't going anywhere. I looked at the mountains, back at the grave, and finished my walk. On my way back into the cabin area, I ran into Jack walking toward Bill's house.

"I'm going to go see Bill here," he said. "Did you see Spot's grave?"

"Yessir, I did."

"Did he say anything to you?"

I shook my head. "Not much."

Jack smiled. "He was always a quiet dog."

Time seemed to stop out there in the desert, or I was moving through it differently. I never knew what time it was. I woke up at dawn and ran five miles, took a dip in the hot springs, did some typing, and drank and ate with Jack in the afternoon. Typed and read some more, and hit the sack, sleeping better every day. A young couple showed up at camp one morning, Chip and Trish, two nice, smart people who ran Outward Bound type programs for poor kids in their off-time. They were on their way to Mexico, camping in their V.W. van at the hot springs with their dog. They were a nice break in the routine and I enjoyed visiting with them both.

One afternoon, on my way from taking a sulfurous hot bath, I stopped at their van and noticed they had left their dog there tied up, all alone. This was odd because their large Akita was always with them. I looked around and saw Jack running from his store as fast as his bent legs could carry him. Sensing something was wrong, I ran up the hill. Jack saw me, a look of panic in his eyes.

"What's wrong?" I asked him.

"Bill's hollerin' for me."

We ran to Bill's cabin and the old man came out walking unsteadily.

"Dot's had a heart attack," he said.

"Oh no," Jack said.

"We called the ambulance but, I don't think she's gonna make it," Bill said matter-of-factly.

Jack and I followed Bill into his small kitchen. A chair had been overturned and a foul smell permeated the room. I saw vomit all over the table and floor. Chip was breathing into Dot's slack mouth, and Trish had her shirt open, pumping Dot's white chest, the old woman's breasts shaking with each push. I asked if one or both needed me to spell them and they said no. Bill seemed shaken and confused.

"She'd just gone down to Presidio," he said, "to get some Fritos for some chili pie I made today. She bought a big bag and said she felt this pain in her side when she was coming home. I thought she was just hungry. She ate a whole bowl of Frito pie an' then just threw it up all over the table. Then she just fell over and died." He shook his head. "I don't know what to do," he said sadly.

"Come on outside," Jack said. "Come on outside, Bill."

They both shuffled out of the kitchen. The ambulance took another thirty minutes to arrive. Chip and Trish maintained CPR the entire time, only stopping as Dot was loaded into the ambulance, and then started it up again once inside. The ambulance sped away, up the hill.

Jack was worried about Chip and Trish being stranded at the hospital so far away. "Those kids jumped in that ambulance an left their car here," he said.

I told him not to worry, I was on my way to get them. I made the forty-five-minute drive to the hospital and found them in the emergency room. "She didn't make it," Chip said. "It was a huge attack."

"I think she was completely dead back there in the kitchen," Trish said.

Chip said they'd forgotten they didn't have a car and thanked me for coming. I told them that Jack was watching their dog and they were relieved. Both went to wash up.

"My beard's still full of chili vomit," Chip said.

Once in my truck, the young couple, who were seriously healthy eaters, confided in me that they sometimes came in from the wilderness and headed for a Dairy Queen. There was one in town, so I took them there and treated them to a couple of giant sundaes as a reward for their efforts. I'd never seen people enjoy ice cream more.

Trish and Chip left the hot springs the next day. All of the sudden I realized I'd been there for over a month and started to feel restless. Bill thanked me for my help and I told him I hadn't done anything. I gave Jack a carton of Camels I'd bought in town and he thanked me profusely, as though I'd given him gold. Bill talked briefly of Dot and seemed the same as he always was, a little dazed, and went off to open fifteen cans of dog food for the cats.

The next day, he and Jack and four other friends, all over seventy, sat on the porch of Dee's place and discussed arrangements for Dot's funeral, trying to decide what she should wear in the casket and who would bury her. There was some controversy over the latter, for they knew a man with a backhoe, but he was "retarded now" Jack said and might not be able to dig the hole in the right place. As they spoke, the afternoon sun struck the porch, warming us all up, and each person, slowly, one by one, fell asleep, their chins on their chests. I looked at Jack. At Bill, his wild, white hair blowing around his sleeping head. It was time to go home. That evening, before the sun set, I packed my things in the truck and said my good-byes.

"You come back an' see us," Jack said. "We like you. You can stay as long as you want."

I thanked him and drove away, making the long trip home, back to Austin, not ready to go to sleep just yet.

—8—

I did go back to the university and got my degree, but I never completely cut myself off from the movie pipeline, in the off chance that I'd need the money and have to jump back in and eat all my lofty words. After eight months of being a broke college student, I began my last word meal and picked up the phone, calling my contacts. The first thing I did was the wrap or restoration painting in Lockhart, Texas, for a terrible Sissy Spacek movie called, I don't know what it was called. Thoroughly broke, my only transportation a broken down truck my co-worker Rodney Brown had given me, I charged a pay phone call to my parent's phone number to call Cary White and ask him for a job on *A Pair of Aces II* . By some accident of programming, the first *Pair of Aces* had done unusually well in the ratings, enough to warrant a sequel. Cary was the designer, Dave Wilt the construction coordinator, and they hired me as their lead scenic, advancing me enough petty cash to get my tools out of the pawnshop.

My primary project on *Pair of Aces II* was to paint about three hundred feet of tall wooden and plastic doors to look like rusty steel and tin so they could be exploded for the big, I guess, explosion scene. I had lots of other things to paint as well and paint I did. When the big scene came around, I stayed on the set late into the night and watched them explode my doors, all my work all over the parking lot. The director was Bill Bixby, one of the nicest TV directors I ever met. He took pains to make people feel comfortable and I liked his politics, especially when he stopped shooting for an expensive moment of silence on the set, when we heard the Gulf War had just started and we were bombing Baghdad. Then, war or not, it was back to filming. I felt that night, and on many others, that somehow life was somewhere else. A nuclear war could have started in China, or Europe, even Iowa, and we would've kept shooting. There was simply too much money on the line during filming to stop for decapitated children, burning artists, or World War III.

After *A Pair of Aces II* , I called John Burson, a carpenter foreman from *Lonesome Dove* who was now a construction coordinator. I found out he was doing a low-low-budget movie of the week for CBS called *Seduction in Travis County* starring Lesley Ann Warren and Peter Coyote, both making several hundred thousand dollars for their noble efforts. John Frick was going to be the production designer. He hired me as his lead scenic and I dutifully painted what I was told. This was difficult since pulling John Frick's teeth out with my left hand would have been easier than getting directions from him. I had whole houses to paint and a huge police station (yes) interior to do, and with them all shooting in a matter of days, I couldn't find my designer. When I did manage to corral him, Frick was more worried about whether paint was visible on the bottom of a door than about the whole set. Every day for me was fraught with work and worry.

The worry was unnecessary . This movie was so cheap it almost didn't matter whether we finished the sets or not. The producers were Casey Justice, the former stuntwoman, and Debra Simon , the former a.d., both from *Gideon Oliver.* None of us knew how they were suddenly our bosses, but it was a fact one had to be aware of in the movie business. At any time, you never knew when someone who once worked for you could be your boss, for any number of ridiculous reasons, few of them being merit. A good side-effect was it forced you to be nice to people. The other producer on the show, the real money man, was a guy named JC Hogue, or, as he liked to be called, "Doc."

Doc seemed like the quintessential low-budget sleazy producer. He took out ads in our local papers advertising his occupation and asking for an attractive Latin woman to be his escort. The crew found this out and set up a date, and one of the local male Teamsters, dressed as a woman, showed up for the disappointed and embarrassed Doc. I had the misfortune of sitting at a table with my producer at a party at a local overpriced restaurant in Austin called Katz's where Doc explained his nickname to me and a completely married friend of mine named Gail. He gave us, unasked, his whole story as he tried relentlessly to pick up an uninterested Gail. One of the most bizarre things about Doc was his

hairline that started across the center of his forehead. Worried about
hair loss, he'd had his hairline lowered or his forehead raised, something, the result being freakish and hard to view. He invited himself
over, after first sending a drunken John Frick over to ask Gail if she
wanted to meet Doc, and she had said no. Once at our table, he sat
much too close to Gail and ordered a glass of milk.

"I only drink milk in bars," he told Gail, as though his chastity
would impress her. "No alcohol for me."

"We don't have any milk up here," the waitress said, referring to
the upstairs veranda where we sat.

"Oh. Hmm. You don't have any milk?"

"We have some half and half," she offered.

"O.K.," he said, relieved, "a glass of half and half." He then
launched into why he was called Doc again, trying to impress Gail.
"You see, I'm not just a Hollywood producer. I know you probably
think I'm all about glamour and the movies and money and movie stars.
Don't get me wrong, I know a lot of movie stars. I've met several I can
call friends. But you won't catch me throwing my weight around.
That's not me. You see, Jane, can I call you Jane?"

"You can, but my name's Gail."

"Of course, of course," he said laughing. "I know that. It's a beautiful name. You see, Gail, what I'm interested in is real life. Are you
interested in real life?"

"Yes, I have to be, and you can take your hand off my knee now."

"Oh, I'm sorry. This place is so cramped. I guess I'm almost too
friendly sometimes. "

"I guess."

"Real life is what gets me, not all this movie stuff. You see, I used
to be, I mean I still am, a war photographer. In fact, I'm known around
the world as one. I was with the Contras down in Nicaragua and I was,
I can say now, helping them get weapons, setting traps, things like that,
recording everything with my camera. Yeah, it got pretty rough out
there. I remember once kneeling before a church and seeing a cow crying. The cow had seen so much hardship, she was crying her eyes out.
She was weeping. I thought it was a miracle and that was when I started drinking milk. I saw things you wouldn't believe. Lots of injuries,
death, uh, bombs and stuff, lots of injuries. I started patching up my
comrades out in the field, you know, a splint here and there, digging out

bullets from some poor freedom fighter with my combat knife. I became known to the peasants as El Medico, that means 'the doctor' in English."

Gail nodded, smiling. "Is that right?"

"Yeah, the Americans down there called me Doc, short for doctor. Soon, all the mercenaries throughout Central America wanted to know who Doc or El Medico really was." He chuckled and sipped his half-and-half. "I don't mind saying, I was quite famous. I wanted to stay and help with the war but I had my photography always calling me to leave. You see, I'm an artist first and. . . "

Because El Medico was ultimately my boss, I had to listen to his bullshit all night, nodding my head every now and then, smiling, trying to keep his grubby paws off my friend.

The wrap party for *Seduction in Travis County* was held in Bastrop where we had several sets, including a bar exterior that I'd spent days painting and we'd just burned down for a shot. The party was held in another, real Bastrop watering hole, the Oyster Bar dance room. It was O.K., except for when Peter Coyote decided to get up onstage with the band, grabbed a guitar, and entertained us with his musical talents. See, he was a musician as well as an actor (who knew?). After several terrible songs, he left the stage and danced with one of a few local, oh let's say, party girls, who seemed to show up wearing practically nothing at almost every wrap party I've ever been to. At the end of the night, in a gesture of magnanimity few could argue, Mr. Coyote (if that is your real name, Colonel Bat Guano) bought the crew a case of cheap champagne. To his embarrassment, there was some law against bringing alcohol into the Oyster Bar, a law that wouldn't be broken even over the loud protests of Peter Coyote. Not wanting to upset our star, and looking for yet another free drink, we dutifully followed him outside. He popped a few bottles open, passed the plastic cups around, and we all had a drink. Friends forever, he told us how great we and Austin, Texas were and promised he'd be back to work here soon. To neither mine nor, I'm sure, his chagrin, I haven't seen him since.

−9−

You have to be very careful around your superiors, not necessarily the actors, when the promise of "I'll be back soon with another movie" comes up. This is more often than not a ploy or warning sign, that you're going to be asked to bust your ass in a way you haven't done yet. Only interns and first- or second-time movie workers fall into the trap of "do this now and I'll be back later to give you a better job." This tactic goes right on up the ladder, to the top I'm positive: "do this (nude scene, dangerous stunt, horrible script) now and I'll gladly repay you for a hamburger on Tuesday. . . "

I was lucky, though, and had a few local movie patrons such as Cary White in Austin, Brian Stultz in Wilmington, Ed Vega in Santa Fe, Barbara Haberecht in Houston, people who were higher up or had more experience than me, who were always going to be working and could thus give me a lead. Unlike many other people in Austin, I didn't want to completely hitch my career wagon to the Cary White train, but when push came to shove I would. I was still broke, trying to procure tools and keep my truck running when the rumor mill started flowing about a new western series called *Ned Blessing* that would be penned by the successful writer, producer from *Lonesome Dove* , and local Austinite, Bill Wittliff. Mr. Wittliff had also written other good scripts for such movies as *The Black Stallion* and *Raggedy Man*, so we all had high hopes *Ned Blessing* would provide the much longed for steady work in our state. There was talk of a pilot for CBS. There was talk that this would be the next *Gunsmoke*. There was talk that we (the Austin art department) would work for six months straight. Mainly, though, there was talk.

Because of such talk, I turned down a cable movie that was to start in Brenham, Texas, called, and this is true, *The Last Prostitute Who Took Pride in Her Work*. It was to star Sonia Braga and that kid Will from *Star Trek, The Next Generation*. John Burson was the construction coordinator, John Frick the art director, and the production designer a flamboyant man named CR Holloway from New Orleans. Waiting for *Ned Blessing*, I recommended Karen Luzius for the job and she was hired. A few weeks later, because of fights with the network , *Ned Blessing* was pushed back, way back, and I was out of work. I called Karen to see if she needed any help and she asked me to come down as she was having trouble with the designer, CR.

I packed up my tools and went to Brenham, where I quickly saw the problem wasn't Karen or her work, but a bitchy CR. The man hated Karen for some reason, which is odd, because she's probably the nicest person I've ever met in the movie business, which made it all the more difficult when CR had John Burson fire her a week and a half before shooting was completed. Needing the money more than feeling good about myself, I went along with it, lamely taking up for Karen with CR when he told me she'd be leaving.

"You're in charge now," he said.

"CR, there's no need to do this. Karen hasn't done anything wrong and I'm going to probably leave the show early anyway."

"You are? Why?"

"*Ned Blessing* is supposed to start. We're only talking about a week or so."

"I guess I could fire both of you then."

"Yeah, you could, or keep us both on."

"It's you or her," he said. "I don't have the budget for both."

I thought about it for two minutes and decided: better her than me. Karen was told she was fired with no warning and she approached me that day, her last, with tears in her eyes, asking me if I'd known she was on the way out. I had for days but told her, no, I didn't. I was becoming movie slime.

The work on *The Last Prostitute* was arduous and hot. We painted several barns, houses, the usual. The star, Sonia Braga, was around the set often. A rather earthy woman, she wore little clothing, a slip, a bra and panties, loose halter tops, her breasts falling out regularly, entertainment for the crew. She was talking to me one day on the set about horses, a sick colt she'd bought and was lighting candles for, when John Burson's dog, Mattie, walked up and began to urinate. Mid-conversation, Ms. Braga stopped. "Oh, look at this little dog peeing," she said, and squatted down on the ground and simulated urination, walking away, oh, ten feet, in this squatting urinating pose. When she began to bark like a dog, I assumed we were through talking and went back to my real love, painting barns.

The special effects boys burned that barn down and we finished *The Last Prostitute Who Took Pride in Her Work.* I was ashamed to tell people I'd worked on it for the title alone. When it aired, my shame deepened. Relatives from all over the country called me on this one to tell me how bad it was. I never saw it, but took their word for it.

Ned Blessing finally happened but was far from a blessing. We filmed the TV pilot up in a mock-western town built for the movie *Red-Headed Stranger* on some land Willie Nelson owned up in the Hill Country, near the Pedernales River. We called the town "Willieville." Mr.Nelson also had an attractive cedar cabin up there. A lot of his cronies, roadies, and old friends lived up there in the hills near Willie's house. They seemed to have no job other than the worship of Willie Nelson, who by their own account had done many good things for them. These men helped with security before and during filming and would seem to appear out of nowhere, bearded phantoms emerging from the cedars briefly, then disappearing again, taking a few two-by-fours or the odd piece of plywood or gallon of paint we didn't need.

I say Willie owned the land. I think he still did, but this was around the time he was having serious problems with the IRS and two of their agents showed up in the western town one day to see what we were doing. A mutual friend and former sound man for Willie, Little Joe, introduced me to Willie one afternoon. Willie was there in his jogging outfit with one of his children and we talked for a while in a plastic and plywood bank I was painting as limestone. He and Little Joe asked if I would paint Willie's house up on the hill, spray a sealer on the cedar. I said I would until a few days later when discussing my fee with Little Joe, I got the IRS sob story and was asked to maybe, you know, do it real cheap, maybe even for free, and I said forget it. I said I'd paint Willie's other home in Hawaii for free if he flew me there, but not the one near Austin.

Our producer, Bill Wittliff, had finally settled his differences with the CBS executives. It seems they wanted a no-talent, pretty-boy, Lorenzo Lamas type for the main character, Ned Blessing, and Bill wanted a rough and tumble guy. They settled on the heaviest and least attractive Baldwin brother, Daniel, and we started production. The unit production manager, Robin Clark, was a tightwad, like most u.p.m.'s, and told the art department again and again we had no money to refurbish the old town and then didn't give us any to prove it. Every gallon of paint I ordered was questioned by Mr.Clark, as was most of the wood bought by the construction coordinator, Dave Wilt. Our accountant, Miller, acted as something of a shield between Robin and me, but by the end of the show, the man had become so petty, I couldn't stand it. One hot August day in Willieville I was on top of a thirty-six-foot ladder on a rotten saloon porch, covering a building and myself with paint when I was called off of my work by someone and told I had an important phone call. I ran to the phone in the security guard's RV and was told to hold on by Robin Clark. I waited and waited until he came back on the line.

"Yeah, J.R., I've been going over your gas receipts here and you're spending way too much money. You spent fifty dollars last week on gas."

"Well, I live over two hours away from here Robin."

"Listen, you need to get this straight, I'm not paying for your gas to get to work. It's for supply runs only."

"But you're not renting my vehicle and I'm using the hell out of it up here and on supply runs. Plus, out of four extra hours per day of driving, I'd think I should get some compensation for drive time, like a few gas receipts."

"That's not gonna happen on this show. I'm cutting your gas to twenty dollars a week."

"Oh c'mon, Robin, twenty dollars? How about forty?"

"No way."

"Thirty-five?"

There was a long silence with only the creaking sound of Robin's wallet. "You can claim thirty dollars of gas receipts on your petty cash. And that's it."

"Fine."

"And when are you guys gonna be through? You've been working two weeks. We shoot in a week and then you're all gone, right?"

"I don't know. That's up to Dave Wilt and Cary White."

"No , it's up to me."

"Robin, I really don't care. I have to go back to work now."

"You do that," he said and hung up.

I climbed back up my rickety ladder. This man Robin was making four, five thousand dollars a week and he got a percentage of whatever we came in under budget. Since we had one more week of prep, he'd pulled me away from work to make himself another twenty dollars on my gas receipts. Counting his hourly rate and mine, he'd actually lost money in the process. This is what angered me the most about some u.p.m.'s. Robin played golf every other day and took long mid-day naps in his room, and yet bothered to chase down my puny (and in the scheme of the movie business), low-paid ass to try to save a nickel. There were other areas of waste, such as his salary and the actors' salaries, so huge, I couldn't fathom his actions. It was the same on many movies, though. The u.p.m. was always anxious to get rid of art department personnel, mainly construction, as quickly as possible, probably because we were the lowest on the rung and the easiest to pick on. Robin had no idea how Dave Wilt or I operated, how we purchased our materials as sparingly as we possibly could, buying the cheapest items we could get away with, not so much to save the company money, as to stay within our allotted budgets and at least have enough materials to do our jobs and build and paint a set. At the end of a movie, we could point to where our money had gone if the company asked. Robin Clark could only point to his wallet while taking credit for our work.

Nevertheless, we finished the town and shooting began. At one point, we had to stop and do some reshoots, because Bill Wittliff had chosen a giant handlebar mustache for Baldwin to wear as Ned Blessing. CBS hated it and we redid some scenes and were laid off. All in all, it had been about three and a half weeks of work and we would have to wait and see if CBS liked it and would order more episodes. So much for the next *Gunsmoke*.

–10–

Completely broke, I started to get on the dole again, but received a call from John Burson and John Frick down in Houston where they were starting work on a two-part TV movie for NBC. Debra Simon and Casey Justice were the u.p.m. and producer. The show was another winner entitled *Trial:The Price of Passion*, starring Beverly D'Angelo, Peter Strauss, and Jill Clayburgh. Burson asked me to be the lead scenic and fax a resume to their production designer, a man from L.A. named Paul Peters. I found out later that Paul was actually from San Antonio, but having made his trek to movie mecca, he'd decided to stay there. Not even being a tiny big shot yet, I would have to work as a local, putting myself up, paying my own expenses, cutting heavily into my pay. I drove to Houston, found a decent apartment, and went to meet the designer.

Paul Peters seemed a dapper man, nice but distant, who didn't want to get too friendly with me because I might work for him and he didn't know me. I showed him my book, a collection of photos of my work, and he hired me.

Trial was a relatively easy show, as are most modern, TV productions. You had a lot of bedroom interiors, courtrooms, and, of course, a police station. Paul wasn't too demanding but, not trusting me (I was an unknown quantity), he hired out his two murals and a portrait of Beverly D'Angelo to be used in the film to an artist I didn't know. Paul found a man in Dallas who did the paintings, and when they were all finally delivered late, I had to fight to keep from laughing. Paul's face turned red as we unfurled the largest mural for the Harris County courthouse. It was of two nude men, both touching a torch or law book or something a la Michelangelo. Something had gone wrong perspective-wise and the men were malformed and contorted and frog-like to a noticeable degree. The smaller mural was O.K., though, and because of time, he had to go with them. It didn't really matter anyway because not much of it would be seen on the tiny TV screen. The portrait, though, was the worst. A different artist had done it, and mistakenly using realism, he had accented Ms.D'Angelo's somewhat buckteeth, an honest mistake. The actress took one look and said forget it. I don't know if they snuck that painting in front of the camera or not.

My own mistake on that show came one day as I was riding around with my designer Paul in his rented car. We were talking about pictures we liked and somehow football movies came up. Paul mentioned a feature filmed up in Dallas called *Necessary Roughness*. Had I seen it?

"Are you kidding?" I said. "That looked like a complete piece of crap."

We talked some more about movies. He mentioned a recent release, *Harley Davidson and the Marlboro Man*. Had I seen it?

"No way, you couldn't pay me to see that. It's just another stupid buddy movie and look at the buddies: Don Johnson and Mickey Rourke, two schmucks. I wonder what idiot had the idea to put those two ego-maniacs together? What's that movie about anyway? Are they lovers in it or something?"

"No, just another buddy movie," Paul said.

I'd been talking too much about some of the projects I'd worked on and, wanting to suck up to Paul, asked him what he'd been designing lately.

"I just finished two features," he said.

I had a sudden, sinking feeling. "Oh? What were they?"

"*Necessary Roughness* and *Harley Davidson and the Marlboro Man*."

It was a quiet ride then, back to the art department.

The shooting crew and the a.d.'s were particularly annoying on *Trial*. The director, Paul Wendkos, had a son named Jordan who was the worst kind of movie idiot, one who thinks he's smart and cool. Because his father was the director, Jordan had been made the second a.d., something I don't believe he'd ever done. A good second a.d. should be in touch with every detail of shooting, to the extent that the first a.d. is in control, as the voice of the director, of every aspect of the actual filming. The first, second, and third a.d.'s and their p.a.'s are people in a hurry, people acquiring, retaining, and dispensing a good deal of information, enough to completely take over their lives for the entire shoot. The director's son, Jordan, had not retained his ABC's, much less the actor's call times, the Teamsters' overtime, how many pages we were shooting that day, where the extras were and whether they had filled out their paperwork, filling out the next day's call sheet, who the police officers were who were holding traffic on busy downtown streets, and on and on. It was not a job for the faint-minded. But put a walkie-talkie headset on a monkey, stick him on a movie set, and he turns into a Gestapo officer, especially if his father's the director.

Jordan's main preoccupation on *Trial* was throwing people out of the food line at the caterer's wagon, especially people from the art department, if he could. Teamsters eat first, and construction and art along with them, allowing the more hurried shooting crew to come in once we're done. Jordan was always running to the line, checking to see if we were who we were in an excessively zealous manner. If he had anybody from the shooting crew with him, he'd try to move him or her in front of us in line. This often happens legitimately with say, an actor, the director, makeup, and the like on a big, legitimate production because of time and money. But not on *Trial: The Price of Passion*, where the entire crew usually ate together leisurely.

One of the members of our crew who wasn't white was almost ejected every day by Jordan. When one of my painters mentioned the man's dark skin color to Jordan and wondered if it had anything to do with his constant ejection, Jordan grew incensed, screaming at her that he wasn't a racist, to the doth-protest-too-much level. Myself, I was asked four times by the boy, who I was, what did I do, and did I belong in line. The fourth time, I might have decked the little bastard, had I not seen that day his sad performance on the set. You may not have to produce, that is, do what you're paid for, all day on a movie set, but when you do, when you're called upon, you better do it. You can fake it and fake it, but not at that moment. Jordan had flubbed that moment so many times he had become an irritating laughingstock on set. It was the reason why he was over at the caterers bothering people who had every right to be there and just wanted to eat their lunch. That day alone, filming was stopped twice, expensive time wasted, because Jordan was actually *in* the shot, just standing there in front of the camera, oblivious to it all. He was the guy who was supposed to be keeping people out of the shot. And yet he stayed on the picture, collecting paychecks, simply because he was the director's son. This was to no one's surprise, because nepotism abounds in the movie business. The Mafia is probably the only place where it is more prevalent.

Houston was a city under siege during the filming of *Trial*. The city has always been violent; I grew up there and had watched the nightly rape, murder, and robbery report grow since I was a child. There was a vicious crime wave going on now and everyone was scared. The head of the Teamsters in Houston, an affable man, and somewhat scary himself, named Ron Kearn was held up a few blocks away from our art department and production office, in broad daylight at a busy convenience store. He had a gun put to his back and his Rolex taken off his wrist. We figured if the head of the Teamsters gets hit so easily, we're all in trouble. It was the reason why John Burson, our construction coordinator, went with me when I had to do some painting in the downtown mission district in Houston, the local skid row. Burson, a still-heavily armed Vietnam vet, always had at least two pistols on him (a Texas construction coordinator requirement). I had a vision of Burson going into a production meeting, opening his briefcase widely to reveal its contents to the u.p.m., a loaded army issue .45 and maybe a few purchase order slips he needed signed, the .45 on top. I considered it a potentially brilliant negotiating maneuver when going over your deal memo with a tight-assed production manager. As I painted the skidrow building, Burson actually had his gun out standing beside me as I hurriedly rolled on my paint, shooing away my belligerent and drunken audience of about thirty defeated men. Sadly, most of the men just wanted a job, not to rob us, and their plaintive entreaties for work almost made the gun necessary. I had to wonder that afternoon about the disparity between the ridiculous amount of money being spent on this phony-baloney movie and the hundreds of destitute men and women lining Houston's streets, being run away from our sets, turned out of our food lines by the likes of Jordan Wendkos, or held at bay with guns by me and Burson.

I went to the wrap party for *Trial* because there was a free bar. The main reason I went, though, was to try out my new celebrity theory: the more you ignore a celebrity, the more he or she will seek you out in direct proportion to the extent of their insecurity. Most actors want attention, not just onscreen, but offscreen as well, offscreen even more. At a social gathering such as a wrap party, or even just on the set, if you are a visible member of the crew, someone they might see every day and notice, and you completely ignore them, they'll usually find you and, at least, make eye contact. I'd seen the actor Peter Strauss several times on *Trial* and at the wrap party made a point of completely avoiding him, but at the same time, talking and laughing with several members of the crew who had been steadily kissing his ass throughout the show. Sure enough, at the end of the evening, I saw him coming. He was working through the crowd, people stopping him. I was parked at that free bar, getting drunk, and having a good laugh at the young Mr. Wendko's attempt to dance on the dance floor. Suddenly, like a springing shark, Peter Strauss was in my face. It was unavoidable. He said hello and introduced himself. I said hello back and shook his hand, not offering up my meager position on the film. I quickly and politely excused myself, and left him standing there. I think the poor guy actually thought I was somebody.

–11–

I went back to Austin after *Trial* to endure a severe dry spell on unemployment. After a few months, a low-budget TV movie of the week came to town and everybody, starving for work, jumped on it. Cary White was the designer, Sully his art director, Dave Wilt the construction coordinator. I was the lead scenic. The film was called *Dead Aim* and was to film at a mansion in the Bastrop area and at a farmhouse between two small Texas towns, Lockhart and Niederwald. The farmhouse we were to use belonged to one of the Spillman brothers with whom I'd gone to high school, and it turned out to be one of the times when a movie came into someone's home and left it in better shape then before. Mr.Spillman got six thousand dollars, a fixed-up house, and a new road for our filming in his house a couple of weeks.

The stars of *Dead Aim* were Marky Post and Mr. TV, Robert "Bang 'em Right Back" Urich. I'd seen Urich some on *Lonesome Dove*, but saw a lot more of him on *Dead Aim*, where he was the main star. I remember being in the main bedroom of the farmhouse one day, touching up the ceiling, waiting for the director and Cary to come in and give me an O.K. on the room so I could leave. They were shooting a dramatic scene at the front door, just outside the room, and I wanted to get out of there. I was waiting in a small bedroom just off the master, trying to stay out of the shot, when Robert Urich came in with two make-up and wardrobe women. Urich was covered in fake blood, his shirt ripped, and one pant leg cut open, his knee bandaged. In this scene he was to drive up in a truck and get out limping weakly and calling for his children, who were waiting with a p.a. inside to be released on cue. I watched a few takes and had the thought that maybe I could do this crap and get rich. Urich would step out of his truck, wince dramatically, and say, "Buffy! Jody!" whatever, and they ran out screaming, "Daddy! Daddy! Are you O.K.?" and Cut! that was it. They did that three times with the sound of money being deposited in the bank no doubt ringing in Urich's ears. But making a creative, Emmy-hopeful call the director (whom we called "One-Take Vince" because of his speedy shooting) thought he needed more blood and bandages. I waited in my room and listened to the actor and the two young make-up women. Both were on their knees before him as he sat in a chair, giggling and laughing at everything he said. One woman had a pair of scissors and cut his pant leg open to the crotch.

"Hey, be careful there," he warned.

She laughed. "I will."

"You don't want to hurt *that* leg."

Both women laughed. One began to wrap his thigh and he moaned in mock ecstasy. "Yeah, that's it. Wrap it higher, sweetheart," he said. "Higher, higher. . . "

The women both laughed, holding his thighs, dabbing on blood and bandages. They all began to talk of fun things to do in Austin. In fact, what are you two girls doing tonight? Maybe we could all get together and. . . I cleared my throat nosily and walked to the master bedroom to find an escape route. Urich saw me and gave me a get-the-fuck-out-of-here look, which I did, exiting the house quickly out the back door, leaving him to go back to work.

I got a glimpse later that afternoon of the bullshit that comes with being a celebrity, watching Urich outside after his blood and bandage scene. I was still waiting for an approval of my bedroom set (were the walls dirty enough? ceiling too white?) and watched several locals bugging Urich for autographs and info. He dutifully signed and talked with several local Lockhartians. After about fifteen minutes, though, he had to get back to work, to change clothes and act, or rather, be filmed in the next scene. One typical small-town Texas woman wouldn't let him go. On and on she talked, her husband standing next to her beaming and joining in the dialogue. After several polite "I have to go" attempts, Urich grew irritated. "Look, I'm sorry, I have to go back to work, alright?" The woman kept talking, oblivious. Urich just shook his head and walked off. The woman turned to her husband and said, "Well, that was just about the rudest thing I ever saw. I wasn't through talking and he just took off."

Her husband chimed in. "Yeah, I guess when you're a big-time movie star. . . " They said this loudly enough for Urich to hear. He turned slightly to look, shook his head again, and, to his credit, kept walking. I would have asked for my autograph back.

The other primary location we filmed at was a large Tara-style mansion outside of Bastrop, owned by a nice woman named Patsy. Her husband, a wealthy Texas businessman into the big three, oil, land, and cattle, had built her the home with its many rooms and giant columns and placed a plaque on the front door stating that this house represented their love. This house turned out to be just that and no more, though, since, as soon as it was finished, he left Patsy for his younger secretary and went to build the new woman her own mansion. The house had never been fully furnished or lived in, save for one small downstairs room where lonely Patsy stayed. Patsy, like so many others, thought the movies were going to lighten and entertain her life, and this time, in a small way, they did. Robert Urich was nice to Patsy, talking with her between takes, complimenting her gaudy home, even expressing interest, she told me, in purchasing one of two bluebonnet paintings she'd done and kept on display in her one furnished room. At the end of the shoot though as I did extensive painting repairs on her home, I saw the two paintings still in her room, while Patsy, the bustling crew now gone, wandered around her cavernous, empty home.

There was a small party at Cary White's house once *Dead Aim* was aired. Its name had been changed to *Stranger at My Door*. Titles of movies, especially those for television, are often changed, usually to something racier and more immediate. The title change didn't help, though. It was typical, melodramatic TV crap. I spent most of the party drinking in the kitchen instead of in front of the TV, not wanting to let it slip how stupid and pointless our hard work on *Dead Aim* had been.

–12–

I endured another dry spell on unemployment, watching the day-time talk shows, which, taken as a whole, seem to indicate that this country has lost its collective mind, waiting for my checks, trying to hang on to my telephone. It was a running joke now with Cary, Dave Wilt, and Burson that I couldn't keep my telephone connected, but it was true. I had to make long distance calls over the state and country maintaining contacts and looking for jobs. By the time I was laid off a movie, I had no money left for my giant phone bills. If I got another job quickly, I could keep it on. My phone was my only link to the movie business and I had to have it.

After several phone calls to Houston, before disconnection, I had another job on a cable movie called *Seven On, Seven Off* about two teenage boys working on an oil rig who get involved with a murder. It starred, among others, an older, much less cute Henry Thomas, the boy from *E.T.* CR Holloway, the former locations manager, now a seem-ingly color-blind production designer, was at the art department helm. John Burson was his construction coordinator. I struggled down to Houston in my now thoroughly beat-up pickup that drank three quarts of oil a day and painted the uneventful show, collecting my paychecks and cashing them quickly. I got tired of CR's bitchy little temper tantrums and forgetfulness, and had a small argument with him one day over wood-graining a door. The next day he threatened to put me on top of a giant oil rig in Galveston, spraying tinted Mop-n-Glo, so I toned down my stand, kissing his ass again. Either way, as far as I was con-cerned, it was the end of our working relationship.

I went to the wrap party, which was held in the cheap hotel where production had set up on Allen Parkway. The bar was free and that was nice, except several of the grips got so drunk that two got in a fight while another took off all of his clothes and jumped into the hotel swimming pool. At one point during the party, the free bar was closed when the hotel manager came out demanding more money. They'd given the hotel a thousand dollars or so and we'd already drunk all that. The u.p.m. coughed up the money and we went on drinking. During the height of the fight and swimming exhibition, I went to the men's room off the lobby and, standing next to a urinal, was surprised by a young man and woman entering the bathroom. They were both handsome and fashionable and had that talkative, and yet secretive, we're-doing-cocaine-and-you're-not aura about them. They excused themselves into a stall, saying the young woman had to go, and I could hear them sniffing loudly. They both left the bathroom close on my heels. Feeling, I suppose, a physical need to talk, the two followed me back to my table yakking and asking me what I did on the picture. I could tell they were dying to tell me who they were (I figured a producer's kids), so I finally asked.

"We're with Henry," they said.

"I'm his assistant," the young man said.

"Oh." I hadn't paid much attention to this show. "Who's Henry?"

They both looked dumbfounded. "Henry Thomas," the teenager said as though I were an idiot.

"Who's Henry Thomas?" I asked genuinely. I was good with actor's names but was at a loss as to who this one was.

My two new friends now seemed angry and stood up from the table where I'd sat so comfortably alone before, with the occasional visit from a drunken and flirty CR dressed in black pajamas, looking not unlike a cross-dressing member of the Viet Cong.

"You really don't know who Henry is?" the teenager asked. I guess being an assistant to a nobody bothered him.

"No, I really don't. Is he an actor?"

"Fuck yeah, he's an actor," the teenager said. "He was in *E.T.*" He said it again for emphasis. "*E.T.* You know, Steven Spielberg?"

"Yeah, right," I said, remembering.

To prove his point, Henry Thomas walked up just then, and the boy grabbed him. "This is Henry."

"Oh, hello," I said and nodded to the young actor.

Henry, looking bored, ignored my greeting and turned to his assistant. "Let's go to my room."

The three kids left, but not before the pretty, teenage girl left me with one last condescending jab. "It was so nice talking with you. Good luck with your. . . what was it you do again?"

"I'm the painter."

"Right," she said smiling, and trotted off behind one of the world's greatest talents whose name I now knew.

–13–

A long, protracted stint of unemployment struck hard after *Seven On, Seven Off* and I lost my phone and many tools to the pawnshop. Reduced to calling from an isolated beer tavern in the country near my home, I heard John Frick had landed a job as a designer on a feature film called *Dazed and Confused.* A man named Tom Dreesen was to be the construction coordinator. Frick had promised Burson he'd get him on the show, but since Dreesen's wife was the u.p.m., that wasn't going to happen. Many designers brought their key crew members with them on a show, especially a local one, demanding some of their own people because these people are known quantities that can produce the sets well and on time. It was partially a display of power on the designer's part, an occasion when he or she could stand up for the art department and secure a decent operating budget. Thoroughly afraid of the hard-nosed u.p.m., Alma Kuttruff, who, in Frick's defense, reminded me of Peter Cushing ordering the activation of the Death Star, John buckled under, hiring none of his steady crew. Working my pay phones, constantly cajoling my new friend Dreesen, and the indecisive John Frick, and desperate for money, I finally got myself hired by playing on Frick's guilt, mentioning a small job I'd once got for him, drafting for Bob Checci on *The Challenger Story* after Frick had called me, desperate for a job, any job, anything, he'd said at the time. I'd found him a few days of work and let him stay at my apartment for a couple of nights. I'd done it to help him as a friend, not to be used as a future marker. When one is hungry for movie work, though, one might call in anything.

Dazed and Confused was to be directed by a young man from

Austin named Richard Linklater. His claim to fame was a movie he'd made for about $30,000 called *Slacker*. For some reason, this sophomoric film did very well. It put me to sleep when I saw it. Linklater had basically filmed all of his unemployed friends walking around Austin. I'd seen everybody in the film doing the same shit they were doing on camera around the U.T. campus and all over Austin when I'd been a student at U.T. I didn't like the so-called "slackers" then. Their being on film didn't change my opinion. Whenever I saw these guys at a bar, club, or coffeehouse, they seemed bored and affected, painfully eager to be perceived as cool artist types, and yet unwilling to expend the effort to do the work that was actually required to be a musician, artist, filmaker, sword-swallower, whatever it was at which they posed so earnestly, if not adroitly.

Linklater was the only one of the bunch who seemed to have any snap, so it was left to him, I suppose, to record the comings and goings of the snapless. A couple of money people at Universal, thinking they had something truly hip for the young folks, praised the maker of *Slacker* to their bosses, who had to love the numbers it had produced, making decent money for such a low-budget film. Somewhere in there, they found five or six million to give Richard Linklater for his next film. Linklater was now in the directorial loop and, unless he pulled a Cimino some day, he could be in it making good money and movies for the rest of his life.

For his first, let's say, real movie, Linklater chose to film a script he'd written about his high school in the seventies. Having gone to high school in the seventies, I thought it was a good idea, until I read the script and saw it was pretty much "Slacker goes to High School." Another ensemble piece, peopled with an idiotic ensemble. Having been told repeatedly by Frick while begging for the job that there would be no painting, I was surprised at how much painting there was, and for the next eight weeks I worked hard with little or no help. Frick had set aside no real money for me in my budget, so every purchase order was a battle, questioned by Alma Kuttruff and her nice, talkative, but somewhat scurrying husband, Tom. Actually, Tom was the good cop more than not, and I felt sorry for him. Alma had much more power than he did and while her career was taking off with the Coen brothers after *Raising Arizona*, she and both men were slowly and then completely shutting Tom out of their projects as a construction coordinator after his work on their film *Miller's Crossing*. Despite this shunning (which soon graduated to a divorce), Tom spent all of his conversation hours with me and my patient ear giving me the highlights of Alma's career, saying nothing of his own.

Tom managed to get the sets built between cheerleading stints, and I soon had several interior rooms to paint as well as lots of bicentennial stuff——mailboxes, fireplugs, posters, an exterior 50-foot water tower to age, and on and on, every day, something new and exhausting. My two biggest projects were painting a 170-foot-by-10-foot bicentennial mural for a junior high hallway, including the lockers, and a large pool hall/game room emporium with a 70-foot-by-20-foot neon-colored mural of the planets on one wall. All this with no money or time.

I enlisted the aid of an old friend of mine, my high school art teacher and successful Austin artist, Steve Swagerle, who got a quick lesson in the ridiculousness of the movie business. I took him to meet John Frick, who was always going off doing I don't know what, and we tried to get him to show us some designs for the murals, since he was the designer and all. What he finally came up with, or rather hired someone else to come up with, was some very simplistic paste-up stuff out of an advertising book. When Steve and I pushed him on an approval so we could start, we were put off while Frick sweated over the childish copy. Finally, tired of painting lockers because he was a real artist and not a set painter, Steve told me either we had to start or he'd leave. We began the mural based loosely on the design Frick had commissioned from an artist much less experienced than Steve or I. Frick would show up occasionally, questioning our changes or saying nothing, just looking at our work silently. Steve, a straightforward normal person, closer to Frick's age than mine, pulled me aside one day in frustration.

"I can't believe this guy," he said. "What the hell does he do?"

"Well. . . " I thought about it. I usually picked my own colors and ran them by John after having ordered the paint. He seemed so afraid of making a decision, the main occupation of a designer, that it could take days to get a color approval for a background bathroom almost off-camera. Most of the conversations between John and me went like this:

"John, why don't we paint it light blue with a dark blue band?" We would be standing in a set, say a future, obligatory police station.

"Huh?"

I'd say it again.

"Oh."

We'd stand there. "John?"

"Huh?"

"What do you think? It shoots in two days. And we have that other set——"

"I can't think about that set now."

"O.K. But this one. . . "

He'd stare at the walls and leave the room. The next day, with one day left to paint and glaze all the walls in the four large rooms, he'd walk in, late in the afternoon. "J.R., I've been thinking about it and I feel we should paint the walls light blue with a dark blue band."

"Great. That's a great idea. Thanks, John."

This happened on practically every other set. He would always act like the idea was his, as though I'd never mentioned it. Just glad to avoid getting caught in a bind and having to work all night, I said nothing. If the set wasn't painted and ready, I had a strong feeling I was the one who would catch the blame and get fired, not John.

"So?" Steve asked me again. "What does he do? I mean the guy just shows up and acts like this pompous artist who's going to give us his almighty approval."

"Well," I said, "that's his job. That's what he does. He shows up and says it's O.K. "

"Meanwhile, we think it all up, do all the work, and he gets the credit."

"Yeah, he's my boss. He gets all the credit."

"But he doesn't *do* anything."

"So what, Steve? He hired me and I hired you. As long as we get it done and the director likes it, he's done his job."

"And how much does he make a week?"

"Probably a couple of thousand bucks."

Steve went back to painting then, only to add, "This business sucks," as he worked.

We finished the mural and it looked better with our additions. Whether Linklater liked it or not, I never knew. I know he didn't shoot much of it. I hung around the set for a few hours that first day of filming at Bedichek Junior High in Austin. After watching the shooting crew work, though, I decided to avoid them at all costs. Nobody seemed to know what they were doing except that they should look cool while doing it. Linklater, probably as stoned as I was, spent precious minutes pretentiously discussing the importance of Twinkie placement during a scene, while a gaggle of smart-ass extras and other kids dressed in seventies garb roamed the halls. It was hard to tell the difference between the extras and all of Linklater's *Slacker* buddies he'd hired on the film. On that first day of shooting I realized (I'd been to busy to think about it before) why it had been so hard to get a job on this low-budget feature: the art department and production office were filled with Linklater's inexperienced friends. None had ever worked on a real film before and didn't know about or enjoy the long hours, hard work, and quick pace that was required. I suddenly found myself working for an assistant art director and set decorator named Debbie Pastor who had no idea what her job was or even where she was. Nominally one of my bosses, I had to wake Debbie up several times when she was sleeping on the floor of a set I had to paint.

Linklater himself was equally in the dark. He would walk into our sets completely surprised, with a "Like wow, this is cool" comment as though we'd all been busting our asses for the fun of it and built a set as a surprise for him, hoping he might wander by and shoot it. Ignorant of the effort involved, he would then make off-hand requests for the removal of walls, or a new color here or there, and Frick would go along, giving me the last-minute changes through Tom Dreesen.

My final big project on the film was the interior and exterior of the kid's large emporium. I brought in Theresa Dringenberg, a local talented scenic artist, to do all the signs, called Steve back for help with the interior mural, and used one of Tom's carpenters as a painter's helper. We all proceeded to kill ourselves to get it ready. Amid all of this, I was called to the art department to fix a horrible so-called sculpture that the partially burned artist John Huke had dumped on us at the request of our propmaster Rob Janecka. I'd known Rob since *Lonesome Dove* . To me, he seemed a shameless liar who would say anything. For instance, seeing me once reading a book on the CIA, Rob told me that his father was in the CIA and that, through him, Rob could have anyone in the country killed, just point at someone, tell his father, and that person was dead. Mention any sport from football to badminton, and Rob was a former champion, winning championships in high school, college, you name it. I'd heard him lie about his importance on almost every show

I'd ever been on. It was on *Dazed and Confused*, though, that I realized this pretentious man would go far in the movie business. He'd found his niche. He lied to me again over the phone, saying the sculptures weren't that bad, could I help? When I saw the faux bronze sculptures of four deformed MinuteMen who looked like they'd been at ground zero of a nuclear bomb drop, and heard that Huke had charged and been paid almost twice my paint budget for the whole movie simply because he was a friend of Rob's and Frick's, I felt like quitting. Instead, I did my best to repair them and went back to work at the emporium, where I had the incomparable joy of meeting, up close, some of the film's young actors.

It seems there was a character named Pickford, played by a teenager named Shawn Andrews, who was supposed to have a mural of Jimi Hendrix on the wall in his room. Frick, eager to please the young actor, called me up at the beginning of the show to tell me Shawn wanted to paint the Hendrix mural himself. He would do it on a large piece of paper and I would cover the wall with it. The boy wanted to get into character, he said. I had plenty of work to do and said O.K. Several weeks later, as the fateful day of filming the poster approached, Shawn decided he didn't have time to draw the poster. Would I draw it, Frick asked, and then Shawn could fill it in? Sure, no problem. I put the large sheet of paper up on the wall in my paint shop at the emporium and drew a picture of Hendrix from a book. But Shawn never showed up. I continued my other endeavors, then received a call from Frick again concerning the poster. I was now to paint it completely, and Shawn was arriving at my paint shop that morning because the featured poster would be shot the next day. I hurriedly ran to the shop and painted Hendrix with purples, reds, and yellows, leaving several blank fields of color with which the busy would-be artist could play.

They didn't show up that morning after all, but that afternoon. Dee, another assistant art director and one of Linklater's nicer *Slacker* buddies, appeared with Shawn and two of his young, quite beautiful, female co-stars in tow, and pulled me off a ladder. She introduced me to them as all three looked at my paint-covered self with open disdain and said nothing. Dee began to run off and said to me quietly, "You're the baby-sitter now." Before she could get away, Shawn stopped her.

"Hey uh, Dee?"

"Yes?" she said backing away.

"I don't see a radio here. Hey man," he said, "where's your radio?"

"I don't have one right now."

"Well look," Shawn said, pissed off, "I can't work without music, man. You dig? I can't get into the groove and do my art."

"The groove?"

"Look," he pointed at me, "you need to get me some music. Right now."

I turned to look at Dee. I'd spoken with her before, so I could tell she was nice and had some brains. She knew I'd worked on more films than she had and probably realized that I was about to put my paint-covered tennis shoe in young Shawn's ass.

"Uh, just hang on a second, Shawn," she said. "I'll go get you one."

I went back to what I was doing and Dee sped off to buy Shawn a radio with her petty cash. She came back with a nice, new, expensive tape deck and Shawn, happy now, put in a tape of the movie's soundtrack and began to dance around with his girlfriend. Their other little friend started to go through my tools. Dee looked at me, apologized, and left. For the rest of the afternoon and evening, my shop was taken over by the Three Stooges. I tried to explain to Shawn about my expensive paint brushes which cost thirty, fifty, sixty bucks a piece and how he could use all of them if he would just sink them in water or paint thinner when he was through. He looked confused (and dazed), so I started to explain the difference between water and paint thinner but gave up when I realized the whole time I was talking to him he was looking at himself in the mirror and playing with hair styles. I'd mixed up several colors for him and his friends. As I attempted to show him where the paint was, he gave me a patronizing little pat on the back, interrupting me to say, dismissively, "Yeah, yeah, yeah, right, man. Look, we'll give you a call if we need you. I like to work alone."

I swallowed my sarcastic comments and left to go to work. Unfortunately, I had to go back into my shop several times to get tools, brushes, and materials and saw the artist at work. Shawn would sit down, stand up, sit down, pondering many, many deep thoughts, staring at the poster of Hendrix intently. His girlfriend and the other girl stood in front of the poster, paint brushes and cups of paint in hand.

"O.K.," Shawn said, rubbing his forehead, concentrating, "I see a train. . . "

One of the girls would quietly paint a childish train.

"Good, good," Shawn said. "Now. . . " squinting and concentrating, "I see. . . a flower. . . "

One of the girls painted a rudimentary flower.

This went on until the poster was ruined and the kids were bored—that is, not very long. Shawn and his actress girlfriend had a reputation for pawing each other openly, going so far as to put a hand down each other's pants while sitting in their makeup chairs. Utilizing an opportunity, I walked into my shop at one point and found him fucking his girlfriend up against the wall, her short-shorts pulled down while her third-wheel friend drew listlessly on the poster. I stayed out of my own shop then until it was quitting time and drove to where I was staying, imposing on a friend in Austin. The next morning, I went back into the shop to find several brushes thrown about, dried and ruined, paint all over the floor, and all the shop doors left open in what was a high-crime area, and the poster gone. I cleaned everything up and went back to work. A few days later, I overheard Frick talking on the phone in the art department, "Did you see that great poster Shawn painted? He did all that by himself. . . "

My last few days on the emporium set, I was extremely busy getting the interior and exterior ready. At one point, the faux bronze sculptures were brought to me again. The gag with the Minutemen involved the kids stealing them and then painting them to look like the members of the rock group KISS. I'd already painted the statues to look like Gene Simmons and the other three, umm, musicians when two were returned, Ace and Gene, with their faces missing. Someone had forgotten to weight the spray foam statues down in the back of a pickup, during a driving shot, and they'd both flown out during filming and gotten wedged face down on the concrete under the following camera truck. I redid their faces with putty and paint, embarrassed and worried that someone might think I'd made the comically deformed sculptures myself. I was back at work texturing and painting several tall interior columns when I saw a small camera crew come in the door. Apparently, Linklater had taken some of his salary to hire these people to make a documentary of his brilliant filmmaking. I wondered if Scorsese had done the same thing on *Taxi Driver*. Anyway, the three filmakers, outwardly convinced of the importance of their job, were talking to and filming people working around the large room. When they reached me up on my ladder, spent of patience and ready to spew vitriol, I practically jumped on them.

"You're doing what?" I asked.

They told me of their documentary.

"Listen," I said, "you want to make a documentary of this movie, you should concentrate on the money because that's all most movies in this country are about. This business is nothing but a scam run by scam artists, and we're all in on the con and preserve it to keep our jobs. You oughta make a movie about the millions of dollars wasted on this and most every other movie, not Linklater having a mental battle with a Twinkie."

They slinked away, their cameras turned off, something for which I was thankful, not wanting to lose my job and needing the money.

I skipped the *Dazed and Confused* wrap party. Having had enough Slacker coolness in a work setting, I couldn't guarantee what I'd say in a social situation. After that first reading of the script, I never thought the aptly named *Dazed and Confused* would make it to the theaters. It did, though, for about a weekend and then promptly sped to my local video store.

–14–

I was still telling everyone I was quitting it all, so much that they'd begun to say, leave already, when a real movie, a feature film called *Flesh and Bone*, came to Texas, and I had to eat my words yet again. Tom Dreesen was applying for the job as construction coordinator with the designer, a hotshot up-and-comer named Jon Hutman. Jon was around my age, thirty, and had just done Redford's *A River Runs Through It* and was being sought after as a production designer. He'd gone to school with Jodie Foster at Yale and had designed her directorial debut, *Little Man Tate* . My old boss, Brian Stultz, had been the lead scenic on *A River Runs Through It* and was, I found out, the lead on *Flesh and Bone*. Brian only did features now, and this promised to be a good one. The producer was Mark Rosenberg, the u.p.m., G. Mac Brown, and the director Steve Kloves, a young man in his early thirties. Rosenberg had produced Kloves's first directorial effort, the successful *Fabulous Baker Boys*. This was his first film since then, and everyone had high hopes for a quality picture. The story was about a bad, thieving father, played by James Caan, who comes back to cause trouble in his now-grown son's life. The son was played by Dennis Quaid and his wife, Meg Ryan, was his on-screen love interest. Quaid and Ryan's characters have a few adventures and then there's a downer ending. It would be filmed all over Central and West Texas.

I heard about the film through Tom Dreesen and immediately called Brian at his Wilmington, N.C., power center. He promised to hire me, possibly using me as his standby painter. Within a few weeks, Brian was in Austin and took me up to meet the famously talented Jon Hutman, a short, pudgy man who looked like a young Don Rickles with curly hair. Jon had an ebullient, loud, in-your-face demeanor with his underlings that turned into little-boy cuteness with his superiors or equals. He also had a large, braying laugh and constantly yelled out what were supposed to be funny little sayings such as "Hell-low!" in the voice of Ed McMahon or, when he gave you something shitty to do, "See ya! Wouldn't wanna be ya!" He was, at times, the worst of all men: someone who thinks he's funny. He reminded me of his friend and mine: Brian Stultz. Hutman's fiancee at the time, Sam Shaeffer, was also his set decorator. As a couple, they were cute and young and smart and they knew it; having fun and getting paid for it. Between them both, they would pull down thousands of dollars on the picture. Both were hardworking, talented professionals who took pride in their sets and deserved every penny. The movie business was their lives. It had to be, if you were serious about it.

Brian Stultz told me he was basically Hutman's main scenic artist and would do most of his pictures. Over drinks that first night at the Austin Radisson, Brian also told me about the movies he'd been working on, talking about the stars and directors, using their first names as though they were close friends who consulted him on their work. We got into films we admired and I mentioned the rerelease of the director's cut of Ridley Scott's *Blade Runner*.

"Oh, well, you know," Brian said, "Ridley was very upset about the way they treated that picture. Of course, he has his *1492* Columbus picture coming out, which, I predict, is going to be a huge hit. See, Ridley's been wanting to do this picture for years. It's funny, I was actually called to do that picture, but I had to turn him down because I was in New York. Let me tell you something about Ridley, he really . . . blah, blah, blah, blah."

I nodded and smiled and listened. Here I was with Brian again, at his beck and call, pretending to like him. Needing the money, I convinced myself we were buddies, or would have to be for the next four months——we were filming until Christmas.

The first sets we worked on were two large farmhouses up in Pflugerville, an old German farming community north of Austin. Hutman knew all of the scenic tricks in Brian's repertoire and pushed him to the limit. It was fun to watch the great, arrogant scenic artist Brian Stultz get pushed around, scurrying here and there to please Hutman with a variety of samples and finishes. For three weeks or so,

I worked hard with Stultz and his talented scenic foreman, or second, Jim Onate. Jim was a friend of mine and I felt he was actually the secret behind Brian's success. He and an ex-merchant marine from Britain, Peter Duran, usually did most of the work and ran the crews. Jim did double duty, busting his ass painting and running around apologizing to the carpenters, the set dressers, people from the crew, the assortment of people Brian offended on a regular basis with his rude behavior. Brian treated the local carpenters, Dreesen's men, like they were ignorant peons who worked for him. When any complained, Stultz could run to his powerful friend, Hutman, and get them in trouble. Even Dreesen, nominally Brian's boss, was afraid of him and catered to his demands. To give you an idea, Brian's favorite response to anyone who disagreed with him was a blunt "Bite me."

After the three weeks of prep, I'd had it with him again and hoped he would choose me over another scenic to be the production or stand-by painter. It meant I would travel with the crew, on their hours, always on set, only answering to my designer, Hutman, the cameraman Tass, the first a.d., Kara, and the d.p., Philippe Rousselot, a tiny Frenchman who'd shot the film *The Bear* and who won an academy award for *A River Runs Through It*. Hutman had already introduced me to the intense Philippe and I liked him. But with Brian, my tormentor, I had to use complicated reverse psychology to get this plum. He'd said I was the standby painter until he saw I was looking forward to it and started threatening to keep me by his side throughout the show. The more he saw I wanted to leave, the more likely the other scenic would get the job. I started pretending I didn't want the job and that I really cared about Brian's opinions on movies, music, and especially writing. All of this was pointless though, because Hutman had already decided he wanted me on set as his flunky. Brian waited until the very last day, though, to tell me I was the on-set painter and did so grudgingly. When I told Jim Onate the news, he shook his head sorrowfully and warned me about Hutman.

"He's a nice guy and a good designer, but he cares so much, he'll have you running hard for weeks."

That was fine with me, I said, as long as I was away from Brian.

Shooting began at the HL Weiss house in Pflugerville. We would be there for a week, shooting late into each night. As standby painter, I was on crew call, arriving for breakfast with everyone else and not leaving until the last shot of the night was finished. I was never to leave early or arrive late. I did arrive ten minutes late one of the first mornings. Though everyone was still eating breakfast, Hutman came running across the hayfield on his stubby legs up to my truck, yelling at me to never, never, never come to the set late, going on and on until I cut him off, saying it would never happen again. I was working as a local in Austin though I lived two hours away from the city in the country. So broke I could rarely afford a hotel room, with the four hours of subsequent driving, I was putting in some eighteen-hour days that week. Needing the money, I said nothing but yessir.

The crew got to know each other that first week. I was introduced to Steve the director, a nice guy; Tass the cameraman; Kara the first a.d., known as the Dragon Lady , tough but nice; and the prop department Trish, Chris, and Greg, three people devoting their lives to the movies. I made friends with some of the other people on the crew; an irreverent electrician named Scott Greene; Derek, a p.a. extraordinaire moving up the a.d. ladder quickly; Jordan, the second second a.d. who had Rosenberg as his friend and patron; and the DGA(Director's Guild of America) trainee, Christine Tope.

Right off the bat, there was a misstep with the first caterer. A guy named Mitch ran the catering crew, and he seemed rather obsequious and short-tempered at the same time. I'd seen him fighting with his guys a few times, yelling at them. He got angry with me one day, the first day I met him, because I didn't have any empty five-gallon buckets to give him. My standby paint kit was packed tightly into my truck and I had only a few buckets, none to spare. Mitch acted like I was holding out on him and stormed off when I said no. Long lines at breakfast even caused our producer, Mark Rosenberg, to jump up in the catering wagon one morning to help cook, not a good sign when your producer's flipping pancakes and yelling at you to hurry. The final straw was when Dennis Quaid didn't like his chicken-fried steak one day at lunch. The stars' approval of your food could be the final word on a caterer's job. If they don't like the food they're going to be eating for three months, the caterer can be gone. With rumors already circulating viciously (from his own employees) that Mitch was partying all night on coke as well, he saw what was coming. Since he used to write not-so-funny sayings with a colored marker every morning on the posted menu, Mitch did so one last time at breakfast before his departure. As

I got my breakfast taco, I saw he'd drawn several tombstones and written, "They died with their aprons on." When anyone asked him about the sign, he said, "Rosenberg fired me. Read the memo."

"Rosenberg's not gonna like this, " I said to someone.

"Wait til he sees the memo," someone else said.

Just then, Mitch came sweating past me and handed me a typed memo. "We really want to stay on the show," he said. "Tell Dennis to give us a chance, please," he said and ran off, passing out paper.

I read the memo which was essentially an all-out, embarrassing plea for his job directed to Dennis Quaid. I read: "Please give us a chance, Dennis, please."

"This guy's dead," I said to no one in particular. Fulfilling my prophecy, several feet away, I saw an a.d. handing Rosenberg the memo.

"WHAT THE FUCK IS THIS?" Rosenberg screamed. "WHO WROTE THIS SHIT?!"

I quickly fled the caterer's wagon, not wanting to see the carnage. Suffice it to say, the quaking Mitch was gone that second, banished from the show and, I heard later, fired from the catering company.

Of all the problems the first few weeks, it was poor Christine Tope, the DGA trainee, so far down the ladder, who would have to deal with the most troublesome one—James Caan. The DGA trainee has the responsibility, along with other p.a. s , of ferrying stars and extras from their trailers to the set, fetching them coffee and breakfast, while also doing paperwork, passing out the next day's call sheets, calling out "Cut!" and "Rolling!" as it's passed down from the director over the walkie, making sure people are quiet during shooting, and a number of other things that come up.

Caan was trouble from the very start. Not coming out of his trailer was the least of it. It was when he came out that the problems started. One of the first days, he called the director Steve, probably the nicest, most regular director around and definitely a talented individual, a "fucking neophyte" on set in front of the crew. Caan talked at the top of his lungs, complaining about everything, especially his job. I watched him walk up to the house past me one of those first days. Jordan, his headset on, walked up to Caan and introduced himself.

"Hello Jimmy, I'm Jordan. Nice to meet you."

Caan kept walking, making Jordan backpedal, waving him off. "Hey Jordan-nice-to-meet-you, who the fuck are you?"

"I'm the second-second," Jordan said defensively.

"Oh Christ," Caan said, "another shit job. Where the fuck am I going Christine?"

Caan was dressed up in his bad-guy outfit, a black coat, hat, pants, and boots. His skin had been pulled back with tape to get rid of his wrinkles and heavy makeup had been applied. The scene he was in was supposed to have taken place twenty years before. Without the hat, he looked like an old woman at a beauty parlor, with it, hiding all the tape, he did look younger.

"Christine! I said where the fuck am I going?"

Christine had been running behind him, trying to hold on to all of her paperwork, while talking into her headset, explaining the delay diplomatically to the first a.d., Kara. "He's coming in now——We're just going in the house, Jimmy."

"I don't wanna go in the fuckin' house," Caan said.

Christine laughed nervously. "Now, Jimmy. . . "

He patted her shoulder roughly. "Just kiddin' ya, kid. Let's get this piece of shit over with. They better have the fuckin' air conditioner on in there."

They went into the house where you could still hear him yelling. It was like that every time the guy appeared. Everybody had to see and hear that Jimmy Caan was there, everybody, even me. Afraid of power like that, I stuck with Hutman and avoided eye contact with Caan. Jon had me busy anyway, painting and repainting the two trucks, that doubling as one, Quaid would drive throughout the film in his role as a vending machine operator. One day I was sitting on my butt, down in the dirt next to one of the trucks working, Hutman standing over me, guiding my every move, grabbing my brushes and jumping in himself, when suddenly a loud, obnoxious Jimmy Caan was squatting next to me, in my face.

"HEY! HOW YA DOIN'?!"

"Fine, fine, thanks." I kept painting.

"Great truck, ain't it!?"

"Yes it is. Great truck."

I looked over Caan's shoulder and saw the u.p.m., Mac Brown, watching us.

"You know something," Caan said, "my brother Larry used to have a truck like this, but it was a '68. He had it all tricked out, took the seats out, and put in buckets and a 454 four-barrel. I helped him fix it all up and then he sold the motherfucker! Can you believe it?! The stupid fuck probably sold it for a couple keys of cocaine! The whole truck went up his fuckin' nose! Know what I mean!?"

I smiled and nodded my understanding and he stood up.

"Ahh fuck. Brothers, you know, whadda ya gonna do?" He looked around and walked off toward his trailer.

Mac stood there shaking his head.

"Wow," Hutman said, "what was that? His brother sold his truck for cocaine?"

"He doesn't have a brother, Larry. Whenever he tells you about his brother I think he's talking about himself," Mac said and left us, chasing after his star.

At the end of that long first week, where everyone went into overtime and there were several third meals served, Mark Rosenberg bought five or six coolers of beer and wine and champagne. After the final shot that night, we all grabbed a drink and gathered around him. The producer was of medium height, had a large gut, thick curly black hair, and a black beard. He drove around in a rented Ford Explorer, chomped on cigars all day, and yelled loudly and often for his assistant Loring. I was scared of both him and the u.p.m. Mac, since I knew, once things settled down, I'd be standing around a lot and would have to avoid their budget-cutting eyes. Rosenberg raised a champagne glass once everyone was there. He said a few words about how talented Steve was, mentioned their good experience on *The Baker Boys*, thanked us all very much for working so hard that week and getting a jump on the picture, and promised a great show to come, all in all—a nice gesture.

However, *Flesh and Bone* turned out to be a hectic and even tragic picture. The actors James Caan and Meg Ryan caused trouble several times, with only Quaid turning up every day with a professional demeanor, always doing his job without a lot of noise. Though I liked his work as an actor, to me Quaid was just another guy from Bellaire High School in Houston. This view led me to make the error of speaking my mind one day at the caterer's tables. The 1992 presidential race was in full swing and everyone was talking about it. Quaid was sitting across from me and going on about H.Ross Perot and how good he was, and how he would cut taxes and so on. A couple of wardrobe people flanked the actor, with one of them, Eva, agreeing with everything he said. Outspoken to a fault on my political opinions, I had to interject.

" Look," I said, "I think anybody who supports Perot is making a big mistake. The guy's a lying billionaire, completely removed from the reality of the majority of people who live and work in this country. He's running against the government and yet it's the lucrative government contracts he secured that made him a billionaire. A demagogue with his kind of wealth is extremely dangerous. We could be living in a totalitarian state before you can say Jack Robinson." I went on to mention Perot's long-ago promise to turn the education system around in Texas, one he'd seemed to have forgotten since it was still below average, and then I stopped talking.

The table grew very quiet. Eva looked at me as though she might stab me with her fork. I saw Quaid's perplexed and irritated face and realized my mistake: I'd forgotten I was a nobody and had disagreed— vehemently, mind you—with a star. What was funny, he was rattled.

"Well then, who are you gonna vote for?" he asked me.

"Who else is there? Bill and Hillary Clinton."

Quaid made a noise of disgust. "Shit. They're not gonna do a god-damn thing but raise my taxes." He stood up and left the table, his tray in hand, to eat somewhere else. Not having any money to have taxes raised on, I had nothing to say.

I met the actor's wife, Meg Ryan, on the set not long after that. She was very pleasant and talked to me about their ranch in Montana and their new baby. She was so nice and talkative, in fact, I had the brief delusion I could say hi to her when I bumped into her a few hours later at the craft service table. The near-lethal, go-straight-to-hell look she gave me, brought me quickly back to reality. For the most part, no one got much of a chance to say hello to Ms.Ryan. The story was, there was a stalker after her necessitating a bodyguard by her side at all times. The first bodyguard lasted only half of the movie because he was too nice. At least, that was the rumor; that she thought he was talking to people too much, not sticking close enough by her side, or looking mean enough. The guy she replaced him with was another nice guy who, like the other guard, smiled often, but this one would get a somber, mean look on his face whenever he escorted the actress from her trailer to the set. Though stalkers are a real and frightening threat and not something to make light of, our sets were mostly closed or in obscure, empty, eas-ily guarded watchable small towns, and the stalker was reportedly in another state being tracked by the police, so many on the crew thought she might have been overreacting a bit. The bodyguard was mostly looking at us and we weren't going to stalk her, even though her arguments with Steve could drag out the day's schedule longer. While shooting in an abandoned house in Coupland, Texas, Ryan held everything up before a big scene where she and the actress Gwyneth Paltrow were supposed to run through a virgin wheat field. I was standing next to Cecil, the Teamster captain, listening to the first a.d.'s frustrating conversation with a p.a. and the bodyguard over Cecil's walkie. The p.a. had been trying to coax Ryan to the set, but she wasn't budging.

"I don't believe what I'm hearing," Cecil said and turned his walkie off. I turned my walkie to another channel and eavesdropped on the conversation.

"What's the problem?" Kara was asking. Any hold up fell on her shoulders and she had to solve it quickly.

"I'll let you talk to her bodyguard, " the p.a. said.

"Kara?"

"What's the problem?"

"Meg has some concerns about the wheat field."

"The wheat field?"

The field behind the house had been cultivated months before, especially for the film. The whole point was that it was this perfect, untrampled field and they would run majestically through it. It was surrounded by miles of empty farmland. Police were at every crossroads, halting what little traffic might encroach on the scene. The only people for miles were the crew.

"She would like me to check out the field," the bodyguard said.

"What do you mean?"

"To make sure that nobody's hiding in it. She wants me to run through the wheat field ahead of her."

"That might mess up the wheat, and it would certainly be difficult keeping you out of the shot."

"She's very concerned."

"Will she at least come up here with you?" Kara asked, exasperated.

"I'll try. It's just she's very concerned and I can agree with her."

"O.K., O.K., we'll work it out if you can just come up here."

"I'll do my best."

Eventually, she did come to the set and her bodyguard looked around the field before she ran through it with the other actress. The man kept looking around the wheat, a gun in a pouch around his waist, looking and looking . . . Well, I don't know what he was looking for out there, but I couldn't blame Ms.Ryan for being worried about her fans. As everyone knows, the word does come from "fanatic," after all. Strangely, there was just something weird that happened to people when they were around celebrities, something that, frankly, made them scary.

A prime example of crazy fandom occurred while we were shooting in a small, rundown home in a bad neighborhood outside of San Marcos, Texas. The house was supposed to be Ms.Ryan's tacky home in the script. The tacky people who lived there in real life were a put-upon, brow beaten woman and her insanely, hot-tempered unemployed, security-guard husband, who, as I saw in his garage, liked to collect pornography and guns, an odd but all-American hobby. There were many problems with this couple, the main one being they had no idea how much they were completely losing their home to the company. Though they were being put up in a hotel, they insisted on hanging around and trying to get near Dennis and Meg.

One horrible, hot, humid afternoon, the wife kept hovering around her back porch trying to get a look at Meg Ryan shooting a scene in her kitchen. Derek, the hardworking p.a., was having a hell of a time telling her, more politely, I noted, than I would have done, to stay farther away since they were rehearsing.

"I just wanna say hi to Meg," the chain-smoking woman said.

"Please, ma'am, that's not possible right now," Derek said.

"I just wanna tell her something!"

"If you could please just lower your voice. . . "

A call came over the walkie then from Kara warning that the woman was in Meg's eyeline and had to be removed from the set. Though people were constantly in Meg Ryan's eyeline (the actress seemed to have the eyes of a hawk), this woman was definitely in the way. When Derek told the woman she would have to get out of her own backyard, she started to cry. As Derek tried to move her delicately along, she threw down her cigarettes and pitched a sobbing, screaming fit, running away from her house. Even though the company was in her kitchen, she'd signed a contract and essentially given up her home.

Not long after this incident, Quaid was standing on the back porch of the house smoking a cigarette between scenes. He flicked his cigarette butt out into the yard and went back into the house, not noticing the irate owner, the unemployed security guard, watching his every move. The skinny little man went berserk, shouting and yelling and screaming that he didn't appreciate the way he and his wife were being treated. Ms.Ryan's bodyguard held him back while several locations people tried to soothe him after calling the police.

"That son-of-a-bitch Dennis Quaid threw a fuckin' cigarette butt out in my yard!" the man screamed. "Who does that bastard think he is?! He's too much of a bigshot to say hello to me an' my wife! This is my house! This is my house! I'll throw every one of you bastards out!"

The large bodyguard made sure he stayed between the house and the little man who was now pointing up at his chest.

"So help me God I guaren-fuckin'-tee ya, it's gonna take a lot more than a gorilla like you to stay between me an' Dennis if I see that bastard throw one more cigarette butt on the ground! Five of you bastards ain't gonna be able to stop me! Motherfucker don't respect my goddamn house. . . "

The locations people finally calmed him down, one of them making a big production of putting a bucket on the porch for Quaid to throw his spent cigarette butts into—which, I also saw, Quaid was now dutifully discarding. Even though Quaid and Ryan had been friendly enough to the homeowners, it hadn't been enough. They had to get some more of that celebrity.

–15–

Most of us working on a movie aren't concerned with the actors. The worst thing they could normally do is make the working day longer. The crew is usually busy doing their jobs, or hanging around the boring set, eating at the craft service table, and waiting to do their jobs. I had a walkie on me at all times, which gave me the freedom to walk around or hang out at my truck where all my paint was and where an a.d. could call me if needed. Everyone near the camera rushes around urgently between shots, so if you don't have something specifically to do there, it's best to stay away. When they did call me, it was usually for a shiny spot on something or an unwanted reflection. For almost every project, I used a little tin of paste wax and some tint. In fact, Mac, the u.p.m., might have saved himself fifteen thousand dollars, my salary for the film, if he had simply bought a five-dollar can of paste wax and given it to props. Other times, though, I used touch-up paint from the stand-by kit Jim Onate left me on each set, or pulled out a trusty can of Streaks-n-Tips, colored hair spray. No one seemed to know about the few little tricks I had, so I came out looking like I was worth something.

One night there was a big scene with a fake staircase and Caan was to roll down it. The staircase was built horizontally, and all the actor had to do was a couple of tumbles, three or four times, and that was it. Caan made a huge deal out of it as usual, acting as though he were rolling down a real vertical staircase, so it took much longer than necessary. After a practice run, someone noticed the paint was chipping off the steps, which were made of soft Styrofoam. As this was a close-up, the chips were obvious. An urgent call for JR Helton went out. I ran up and found the first a.d., Kara, in a panic. I had one minute to touch up the steps. I said O.K., nonchalantly.

"Listen to this guy," Kara said. "You don't understand, we're running out of time. The paint has to be dry this instant. Right now."

"O.K., Kara."

James Caan was standing there looking at me. "Yeah, I don't want any paint on my fuckin' shirt."

I had two cans of Streaks-n-Tips, brown and gray, on me. I sprayed the steps with brown and fogged the gray on as an age effect. Like most hair spray, it dried instantly. Kara kept touching the steps to see if they were dry.

"Don't worry, Kara, it's dry."

"Wow," she said. "JR, I'll never doubt you again. Now get out of the way—let's go everybody, picture's up!"

I stood by to touch up the steps periodically, with each take, and then went back to my truck and threw the spray cans inside. Another movie saved, I got inside my truck and went back to sleep.

Other days, my job was more ridiculous. I did a lot of work for props, glad to stay busy during the long days. One of the vending machines serviced by Quaid's character was a big glass and wooden box I had stained and aged. A colored chicken would stand inside the box surrounded by blinking lights and the sucker who put a quarter in played tic-tac-toe with the bird. The gag was, the chicken had died and Quaid had to replace it. Therefore, we needed several dead, colored chickens for each take. I was in charge of dying a few of them to give the director a color choice. I remember sitting there on the ground, my hands purple from the dye, carefully blow-drying the feathers of a dead blue chicken when Dennis Quaid walked past me. He stopped to look at what I was doing. I started to say something and he just shook his head, muttered "Jesus", and walked off. I didn't know if it was a low point in his career or mine.

The real live chickens that would be carried around the entire show in cages on Quaid's vending-machine truck were watched over by Karen Prince, a Teamster and animal wrangler. I saw a lot of Karen, she being the only person who probably sat around more than I did. Her primary job, after dying the live chickens green, blue, and red, was to then watch them for the whole show as the chicken wrangler. I'd seen her as a duck wrangler on *Gideon Oliver*, so it didn't surprise me. I'd also seen goat wranglers, rat wranglers, and even bug wranglers. Karen was forced to do a stint as a fly wrangler on *Flesh and Bone* as well. A good person and animal lover, she caused our u.p.m., Mac, no end of aggravation with her humaneness. I remember watching him walk around in frustration when, before a scene that called for a bunch of flies, Karen wouldn't just swat the flies or let anyone else do it or catch them. She had to capture them alive, not hurting them in any way. On two different locations, I felt sorry for her as she ran around with an empty jar trying to good-naturedly kidnap some flies while the expensive crew waited. Another evening, in another small town, Mac had had it with her and he said so.

"I've had it with Karen Prince," he said to Jon Hutman, who was standing next to me.

"What?" Hutman asked.

"We've got this horse," Mac said, "standing out there in the field. Her job is to just get it to walk over to Dennis and Meg. No big deal. But no, she can't do it. So when I tell her she absolutely has to do it, she makes me and everybody else turn around, close our eyes, and either send the horse positive energy to make it come to us or I don't know, shame it into coming to us."

I looked over his shoulder and sure enough, Karen and several others had their backs turned on the immobile horse.

"That's it," Mac said. "I'm going over there and telling that horse I'm gonna turn him into dog food. That oughta get him going."

He must have, for shortly afterwards, they got the shot off.

Jon Hutman was doing his damnedest to keep me as busy as possible. Try as he might, though, I had a lot of slack time, which made him angry. When he first introduced me to Kara, he told her, "You gotta watch him. He's lazy." I'd come through now for Kara a few times a day with only two or three minutes to do my paint job, with the whole crew watching and waiting, enough to let her know she could count on me when she called. I'd done the same for Tass and Philippe (who forced me to paint a green summer landscape on a white screen in four minutes for one background shot). The triumvirate around the camera (Steve was busy with the actors) now knew of me and my abilities. Because I was in fact needed a few times a day, I became more a part of the shooting crew than the art department, which was really the way it should have been. This aggravated Jon, who knew from those first few weeks of prep with Brian that I was a painter who could get a lot done for him. Being a good designer, Hutman wanted to utilize my manual talents by yanking me off the set whenever he felt like it, to go bust my ass on a set we were yet to shoot, rather than sitting on it like I was doing. Not wanting to leave my cush job, I ingratiated myself so much with Kara that she told Hutman he couldn't take me away from the set anymore and he had to obey. I made sure to rub it in afterwards, playing big games of touch football with the electricians and sound guys whenever Hutman came by.

We had a good time playing football and Hutman could say nothing about it, especially when Quaid started throwing the ball with us. On one set, the actor played catch with Scott Greene and me and another electrician whenever he got a chance. In one small town, Quaid seemed to be uncomfortable with the fact that he had to act and would run over to where we were and even throw the ball between takes . This brought Mac and Mark Rosenberg over seeing their high-dollar boy playing catch. Quaid drilled a pass at Rosenberg that went through his hands and bounced hard off his chest, almost knocking the cigar from his mouth. Rosenberg gamely tried to throw it back to Quaid, who then threw it to Mac, and all of the sudden there were several people making several thousand dollars a minute throwing a football around, much like the NFL, I guess. There was a weird period when many people on the crew were playing sports any chance they got. Even the director, Steve, was taking the time to throw a baseball with one of the sound guys. Being on set is so monotonous, starting and stopping all day into the night, you'll do anything to break it up.

I broke up most of the monotony by reading and writing and smoking dope, while Quaid did it by playing chess. Between every shot, throughout the show, the actor was sitting with his makeup guy, Leonard, playing chess all day long. It was, I thought, a good way to keep busy and avoid talking to people who always want to talk to an actor. I thought my fellow crew members were going a little far with the suck-up factor, though, when some of them started watching his games and cheering him on, as if chess were a spectator sport and interesting (yes, I'm sure it is.)

One of the best things about working on a movie are the free phone lines. They weren't free for Mac or Mark Rosenberg, but they were free for us. The nature of the shoot had us all over West Texas using a number of run-down motels as our sets. On every motel set, besides the interior room we were shooting, there were a few rooms that had been reserved with phones and TV's. There was usually a production room for Marge, the second a.d., to do her call sheets in and for Kara, Jordan, Derek and Christine to put all their gear and paperwork in. This room was also used by Mac and Rosenberg to make phone calls. The other rooms were used by the crew—wardrobe maybe, or special effects—to stock items or just get out of the cold that winter. Myself, I hid in these rooms often, watching cable TV and occasionally using the phone to call home. Because of my paranoid feeling that I could be fired any instant, I tried not to abuse the phone privilege too much. I'd had so many low-paying, shitty jobs in my life that I still hadn't managed to acquire the movie-worker attitude that I deserved all this money I was making. Even when working hard, I always felt guilty thinking about all the old housepainters I knew, fifty-five-year-old men making in a week what I made in a day.

One can get used to money quickly, though, and others on the crew had no difficulty sitting on the phone for up to an hour between shots. I saw many people gabbing, but mainly it was makeup, hair, and wardrobe. One woman in particular was on the phone throughout the show, when she wasn't sitting down on the set. Building a new home in Mexico, she was on the phone often to the foreign country, haggling with Mexican contractors over plaster, plumbing, and tile. Likewise, Leonard, in charge of Quaid's looks and losing to him at chess, was constantly on the phone. He had recently done an info-mercial with Cher, one of her first info-mercials I believe, and was making gobs of money on his products, using the company phone to check on shipments of thousands of jars of wonder makeup.

Primarily, most of us were in the rooms to get out of the cold. When we reached the small West Texas town of Big Lake for some night shooting, the winter, for Texas, had grown severe. The water sprinklers for a rain shot froze at one point, forcing special effects, Randy Moore and company, of exploding coke-filled duck fame, to turn several fire hoses gushing cold water into the air, falling like rain on

Quaid as he ran back and forth in the scene from his truck to the hotel room, earning his money that night. I spent most of my time across the street inside a bar/pool hall that Mark Rosenberg had rented from a local to hold crew and extras and to give catering a warm spot to set up for lunch and dinner.

The bar was a typical West Texas hangout full of rednecks, roughnecks, racists, and deer hunters. Big Lake was an oil and deer hunting town. A large dry lake bed could be seen from the highway on the way into town. A tall billboard posted at its edge posed the eternal question: Who pulled the plug on Big Lake? Being from the state and having several relatives not unlike the bar's occupants, I knew these people and their particular brand of meanness and wariness of outsiders. I watched them closely as they reacted to the movie crew filling their bar, which had, among other charming items, a flashing message board running a repeating string of racist and homophobic jokes. Rush Limbaugh was constantly on the TV set, his pasty, elephantine face moving freakishly on the screen. I realized that these people saw me as one of the movie company, rather than as a Texan, when I ate lunch across from the local sheriff. The presidential election was going on and no one knew who would win. I mistakenly brought up politics and George Bush and the man grew angry at my opinions, especially when I let it slip that I was for the Brady Bill and gun control. He stopped eating and looked up at me as though I'd said I was for child molestation.

"Well," he said, standing up to reveal the .45 on his hip, "around here, we like George Bush. An' we sure as hell ain't for gun control. Maybe in California it's different."

He left then. I knew what he said was true. Everyone in the bar was probably packing. Our own governor at the time had to go hunting, killing animals occasionally, just to get elected. My own sweet little mother had a .38 under her car seat down in Houston. I finished my food and went up to the bar, ordered a coke, and watched the election results. Quaid came bustling in and out from time to time to use the production phone near the bar. A pinched-face woman, her husband, and another man, all local extras, watched the actor come and go. I listened to them.

"That was him right there," the woman said.

"Yeah, I seen him," her husband said. "Mr. Movie Star."

"He really is a snob, ain't he?" the woman said. "See how he just completely ignores us."

"Whadda ya expect?" the other man said.

"His wife is as rude as hell," the pinched-face woman said, adjusting her green camouflage windbreaker. "I mean a B-I-T-C-H bitch. I tried to say something to her on the set an she ignored me. I just can't stand those people. Did you see the way Dennis Quaid looked at us? Like we were nobodies."

"That's right," her husband said. "An' this is our town. We live here."

"If they don't like it," the other man said, "they can just leave. We don't need 'em here."

I began to feel sorry for the actors of *Flesh and Bone* —all actors really. They couldn't win for losing. If they ignored people, they were snobs; if they stopped to chat, they could be inconvenienced and bothered for hours, days; sometimes they were even stalked and killed. The only avenue I could see was to avoid people at all costs.

The three locals began to speak of the abundance of deer that season on the highways. It was true. Between Ozona and Big Lake, I had counted forty-five live deer one morning running across the road or grazing beside it. Several more, as dead carcasses, littered the highway, hit by trucks and cars. On the road at night, I always had to creep along in my truck, trying not to hit any. That evidently wasn't the Big Lake way. Attempting to make pleasant conversation, I brought up my driving difficulties.

"Oh, I know," said the pinched-face woman. "I've seen so many this year."

"It really is getting out of hand," her husband said. "I'm afraid I'm gonna wreck another truck hittin' one of them dumb-ass deer."

"I tried one of them deer whistles," the other man said. "you know, on my truck, but they don't work for shit."

The woman lit a cigarette and smiled at me. "You shoulda seen what happened to us yesterday."

Her husband smiled. "Yeah, tell him that."

"Well, I was drivin'. . . " she picked a piece of tobacco off her tongue, "an' all the roads were frozen over——"

"We got some sleet the other night," her husband added.

"Yeah," she said, "so the roads was real slick. So, this momma deer comes out, just a trottin' over the road, pretty far ahead of me you know, so I wasn't gonna hit her. Then, her little baby, this little fawn came out of the brush an' she's tryin' t' follow her momma you know?" She smiled and chuckled. "So, she gets in about the middle of the road an' starts t' slippin' an' slidin', she just can't get up on those little tiny legs. An' her momma's still standin' there on the side of the road like she's sayin, 'C'mon baby, let's go.' It was hilarious. She was about fifty yards away then, still strugglin' an' tryin' to stand in the ice, so I just gunned it an' Bam!——flattened her out all over the road."

Her husband laughed. "You shoulda saw the look on that little fawn's face. I mean she just knew we wasn't gonna slow down."

Not a fawn killer myself, the woman must have seen the look of horror on my face.

"See, you gotta understand," she explained, "there's so many deer out here they're like pests."

"Yeah, like rats or something," her husband said.

"Oh."

I turned back to the TV. *Nightline* was on and Ted Koppel and his hair were interviewing Ross Perot and his ears.

"Turn it up," the woman said to the bartender. Then to me, "I love Perot."

"We need a man like him up in Warshington," her husband said.

Our producer, Mark Rosenberg, came loudly through the door then, followed by Mac. Rosenberg, having rented the bar, essentially owned it for the night. He looked up at the TV and said loudly, for all the room to hear, "Oh shit, it's H. Ross Perot. I hate that bastard. What's with him? He can never make up his mind if he wants to run. He's in, he's out, he's in, it's like he's fucking somebody."

The three Big Lake residents at the bar looked at one another, then to Rosenberg, with disgust.

"That man uses the most foul-mouth language," the woman whispered to her husband.

"New York Jew," he said quietly, as if that explained it all.

To their dismay, Rosenberg and Mac pulled up two barstools and sat next to them at the bar. They began to watch the election results with the rest of us. As more came in and the projections predicted Clinton's victory, Mark grew more gleeful, especially whenever George Bush's face came on the screen.

"Ahh, Bush," he said, "you stupid son-of-a-bitch. One term, you stupid bastard. Look at him. Bush is gonna cry. What a miserable fuck."

I watched the sheriff and the many locals in the bar and wanted to tell Rosenberg to watch his back. Then the two producers began to talk about adoption. I'd heard Rosenberg and his wife were trying to adopt and the conversation grew into a heated argument when the subject of qualifications for a good parent came up. Mac started saying that gay or lesbian couples could never be good parents and Rosenberg disagreed. As for the locals, they just kept staring quietly at the jokes flashing across the light bar over the liquor bottles: These two lesbians. . . These two lesbians. . . These two lesbians. . .

"Look," Mac said, "you can't tell me that some guy in New York, some guy who goes out at night and sticks his dick in a hole in a public restroom and lets total strangers suck him off and then he sucks off a bunch of other guys' dicks, is going to go home and be a good parent."

"People shouldn't be having anonymous sex with AIDS, I grant you that," Rosenberg said, "but the government can't go around telling people where to stick their dicks. A homosexual is the same person as you or me, and it's none of yours or my fucking business where he puts his fucking dick either."

The pinched-face woman's face turned in on itself even further. She nervously plucked at her hair.

"I'm surprised at you," Rosenberg said.

Mac shook his head. "I know homosexuals are great and all. I have friends who are gay—I mean, I live in New York. I'm just saying the best, most ideal situation is a normal father and mother."

Rosenberg laughed. "I'm not gonna argue with that, nobody is. All I'm saying is, we don't live in a normal world. Who's to say what's normal or not? I'm not, are you? Lots of normal mothers and fathers have produced serial killers and turned out to not be normal after all. If I should die tomorrow, God forbid, I would hope that a person, any person, no matter what color or sexual preference, but only a loving, intelligent person, would take care of my child. I'm just saying the government should relax some of the restrictions on adoption. Look at all the trouble we've had trying to adopt and I'd say we're fairly successful dependable people."

The argument went on and Mac made the mistake of bringing up the law—the legalities of adoption and sexual preference.

"Oh," Rosenberg said happily, "you fucked up now. I got you by the short and curlies, Mac. I got you by the short and curlies. . . "

He then proceeded to rip Mac's argument apart, limb by limb. I listened intently to Rosenberg. Before that night, I thought he was a typical blowhard producer who yelled at people. I knew he scared me. Just that day, at the catering wagon, I had made a joke about some questionable potato salad and he got right in my face.

"What? What?" he demanded. "What's wrong with it? Is there something wrong with the food here?"

I immediately said no, I just didn't like potato salad, and left it at that. I detected a hint of humor, though, in his rebuke. Listening to him speak amid all my fellow Texans, disturbing them deeply, going on about the right to be an individual, to be different, to be free in this country, all the ideas the United States were supposed to be founded on, I had to respect and admire him. I suddenly had this vision of him as the last real liberal and, to me, American, isolated out here in the West Texas desert, in the heart, or the spot where a heart might be, of conservative America. I got a call on my walkie—I actually had something urgent to do—and stood up to leave. Before I left, I felt I should lend my support, and stopping next to Rosenberg, I told him I was on his side . Mac frowned at me, but Rosenberg smiled, saying, "Well, thank you very much," and went back to arguing with Mac, who sat there quietly, obviously losing the debate.

We traveled to Midland the next afternoon to film some scenes in the nearby town of Stanton. The first day of shooting there, we gathered around the caterers for a late breakfast. Tom Katz was the new caterer and had a well-deserved reputation for quality. Quaid had liked them so much on *Great Balls of Fire* he specifically asked for them after the other caterer was fired. To me, their food tasted like a lot of movie-catered food, but they had this great thing called service, filling your plate in quick buffet lines, filling your glass with tea, taking your tray, things you remembered afterwards. I was standing before their open catering wagon, through with my breakfast, talking for a moment with the busy Kara. I noticed Rosenberg was standing next to the coffee dispenser on the wagon, when he began to stumble and fall on some people, holding his throat as if he were choking. A man of great girth, no one could hold him up and he fell down on the ground, rolling and writhing on his back. The man seemed to be either choking or having a seizure. Kara called quickly for the on-set medic, Annie, and she wasn't there. As it turned out, she was at the hotel, checking on Rosenberg's assistant, Loring, who'd contracted a case of salmonella poisoning the night before. This was bad news for Rosenberg, who was writhing in pain. Mac and Steve Kloves were now kneeling over him, speaking calmly, reassuring him, "It's gonna be O.K., Mark," Steve said. "It's gonna be O.K."

An ambulance had been called and many of us stood around helplessly and quietly waiting. Several extras had wandered out of their holding area to watch the spectacle. Two blue-haired, bee-hived, polyester-clad women stood behind me, talking loudly, laughing and complaining.

"When the hell are we gonna start this show?" one said.

"I don't know, but I'm ready to go home. Hollywood can make it without me," the other said. Then she pointed to Rosenberg. "What's wrong with him? What's he doin'?"

I looked back at them and then at Kara, who'd heard the same thing. She quickly ushered the two women and the other extras back inside the building, and went to Rosenberg's side.

The ambulance finally arrived and I knew he was really in trouble. Two befuddled men jumped out and fumbled around with their equipment, seeming to be confused and not knowing what to do. When they finally got an oxygen tank and mask ready, it turned out the tank was empty. The set medic, Annie, showed up then, immediately saw the seriousness of the situation and took charge. They loaded the writhing and struggling Rosenberg into the ambulance and sped away.

Not fifteen minutes later, we were working. The first shot was a crane shot. Steve and Tass were up on the crane ready to go when, suddenly, they lowered the crane and everything stopped. I saw Steve's shoulders slumping, people hugging each other, and then someone walking past said, "Rosenberg's dead. He died on the way to the hospital."

"What?"

"There was only like one doctor there when they got him there and he was in surgery."

The second a.d., Marge, walked past. "Mark Rosenberg just died," she said. "Steve can't go on today."

"What do we do now?" I asked.

"We're all going back to the hotel and figure it out from there."

Back at the hotel, I walked in a side door and found myself passing the production office. Steve and Mac, both friends of Rosenberg, were standing in the hallway with tears in their eyes. Not knowing what I should say, or if I should say anything, I gave a somber nod and kept walking to the hotel bar. I met the electrician Scott Greene in there and we had several drinks. We went back up to my room and drank some codeine-laced cough syrup I had for a cold I'd contracted and smoked some dope. I was also taking a synthetic morphine called Lortab I'd procured from the medic for a sore throat, so I was feeling pretty comfortable. Scott and I talked about Rosenberg.

"So what do you think will happen?" I asked him.

"Ah, we'll take a day off and go back to work. We're too far along in this picture to stop now. Everybody will say shit like 'This is what Mark would have wanted' and we'll go back to work."

"Only one day?"

"Hey, look at Mac's position: thousands of dollars riding on every lost hour. What would you do?"

"I guess I'd get everybody back to work. Still though, one day. . . "

"Fuck it, man. You didn't know Rosenberg, neither did I. Probably none of these people did except Steve and Mac. I mean, I'm sorry Rosenberg's dead, really, but how much time do you think they'd take off if one of us died? Me or you?"

"Zero."

"Exactly, dude. They'd say, get that dead painter out of here."

"Right."

That night, the caterers threw a special memorial dinner at the hotel in an upstairs dining room. The whole crew was packed in there. Quite a few of the women were crying their eyes out, telling Mark stories and acting as if they had been childhood friends with the producer. This canonization of Rosenberg would amplify for the rest of the show until, at the end, Mark had many good friends. One real acquaintance of his, the second-second Jordan, whom Rosenberg had helped get on the film and had patronized for years, took the Rosenberg homage to great lengths, going as far as telling me one night, when we got stoned in his motel room, that this was Rosenberg's old pot pipe we were using, that this was even his lighter, as though it were something holy. Jordan had always been a snobbish jerk, flaunting his powerful connection before Rosenberg's death. After the passing of his benefactor, all of us, his cut-throat colleagues, began to wonder out loud how long he would last. Almost overnight, Jordan became much nicer, suddenly needing friends. I know he kept asking me for days afterwards to watch the videotape of the funeral. "I spoke," he kept saying, "I spoke at the funeral."

Before we all went to serve ourselves dinner, Mac stood up and said a few words, basically that the show would go on and that Mark would have wanted it that way, which was, I would think, completely true. "So, all of you," Mac said, "let's just eat dinner tonight and try to have a good time and think of Mark."

Almost before he was finished, at least before there was a proper period of somberness, my friend Scott jumped to his feet to go eat. Everyone in the room, seventy people or so, stared at him. He looked at me.

"What? He said, let's eat. Right?"

With that, I stood up, as did everyone else, to get our food and eat it, amid the sound of sniffles and fond remembrances that could no longer be refuted by their subject. We went back to work the next day.

Before we left for Marfa, Texas, James Caan was shot out of the picture at the wheat-field house in Coupland. The last gag involved a stuntman doubling for Caan, falling down a real vertical flight of stairs. Caan would replace him at the bottom of the stairs on the floor. The stuntman, a wild-eyed person who couldn't stop talking to all of the women on the set, had to fall down the stairs four times at Steve's request. Each time, he got up a little slower, and with a little more money—at five hundred dollars a tumble. And each time he fell through the balsa-wood railing, breaking it into pieces, a carpenter and

I were there to quickly put the staircase back together.

Caan, as usual, took forever that day. When he was finally through with his last shot, Kara called out loudly to everyone, all of us huddled in a downstairs room for warmth, "That's it for Jimmy!"

The entire crew cheered, "Yeah!" letting him know how sad we were to see him go.

Caan was standing two feet away from me and waved us away with his hand. "Ahh, fuck all you guys," he muttered and then began to mumble a strange, garbled thank-you to the crew. No one was listening and he gave up trying, his voice trailing off. I watched him and he seemed vaguely old and alone at that moment. He left the set and was driven away by a Teamster, out of our lives.

Hutman made a point of telling Mac he needed me as a slave in Marfa, so I went with the crew out there for the last week of shooting. Most all of the crew stayed in Alpine, a small town centered around cattle ranching and a rodeo college called Sul Ross that sits on a hill in the center of town which Texans call a mountain. We made the thirty-minute drive to Marfa every day while the other higher-ups stayed at the hotel in Marfa or in Fort Davis.

The first day of shooting, it had snowed thirteen inches the night before. Since the scene was supposed to be in the summer, it posed a slight problem. The whole reason we'd all journeyed to Marfa was so Steve and Philippe could shoot the beautiful, stark West Texas vistas, now covered in snow. Hutman and Mac were running everywhere trying to figure out how to clear the snow. Several of the locals standing around said not to worry, it would melt off, all of it, by the next day's sun. Mac didn't have time to wait, though. It was almost Christmas and he did not want to bring everyone back after a holiday break. An army of locals with makeshift flamethrowers were hired to melt snow while people like me and the set dresser, Marcus Brown, grabbed a shovel. I became the standby shovel guy then and Mac began to direct my shoveling so we could clear background grass and roofs. With the interior shots as filler, we were able to work around the snow that day. Soon, as the locals promised, it all melted.

That last week was the most enjoyable for me on the whole movie. There was very little for me to do, frustrating Hutman. I was no longer running up to him trying to find something to do, either. I hung out in the motel rooms watching TV, eating sunflower seeds, and drinking hot apple cider and rum, being called to the set once a day. Kara called me over to the set for something one day and, after doing my little job, I stood around too long and noticed Kara staring at me.

"I want your job," she said smiling.

"I don't want your job," I said back.

"JR, I'm putting you in this next scene for that."

I was sent over to wardrobe where Tania put a cowboy hat on my head and a vest on me. I walked by in the background behind Quaid, three times in the cold. Jordan had me fill out some paperwork and told me I would be paid seventy-five bucks for the ten minutes of work. Coupled with my salary, it was an easy-money day.

At night, I hung out with Scott, Derek, and Christine, smoking dope and chasing the Marfa lights across people's ranches. I saw the fabled, mysterious lights almost every morning and night. Some of them were probably headlights in the distance, but there were other phenomena I saw often and couldn't explain, such as floating, darting lights and a solitary flame lighting up, disappearing, and reappearing quickly in several different locations on the horizon. Kara, who seemed as skeptical as I usually was about things, told me one morning, on a drive to the set in a Teamster van, what she had seen. It coincided with the flame-like light I'd seen. There was something strange out there in the desert, and it wasn't just our crew.

The shooting went fairly smoothly and quickly. Because we had to finish up, Mac arranged walking lunches for the last day, which meant—grab some food and keep working. The last shots of Quaid and Meg Ryan saying good-bye, the sad ending, were done and that was it for the two actors. We gathered for a crew photo and Quaid asked for a moment of silence in memory of Mark Rosenberg. Then, as soon as the shutter had clicked on the camera, the two actors, our king and queen, hopped on a plane and got the hell out of there.

Later that evening, in lieu of a wrap party, we had a lobster dinner at the El Paisano Hotel. Before it was ready, several people were milling around the lobby near the production office bitching about a meal penalty; because of the walking lunch they wanted more money for the day. Mac overheard the grumblings and I watched him get pissed out on the street. "Goddammit," he said, "I have bent over backwards to accommodate everyone on this picture and now they're gonna bitch about a meal penalty? Fuck this shit!"

I couldn't blame him a bit. He'd been generous to me, paying me well, renting my vehicle and tools, and I'd seen him transporting other crew member's motorcycles so they could ride around, putting up with complaints, the death of his producer, a foot of unwanted snow, the coming of Christmas, and now people were getting petty. I could tell he was tired of dealing with all of us on the picture. In one revealing moment the night before, one of the hairdressers, a demanding old woman who reminded me of a sea turtle, and always walked around with a tiny dog in her coat, bitching about people sitting in her special chair, slipped and fell on the sidewalk outside of one of the hotel room sets. The woman really went tumbling and after Mac helped her to her feet, I watched him throw back his head and laugh heartily at her fall all the way to his office.

I went back inside the hotel for the lobster dinner. After we ate, there were several heartfelt speeches about how wonderful Steve was. In fact, we all stood up and gave him a standing ovation when he walked into the room. As the dinner broke up, everyone walked around the tables hugging and saying some real and phoney good-byes. Steve was stopped and thanked and congratulated by everyone as he toured the room. When he stopped near my table, I couldn't think of anything congratulatory to say. I'd read the script and watched the scenes and yes, Steve was a nice guy, but I thought his movie was boring. Scott didn't say anything either, except "Hi Steve." That was all I could muster too. Steve stood there for an awkward moment, a pleased smile on his face, and walked away to be lauded by others.

I stood up and went into a large den where comfortable couches surrounded an active fireplace. Warming myself in front of the fire, I noticed Jon Hutman sitting across from me on a couch, eating another lobster off the plate in his lap. If I was to say a sincere good-bye to anyone, it would be Jon. He was the man I'd spent the most time with, for whom I'd worked. He made a point of proving it that last day, on the very last shot, making me run to the set and paint something inconsequential, touching up a background sidewalk. When he got Steve's indifferent approval of what I'd done, he turned to me and said,

"Alright, JR, that's it for you on this movie. Get out of here."

I stood across from Hutman and thought of how much he reminded me of Brian, except for having more intelligence. It was Hutman's intellect that had impressed me more than anything, and I felt I should say something. Though he had been openly disdainful and patronizing of me at times, he had been complimentary as well, he and Sam even buying me dinner one night, and had kept me on for the entire picture.

"Well, Jon," I began, "I guess we did it. . . "

Hutman set down his plate, looked at me, and let out a long, loud fart. His way of saying good-bye, I suppose. Saying, or rather, emitting nothing else, he stood up and left, his empty plate still on the coffee table.

–16–

Back home, after a month or two of unemployment checks, I heard they were putting *Ned Blessing* on the rails again. Someone at CBS had given Bill Wittliff and Bill Scott some money and we were to do six episodes in hopes that it would get picked up. We filmed again at Willieville, adding several new buildings, including a few jails, a cantina exterior, and a couple of quite large barns. Episodic TV moves at a very fast pace and, being the only painter, they killed me. Cary White was the designer, Sully his art director, Dave Wilt the construction coordinator. The first two episodes had the same director, a demanding s.o.b., who had Cary and the rest of us hopping, doing things like building an interior Styrofoam cave in three days complete with forty giant boulders for a cave-in gag. Every day there would be an impossible, new set to build and every time, we'd do it and do it well, getting little or no appreciation from the director. With no time left, he'd have to shoot it. Every set was such a rush to finish that I found myself more than once painting in the rain, slogging around in the mud with a forty-foot ladder and eighty-gallons of raw umber wash, putting it on a building, only to watch the rain make it disappear.

The production company was very cheap and thus, so were many of the people they had hired. It was no *Flesh and Bone*. Our craft service was the worst. Craft service, usually run by a helpful sort of person, is in charge of keeping snacks and drinks on the set for the crew. As I was also being called to the set for standby painting jobs, I had a right to grab some food and drink occasionally. The rotund little man who ran the craft service truck didn't like me eating potato chips he felt were destined for more important people's stomachs. When the direc-

tor walked by, the man would chase him around, trying to run and kiss
ass at the same time, practically throwing food at him. When I grabbed
a few Cheetos, he would stand there and stare at me. "Are you gonna
eat all of those? Are you with the shooting crew? You look like you're
with construction. I really don't like construction or anybody from the
art department around my truck. I don't have to feed you guys."

After about three incidents like that, I told him explicitly to keep
his shitty food for his own fat ass and stayed away from his truck.
Nothing particularly memorable happened for those six episodes. Well,
maybe a few things. One day at the catering wagon, Brad Johnson, the
star of the show, after stupidly throwing away his per diem with his
lunch, grew angry and frustrated when no one would dig through the
trash for him and fish out his money. After standing there for a minute,
he did it himself. I had a particularly lovely exchange with the actor
Bill McKinney one afternoon. Bill was famous for only one thing that
would haunt him probably for the rest of his career. He was the guy
who sodomized Ned Beatty (on screen) in the movie *Deliverance*.
Apparently proud of this, I heard him more than once scream out those
tell-tale words, "Squeal like a pig!" I don't know what it was, maybe
because I was always covered in paint, wearing seemingly dirty clothes,
but people didn't seem to care what they did around me. I was painting
and repairing a Styrofoam chimney on a background cabin off the main
street when the actor came over in costume.

"Hey, Mr.Painter," McKinney said.

"Hi, how are you?" I answered, pumping my Hudson sprayer.

"Fine, fine," he said, and unzipped his pants and pulled out his
penis in front of me. Was he a flasher or something? Was I going to
meet Ned Beatty's fate?

"You don't mind if I take a piss over here do you?"

I said that was O.K., politely moving out of his way, but wanting
to say, no, by all means, come stand two feet away from me and take a
piss in my direction, I've been waiting all day.

As he urinated, he let out a long, loud, Hutmanesque fart.
"Whew!" he said. "That felt good. Here comes another one," he
announced and had flatulence again. "Much better!"

He thanked me then, just for being me I guess, and walked back to
the set. Playing a crass lunatic in this episode, perhaps he was in character.

I landed another movie job before the last episode even started filming and broke the news to Cary while we sat on the porch of the sheriff's office painting a sign. He'd just mentioned several other people who were leaving for other shows when I told him.

"Like rats from a sinking ship," he said and then mentioned a show he might have in the works. We parted amicably, even though I left an intern in charge for the last week, skipping the last episode. CBS decided to skip the last episode as well, not even airing it, and the series did indeed sink like a rock.

–17–

I'd left *Ned Blessing* to paint the sets on a feature in San Antonio called *The Lane Frost Story*, which became *Eight Seconds*. Directed by John "Rocky" Alvidsen, the film was a true story about a young champion bull rider who gets gored by a bull and dies a hero. The young television actor Luke Perry would play Lane Frost, and yet another Baldwin brother, Stephen, would play his best friend, Tuff Hedeman.

John Burson was the construction coordinator, John Frick the art director, and an overweight, cantankerous man named Bill Cassidy was the production designer. By all accounts, I should have and would have been the lead scenic had my good friend John Frick pushed me for the job. Instead, he didn't, and over John Burson's objections, another scenic was brought in as lead and I was to be his second. The scenic's name was Cole Lewis, and when I met him the first time, my stomach sank in depression. I was about to spend twelve hours a day for six days a week for three months under the command of a complete, even by his own admission, flake. Cole was a true scenic artist from L.A., but a compartmentalized, union guy, he'd never really run a feature or TV show as a lead and was not, as he told me, a set painter. Somewhere down the line, as he poured out his story over lunch the first day, he'd done way too much coke and lost everything, having only weird facial tics to remind him of successful days past. Now his third wife was leaving him for a waiter, and he was bankrupt and spiritually broke. As I listened to Cole's sad story I wondered, since he was ten years older than me, whether I was getting a glimpse into my future as a scenic. If so, I might as well have killed myself with one of the salad forks on the table. The saddest part of the story was this: Cole had a secret wish, a fantasy we'll call it, that he was going to be a producer someday. After a week of watching this forgetful buffoon try to paint, I wanted to tell him to hang up that producer thing. But no, as I soon found out, Cole even had an attitude. He actually thought he was a cool producer because he had made a video back in L.A. called "Hollywood Dumpster" that he kept pressing on me to watch.

"I spent $25,000 of my own money on it," he said proudly.

After watching five minutes of the short video, I saw it was appropriately named and belonged in a Hollywood dumpster, or any dumpster. Of course, when I brought it back the next day I said it was great.

He brightened. "Really? You liked it? I'm trying to make a sequel if I could just get the money together. . . ."

Between Cole's frantic, but vacant, actions, and Bill Cassidy's and John Frick's absent directions, I thought I might quit. Needing the money, though, I stayed on and tried to discern what they all wanted. Cassidy was so old and out of it that he would show up every once in a while, be cantankerous, make a few meaningless suggestions and disappear. He was so overweight his every utterance or movement took all his energy and breath, leaving me to think he might die before he finished his sentence and told me a paint color. Bill did have a heart attack one day while driving in Austin, and a wreck. He was flown to L.A. for open-heart surgery and survived but was off the picture. This forced John Frick into the day-to-day decision-maker role, worrying himself and all of us greatly. Early on in the show, I had hired another painter and quickly moved Cole out of the picture, for which he seemed relieved, even telling me several times, "I'll leave early if you want to take over, I'll leave early." I needed him, though, to do signs and tried to act like we were buddies.

Trying to get the sets out of Frick was as difficult as usual. He had a habit of disappearing for days, giving me no input, and then showing up at quitting time on a Saturday, fully expecting me to stay until Sunday, making gigantic last-minute changes that mattered for nothing. I followed his orders, but could feel my resentment growing. The problem was, though we were supposed to be friends, I didn't think Frick was production designer material. What I felt he really was was a set designer or art director, what he'd been on *Lonesome Dove*. It was obviously what John was most comfortable with and enjoyed. He loved to sit in his office at his drafting table with all of his pencils and drawing tools, drawing all day. A quiet, soft-spoken man, he wasn't meant, in my opinion, to skipper the Titanic-like ship that was a movie. Tired and exhausted almost every day, painting a mural with Cole on a house trailer or painting many rodeo arenas and their stalls filled with cowshit, I came to the point some evenings where I'd had it with him, showing up at the set just in time to tell me to do what I told him I'd do the night before. Somehow though, we remained buddies and got the sets ready.

Our art department problems looked small compared to the production and shooting crew problems. Luke Perry and Stephen Baldwin were young and eager and seemed to pose no problems on their front. Perry, in fact, went a little overboard with the aw-shucks, good ol'boy act, but on the whole, he seemed genuine, taking notice of others around him and being nice. The problem resided with other cantankerous people, the director Alvidsen and his right-hand man, the primary cause of chaos, Cliff Coleman, his first a.d. Cliff was a tall, partially bald and white-haired man who looked like Brian Keith with a mustache. Whereas most first a.d.'s used a walkie-talkie or a headset to communicate with their p.a.'s, Teamsters, key grips, and other crew members, Cliff preferred to walk around with a Mr.Microphone and scream into it at people he needed. I felt truly sorry for his p.a.'s and a.d.'s and avoided him whenever I was on set.

I remember one afternoon, up at a rodeo arena in Boerne, Texas, the whole crew was waiting for a p.a. to arrive with black tempera paint for painting a live bull. They had someone else, a taxidermist, doing the painting, so I watched and waited near him, offering my help if he needed it. The man's name was Tiger and he was part of the local wrangler, rodeo, country-boy crowd, the same kind of guys I'd gone to high school with, who were working on the movie and who viewed the shooting crew with disdain. Thinking I was with them, he gave me a rude brush-off when I offered to help, not giving me the chance to tell him I had some black tempera paint in my truck. Cliff wouldn't let me get near him either, so I figured, fuck 'em, and stood there while the whole crew waited for thirty minutes. Cliff was screaming and yelling at everyone. There were many large crowd scenes in the film and Cliff used his mike to cajole and entertain them. All the local extras were working for free—well, for a T-shirt and a cold hot dog, so Cliff had to keep them there in the Texas heat. He did so by playing little patronizing games and giving away a beer mug or a cap.

"O.K.! I got a buffalo nickel here in my hand!" he would yell to the crowd. "Who can guess the date on this nickel? Whoever can gets a free cap!"

The main incentive for the crowd of uncomfortable extras was a small trip to Hawaii that would be raffled off. This trip and other prizes (the T-shirts and caps) were advertised in local papers and radio stations in San Antonio to bring in crowds. What the people found out when they got there was the trip wouldn't be raffled off until the end of the show in the Hemisphere Arena during the big National Rodeo Finals scene. They would have to come back at the end to win.

"We're waiting on a young girl with black paint!" Cliff said to the impatient crowd. "She's speeding to the set as we speak! Who wants to try for another cap?!"

Cliff's rattled second came running past just then and called out, "She's already here!" and kept running, probably on his way to get her. Cliff, an ex-stuntman motorcycle rider, had a limp, but ran after the second and grabbed him, screaming into his Mr. Microphone.

"GODDAMMIT, YOU STUPID SON-OF-A-BITCH! YOU WERE SUPPOSED TO TELL ME WHEN SHE GOT HERE!"

"I am," the man said weakly. "I just told you."

"YOU STUPID SHIT!" Cliff screamed into the mike. "YOU ARE SUPPOSED TO KEEP ME INFORMED AT ALL TIMES OR YOU'RE FIRED! NOW GO GET THAT GIRL!"

The man slinked away on the quiet set. A wrangler standing next to me shook his head and said, "Boy, that skinny bastard better not ever talk to me that way. I'll kill him." I saw Cliff ream people out in this manner almost daily while Alvidsen said nothing, except to do a little yelling of his own. As I said, I avoided Cliff, but caught what I felt was a revealing glimpse of him one day on the large makeshift warehouse sound stage where we'd built four sets. A black four-door Mercedes was parked inside the warehouse. The on-set nurse, who was Cliff's wife or girlfriend, was seated next to it. Cliff made several time-consuming and obvious trips over to the expensive car to wipe and polish it with a rag, quite proud of it. I was standing there getting some Rolaids from the nurse when I noticed his Mercedes had a large trailer hitch. I suddenly had an image of the carny-barker Cliff, traveling around the country in his fancy Mercedes, pulling a beat-up trailer behind him, and he seemed less forbidding.

With men like Cliff in charge, who had no respect for or knowledge of the locals, problems had to ensue. I watched the crew treat several ranch house locations poorly, throwing trash around, leaving cattle gates open, pissing off the ranchers with their rude behavior. The main problem was with the crowd scenes. Cliff and company had pissed so many people off they weren't getting enough extras. The crew went down to Del Rio at one point to utilize an existing crowd at the George Paul Memorial Bull Ride, a serious annual rodeo event in Del Rio. The crowd was supposed to stay after the real rodeo for a few shots. Cliff started ordering the crowd around, not something you do with tough Texas bull riders and their drunken friends, who were growing restless. When he tried his "O.K., I got a buffalo nickel here" bullshit the crowd stood up and left, all of this forcing the art department to recreate the Del Rio rodeo arena to be shot on a different location. The producers then pissed off the PRCA by asking them for more money. They subsequently pulled out all of their support for the movie, including their permission to film at the real National Rodeo Finals. This was a dumb move on the company's part since it's hard to make a realistic movie about professional rodeo cowboys without the help of the Professional Rodeo Cowboy Association.

Alvidsen then did what he had to and made a soap opera with a lot of head shots and crowd scenes you shouldn't look at too closely. There was practically no one in crowd terms at the mock National Finals at the Hemisphere Arena when we were filming in one of the most populated cities in the US. There was even a story about the scene on the local news that included several interviews with disgruntled extras, complaining about their treatment from the show. I've always figured if you were an extra more than once, you were either a sucker or an actor and deserved what you got. But these Central and South Texans whose homes, arenas, and ranches we'd used were pissed which made things difficult for me as I tried to repaint their homes. As I painted the roof of one rancher's home, his mother's home actually, as appeasement, he assured me Hollywood wasn't welcome on his land again.

Lane Frost, or rather *Eight Seconds* was so chaotic, I kept thinking they were going to pull the plug, something which can definitely happen on a picture. Every movie worker knew a story about someone or other who had saved all of their paychecks only to have the movie fold and find their checks worthless. In Seguin, several bull riders suffered injuries, including broken legs and arms. In the Helotes rodeo arena we were rained out with no real cover set plan, losing valuable time. In Boerne, because of poor planning, we'd actually shot all our cover sets and were forced into a hiatus for a few weeks until Perry could come back and finish his last scenes, all of this costing a lot of money. Someone told me, though, this was the way Alvidsen operated and when he did *Rocky* and *The Karate Kid* it was the same way, by the skin of his teeth. *Eight Seconds* was finally finished and released, but it was no *Rocky*. It now safely resides in your local video store.

–18–

Another schlocky television production moved directly into the *Eight Seconds* San Antonio warehouse after it wrapped. Like most movie warehouses, it was in an economically depressed neighborhood. Many a morning we came in to find car windows smashed, things stolen. Prostitutes, alcoholics, and crack addicts were around every corner, defeated poverty-stricken people who would never join the system. Myself, I had to take time off from work one morning to stop a guy from beating the shit out of his wife in the street in front of his two screaming children and to call the police. Amid this squalor we were to begin a miniseries for ABC entitled *Heaven and Hell,* staring such luminaries as Robert Wagner from TV's *Hart to Hart* and Marriet Hartley with a cameo appearance by Peter O'Toole. The production designer was a nice elderly gentleman named Roger Maus who had done a lot of television over the years, including one of my favorite childhood shows, *Land of the Giants*. He'd also designed many of Blake Edwards's pictures like *Victor, Victoria* and *S.O.B.* Mainly concerned with playing polo now, Roger surrounded himself with competent people and sleep-walked through various assignments like this, collecting paychecks and buying more ponies. We mainly dealt with his art director, Christa, for instructions, a role she didn't mind. The few times I found Roger in his office he was straightening all the pens and pencils on his neat desk, but he did seem to show up in the shop at all the perfect times. He knew that we knew what we were doing and only stepped in when necessary.

Christa turned out to be easy to deal with except for her tendency to take things a little too seriously. We had a hundred sets to produce in eight weeks and she kept pulling me aside during projects to quiz me on my techniques and give me pep talks, saying, "You can make this one a showpiece for your portfolio," when we were struggling to get the set ready before a shoot the following morning. Her and Roger's planning was excellent, though, and it had to be. These weren't small sets. There were large insane asylums, several complete train stations, interior and exterior, completely burned-out streets, stables and barns, several churches, interior mansions, a Mexican hotel and cantina, a giant burned-out mansion of Styrofoam and plastic brick, and many more interior and exterior sets. Only a week or so ahead of production, we were kept busy.

The construction coordinator was a thin, Alfred E. Neuman-looking guy, who was from Texas or California, depending on whom he was talking to, named Lars Peterson. Lars enjoyed the power aspect of his job. Even though I was a lock as the lead scenic, he kept me hanging as long as possible, until Roger, having met me and seen my portfolio said hire him now. I remember Lars having fun with me on our first meeting. First, he acted much too busy to talk to me, forcing me to chase him around the warehouse. When I finally cornered him with my resume, he looked at it, shaking his head.

"I see a lot of TV on here," he said, disappointed.

"Well,I try to stay in Texas," I explained, "so I take whatever show comes to town. There's a lot of TV between features and I'm not very discriminating."

"Still, though, this is a lot of television. I just don't know. . . "

"Well, excuse me Lars, but isn't this a TV show I'm applying for?"

He was a bit taken aback by that. I found out later his resume was primarily TV as well.

"Yes, it is TV, but it's a big mini-series."

"*Lonesome Dove* was a big mini-series with a twenty-something million dollar budget. I've been on a couple other fair-size features there. . . "

"I just don't know. . . " he said and left me that first meeting with nothing more. Roger and Christa stepped in then and I was on the show.

I really enjoyed working with Roger. He was always so polite, saying to me after each particularly big set was finished, "JR, my friend, you've done it again. Thank you, my friend." A few niceties like that from a designer made me work harder. Roger also gave me as many painters as I wanted, up to ten at a time for big rushes, greatly lightening my own manual labor load. Lars protested at first at my fluctuating crew size, even though he had ten carpenters on at all times, and a foreman, Steve, who did every last bit of Lars's work. Construction coordinators, if they hire the right people, never have to do anything much at all except take the blame if the sets aren't ready. Lars, having a solid crew, spent a lot of time fishing in the creeks around Boerne and building a new custom bed for himself and his wife. He had a semi full of new tools, several rented trucks, and plenty of labor. All that was left were the purchase orders and paychecks, and his secretary, Mindy, did that. As for me, it was nice to have plenty of help for once, and, as the show wore on, I found myself following Lars's lead, working less and less, like Brian Stultz delegating more work to my foreman, indulging in two or three margarita lunches at Rosario's and even going to see a few new releases occasionally during the day, turning on my beeper to vibrate in case I was needed. Pleasantly drunk and stoned one afternoon, watching *The Fugitive* in a nice air-conditioned theater and getting paid for it, I thought, maybe this business isn't so bad. Maybe I should be like Roger, become a dignified designer, jumping from big TV to features, playing polo, buying houses, and traveling around the country and world meeting new people. There was still that one little problem I had: Roger had to at least pretend he gave a shit to the director and others about the project, no matter how stupid it was. But then again, wasn't I pretending just as much to Roger when I expressed interest, even excitement, when he told me to construct and paint forty Styrofoam tombstones? Which was harder to lie about? More to the point, which lie paid more?

Heaven and Hell was a sequel, the third installment to the popular mini-series *North and South* that helped launch Patrick Swayze as an actor. They'd tried to get Swayze to do a tiny bit part in this one, but were unsuccessful, reduced to having a stand-in in the shadows for his part. Most of the other actors were minor TV folks, except for Peter O'Toole. I'd always wanted to meet, or just see, Peter O'Toole since I first viewed *Lawrence of Arabia* as a boy in Houston on my parents'

black and white TV set. For years afterward, I had even wanted to be
the man Lawrence of Arabia. I wanted to go out across the world, the
great white leader, and forge a Third World nation. Even up until college, I had a secret fantasy, when finals were especially hard, of chuck-
ing it all and going to help the freedom fighters in Afghanistan (Sly
Stallone must have had the same fantasy for *Rambo III*) or maybe join
the Sandanistas with the Clash and fight against the contras and my old
producer Doc, I mean, El Medico. Most celebrities did nothing for me,
but I simply had to see this actor who'd had such an influence on my
life.

I went over to the set at the Masonic Temple in San Antonio. The
Temple, a beautiful marble structure, was being used in typical TV fashion for about six sets, interiors and exteriors. One of them was a theater, since the Temple had a large, shell-shaped auditorium with balconies and such and a large stage where the Masons performed sacri-
fices and counted money, whatever Masons do. I sat in one of the chairs
next to the stage that afternoon, and watched the director and others go
through O'Toole's scene with him. The actor was not in wardrobe yet
and was wearing plain, baggy shorts, revealing thin white legs, white
socks pulled up high, and tennis shoes. He had on a wrinkled old shirt
and began to rehearse his small scene. Watching the man work, as it
were, I felt discouraged. He looked like a fool, gyrating and screaming
across the stage. He was a parody of Peter O'Toole, not Lawrence of
Arabia. After seeing recent films of his such as *Creator* though, I don't
know what I'd been expecting. As he was being escorted to wardrobe,
a beautiful, smiling woman on each arm, he walked past me and stopped
and stared, as though we might know each other. Trying not to stare, I
glanced at his face, looking for something, and he gave me a large,
friendly smile, said hello, and walked on. I said nothing, remembering
suddenly that I had seen that smile before, on the face of Robert Duvall
at a large party on *Lonesome Dove*. It was indisputable, both times: I
was looking at a happy man. Both actors were having this thing called
fun and as I went to the paint store, fretting over how much money I had
left in my budget, I had to wonder which one of us was the fool.

To say that *Heaven and Hell* was an unwatchable piece of crap is
to do it a great kindness. I do not know anyone, involved with it or not,

who could watch it more than ten minutes, including myself, without ensuing nausea and dizziness. I know our sets looked O.K. to a point, but many of them had begun to deteriorate quality-wise as we ran out of time. There was one fake plaster wall in fact, that we used for about five sets until the director, finally recognizing it, said he didn't want to see that wall again. I repainted it and we used it once more.

–19–

Tired of all this rushed TV crap, and somehow having run out of money again, I was talking to my friend Jim Onate on the phone after *Heaven and Hell*. He told me he was starting a large feature called *The Road to Wellville*, directed by Alan Parker and starring Anthony Hopkins, Bridget Fonda, Mathew Broderick, Dana Carvey, and John Cusack. They would film part of it in a resort on the edge of the Catskills in New York called Lake Mohonk. The rest would be filmed at the studio sound stages in Wilmington. I said I was interested in working on it and Jim promised to talk to Herr Stultz. After I hung up, I wondered what I was doing, trekking all the way across the country to work for someone I didn't like. Needing the money, when Brian called me not five minutes later, I said I was on my way.

I drove across Texas, across the South, to Wilmington, North Carolina, and walked into the studio at four p.m. Brian immediately asked me why I didn't have my paint clothes on. I made up a lame excuse like, I just drove across the country, and offered to work in what I was wearing. He said that was O.K. but to be ready to work hard the next day and meet him on the sound stage at six a.m. It was just our little boss man/slave dance; Brian letting me know if I wanted to stay around, I was at his beck and call.

After a week of extremely hard, bones-tired work, Brian announced we would be leaving for New York in the morning. Myself and another painter named Bill, and the standby painter, Todd, a scenic from Ohio. Todd was extremely eager to work for the great scenic Brian and had been trying to get on one of his shows for a long time.

Todd was a nice, mild-mannered guy and talented scenic whom Brian had already begun to treat with open contempt, telling me on the side, if Todd made a wrong move in New York, he would fire him and let me take over. I said nothing, having no intentions of taking Todd's job.

We took a small dangerous flight up from the Wilmington airport to New York, the plane heavily weighted from all of Brian's new expensive luggage. As always, ever the good consumer, Brian had new houses, cars, clothes, everything, each time I saw him. Once in New York, a Teamster drove us out to Lake Mohonk. I was surprised at how beautiful the place was. A very large, almost gothic hotel, several stories high, was built upon a gray granite mountain next to the crystal-clear Lake Mohonk, itself surrounded by giant gray boulders and filled with impossibly large rainbow trout. Except for Brian, I could tell this would be a nice stay. My room cost almost as much as my daily wage and had a fireplace, nice antiques, and a large bathroom. I could just pick up the phone and have wood delivered, the fire started. Jackets were required at dinner and the food was excellent. It was a far cry from my movies in Texas where I either imposed on friends, put myself up in the cheapest of motels, or was put up by the company in the cheapest of motels. I looked out the window in my room at the changing colors of the trees, the beginnings of the Catskills. Never having seen the countryside of New York state I was again surprised at how picturesque it was. Putting away my things, I received my first phone call.

"Yes?"

"Hey, this is Brian."

"What's up?"

"Where are you?"

"I'm putting my things away."

"Well, you can take a few minutes, but then get into your paint clothes and come on down here to the lobby. We've got work to do."

Fun's over, back to work. For the next few weeks, during the day, I had no life other than orbiting around the black sun that was Brian.

It was cold up there and we'd bundle up every morning. Brian sent Todd and Bill off to do actual work, painting in Mohonk's ancient stables. Because I had some seniority, I was his assistant, which meant, rather than working, I was handing Brian his fitches, mixing up colors and washes, cleaning out his brushes, handing him rags, a general gopher. All of this, though, I was convinced, was only a ploy of his to get me to talk and listen to him. After running up and down stairs and fetching water from the cold lake, he'd have me just stand there like an idiot and watch him paint, listening to him expostulate on making films and writing, two things he didn't do. After a day or two, worried that what we'd painted would freeze, I was ordered to fetch large kerosene heaters and align them with the large deck and railing we were painting, tarp the deck off, and keep the heaters running into the evening to completely dry the paint. This was our main project, an add-on exterior deck with stairs that would play as the entrance to the Battlecreek Sanitarium. I went through the heater routine with Bill and Todd every morning and evening.

Brian quickly confirmed his enemy status with most of the crew up there. Bill Bradford, the construction coordinator, and his carpenters, who were building everything and already hated Brian from this and other shows, seemed to be barely tolerating him. I had to make an effort to show them I wasn't really a friend of Brian's, even though I acted like it, to get along with them. Once they heard me trashing him as much as they did, we were all buddies. Brian's main problem was he felt everyone on any movie worked for him, including the production designer. Rather than trying to actually be a production designer, he played the volatile, put-upon artist and was able to push around many designers this way. Except for this one. His name was Brian as well, which made things confusing, and like a lot of designers from England, he was polite but tough, and wasn't going to let a young loudmouth lead scenic get the best of him. I was with Herr Stultz the afternoon he was put in his place. Stultz and I were standing there painting while the designer watched us work. He had flown up and was quickly finding out from the set dressers and construction that Brian was calling all the shots in his absence. Watching us work on the set, he noticed that some of Brian's colors were a little off and began to gingerly make a few suggestions to his scenic artist for the set's improvement. Brian, not even bothering to look at his boss, blew him off quickly with an I'm-too-busy-for-that reply. The designer tried again. Could Brian help the set dressers paint some furniture?

"Yeah, yeah, I heard about that. I told them we didn't have the time so they can forget it."

I saw the designer stiffen. "Brian Stultz," he said quietly.

"Yeah?" Brian said, still not turning around.

"Look at me."

Sensing trouble, Brian handed me his brushes. I'd seen Brian turn into a remarkable kiss-ass when he had to. "Yes, Brian?"

"Let's get one thing perfectly clear, right now," he said calmly.

Brian appeared confused.

"I tell you what to do, and you do it. Do we understand each other?"

Well, they did. Brian quickly apologized and was on his knees, as we say in construction, ready to make his boss happy.

Our work load increased dramatically after that incident, souring Brian's mood. He took out his anger on his standby painter, Todd, chastising him for everything, criticizing all of his work, going so far one day as to chew him out loudly in front of the entire art department when Todd put in a paint order without his approval. "You don't buy a fucking quart of paint without asking me first!" Brian yelled, a smile on his face, enjoying it immensely. The designer, perhaps sensing the ass he had in Brian, noticed that I was doing a lot of my boss's work now. Being easier to approach, he started giving me little projects to do, which clearly irritated Brian, for he didn't have the authority to pull me away from these projects. He could only criticize them and make me do them again, which he gladly did.

Try as Brian might to keep me under his command, he had to let me off in the evenings. He knew better than to ask me along to dinner with his friends, but he did anyway, and I went along a few times. Dinner with him was hell. He did his routine:talking at a high volume, telling unfunny stories he thought were funny. His friends though, laughed at his tales. He pulled me aside at a bar in the nearby town of New Paltz one evening, put his hand on my shoulder and said serious-ly, "You know, you're always my standby painter if you want to be. I don't like this Todd guy. I'll fire him tomorrow if you want and you can take over." Though it would mean more money for me, I declined the offer and took the opportunity to take up for Todd, whom I liked, telling Brian to give him a chance. I knew for a fact Todd was a good scenic and hoped, in spite of any imaginary missteps, he could survive the show.

"One more fuck-up and he's out anyway," Brian said with finality.

Rather than nights out with Brian, I spent most of my evenings doing a little writing after work, having a nice five-course dinner, getting stoned, and taking long walks on the landscaped grounds, climbing up the granite mountain, or walking back and forth through the long, empty, ancient corridors of the Mohonk Hotel, which looked and reminded me of the Overlook Hotel in Stephen King's *The Shining*. The whole place, to me, was wonderful and relaxing, built for reading and conversation. I would get a cup of tea from downstairs and wander the halls, stopping at one of many lounging areas where a fire was blazing and a comfortable chair and book waited for me.

On one of my walks, I ran into two men around my age. One, named David, worked for the resort/hotel and the other was his friend, Nick Stamper. I'd seen Nick before on set working as a helper for the carpenters. Unlike many of the people I've met in this world, both men seemed to have interesting opinions and some originality. I mentioned that I had run out of pot and was looking for some. David looked at Nick.

"Perhaps we can help you with that," David said from behind his thick glasses.

We went back to my room and smoked some of David's incredibly powerful dope from his tobacco pipe, alternating with hits of real tobacco to kill the smell of marijuana. A small, thin, nervous man, who looked like a cross between Jack Nicholson and George Bush, David kept wiping off the pipe thoroughly whenever I passed it back to him.

"I have a problem with germs," he explained.

Nick was just the opposite of David, tall and outgoing, with a loud laugh. He referred to everyone as morons, which was O.K. with me since I referred to everyone as idiots, starting with myself. Like me, Nick had strong opinions, and we were soon all standing up and yelling and arguing about the ridiculousness of life and all the people in it. This led me to the movie business and I told them all about how stupid I thought it was. How movie companies seemed to be branching out from California and New York now more than ever to go to the other forty-eight states where they could find new suckers—young, eager, and oftentimes intelligent people—to use to do all of their work and where they could find new and different locations to do the same thing to the locals since Californians had caught on to their act. I said it was a business full of misfits, people who had never really fit into normal society, from the actors on down, and that these people started in the movie business for one main reason: they loved movies.

"Movies are made for morons now," Nick said.

"That's right," I said. "Most of them suck. The whole system has been taken over by businessmen who own and control all the avenues of communication, who sell you Product X with Product Y so you'll buy Product Z, all of it owned by XYZ Inc., in the process completely insulting and degrading whatever intelligence you have left, day by day, slowly chipping away at the discerning mind, turning us into sheep and zombies."

"Yeah," Nick said, "It used to only be TV that did that shit."

David then began to tell me Nick's story, acting as if he were his agent. Nick had been a filmmaker and editor at NYU and was, according to David, something of a genius when it came to working with electronics, computers, cameras, and videos. He said that Nick had helped construct the first video-wall at the Palladium, was involved with the beginnings of MTV, and had been friends with Andy Warhol and his buddies. He said both he and Nick spent a lot of time in Woodstock and the surrounding area where, Nick added, he'd hung out with the old beatniks and had met William S. Burroughs and Allen Ginsberg.

I was skeptical about all of it, but the beatniks caught my interest. "You've met Burroughs?" I asked him.

"Yeah man, listen, the beatniks are cool people. Except for the fact that a lot of these guys are homosexuals, including Warhol, they're good people. You see, it's all about freedom, man. Nobody's free anymore. They don't even know they're not free. These guys, these beatniks, they literally wrote the book on it. Burroughs was pretty cool. I showed him some of my videos and he loved them. I didn't really like his books though. They're really depressing. You read one of his books and you feel like killing yourself."

"You were involved with MTV?"

"Yeah, but those guys are morons. They don't give a shit about art or hard work. All they care about is money. That sounds like a cliché but it's true. They just kept stealing all my ideas and making money off of them so I left. That's when I met Warhol and those guys. They liked my little movies. Warhol told me I had an eye, you know what I mean? I had a different way of looking at things through a camera. They sorta took me under their wing. They're alright for homosexuals."

I noticed Nick and David kept running down homosexuals periodically, which was odd, especially since they acted so much like a gay married couple, or any couple, finishing each other's sentences and being so in tune with one another.

"What do y'all have against gay people?" I asked finally.

"It's a crime against Nature," David said.

"It's unnatural, man," Nick said. "They're freaks. All those guys, Warhol and them, were always trying to get me into bed with them, but I wouldn't let them. You should have seen the things these guys did. I made a movie once about a meat market in New York where fags give blowjobs between all the animal carcasses. It was weird."

"That's great and all, but you talk about freedom, and yet. . . "

"Listen, my friend," David said, exhaling a cloud of marijuana smoke, "the Bible says. . . "

He proceeded to go on about the Bible and his own personal bullshit interpretation. As a rule, being an atheist, I stop listening whenever someone begins a sentence with "The Bible says. . . " To me, they might as well be saying, "Peter Pan says. . . " I listened to some of what David was preaching, though, and had to admit he had a funny, intelligent delivery even if it was the same old package. But there was something else there,too. . . maybe that it was all just a big joke.

"Does he really believe all of this crap?" I asked Nick. "Do you?"

Both men just laughed.

"David's a guru, man," Nick said. "A prophet."

I looked at David, who was smiling devilishly. "I'm going to take over the world or just control a lot of people's minds with religion and television ," David said seriously. "I think it should be easy."

" People do whatever he tells them to do," Nick said. "You're the Second Coming—right, David?"

"More like Satan," I said.

"He's a genius," Nick said laughing.

"Nick's the genius," David said.

"Imagine that," I said, "Three geniuses in one room. . . "

The next night, we got together in one of the viewing rooms and I watched a few of Nick's videos. Fortunately, they were indeed good and hilarious, and we laughed the whole time. I asked Nick several times, "Why don't you send this stuff to people? This is good stuff."

"Thanks, I respect your opinion," Nick said, "but those people out there are vicious and they twist you and use you to make money. I've seen it happen. They'll take my stuff and ruin it."

"It's because of greed," David said. "And mindless fornication," he added, smiling.

Nick laughed. "Yeah, right. Moronic Fornicators of Hollywood."

"I think they already made that movie," I said.

The film was about a homeless guy who used to be a boxer. He lived on the streets of New Paltz and Nick and David befriended him and followed him around. The film was touching as well as funny. Nick kept calling the guy a psycho.

"Don't tell anybody this," David said. "We want to start a thing called Psycho TV. You know, movies about real people, real psychos."

"Using our political leaders?"

"Right," David said, "and people on the street. Actually, it's the people behind the leaders, the ultra-rich would be featured as well. I've spoken at length with some very wealthy individuals. A lot of important people from all over the world have come here. You'd be surprised at what they're like. Some of these wealthy people have more in common with the destitute people on the streets than with the middle and upper classes. What you'll find out if you talk with them both is that the world is in a state of physical and moral entropy."

"It's run by greedy morons," Nick said, putting it succinctly.

"No," David said. "The truly rich never let money touch their hands. I try to do the same. Money is evil."

"Yeah right," I said, "but it comes in handy at the grocery store."

For someone who didn't want money touching his hands, David sure managed to get some of mine. I paid him a lot of money, three times as much as I spend in Texas, for a small amount of the said powerful dope. David said he never paid for it, though, since it was grown by special people in Woodstock who didn't want money touching their hands either. He also drove me into New Paltz one evening so I could buy some warm gloves and charged me for the gas and his time. It was snowing that night as we drove down the mountain in his old, giant LTD. David began to speed up, driving quickly and dangerously without his brakes, slipping around on the mountain's curves, dark trees coming much too close to the car. Just as I was about to ask him to slow down, he spoke up. "I'm an excellent driver. Don't be worried. People have commented on my skills as a driver."

I took his word for it and we survived the frightening descent. Once in town, at the mall, David put on a very silly hunting cap when we got out of the car. He must have seen me staring. "I wear a lot of funny hats," he said matter-of-factly. "I'm kind of known for it."

"Like your driving."

We went to dinner at a small health-food restaurant in New Paltz and I realized David wasn't greedy, he was just dirt poor. He inhaled the food I bought him and then ate what I didn't finish.

"Don't they feed you guys at Mohonk?"

He shrugged. "There's an employee cafeteria. It's not quite the same as where you and the movie people eat. It's down in the basement. I know the cooks there and they give me food. I don't have to pay." On our way from the restaurant to the car, I noticed several thugs following us, obviously intent on something. David seemed oblivious to them. Once we made it to the car, they stopped and stared, yelling something as we drove off. I wondered then if David might be one of those people who constantly attract danger.

Going back up the mountain (almost as scary as going down) , we talked about New York City. "If you'll pay my expenses I'll take you there for a tour," David said. "That's what I do here kind of, give people tours. I really don't do anything. The old women who own this mountain love me. I'm their favorite employee and they trust me. So I have the run of the place. I essentially own this hotel and this mountain. Ask Nick, he'll tell you. They pay me practically nothing, but I own this place as much as they do. It's all in how you look at things. You have to be pure in your mind. I could take you to places in New York. I've been in the most evil places in the city, where people are killing each other, and I've stood there in the middle of it all and because I was pure, they leave me alone to observe. If I made one slip toward fear, then I would be dead. Fear and dishonesty will always give you away. You have to go to New York with me. I can introduce you to some cool musicians and interesting homeless people. You'll like it."

The next day, at work, I saw Nick gathering scrap wood for the carpenters. I mentioned David's offer to go to the city.

"Oh man, you don't wanna go to New York with David. He'll get you killed. He'll take you to the worst parts of town. Let me go with you guys and I'll stop him."

As we spoke, Brian watched me angrily. It was starting to bother him that I was hanging out with the locals and not him and his buddies. He didn't like Nick and told me so, as though his being my boss made him a parent who could tell me with whom to socialize. A five-ton set-dressing truck drove up and a Teamster called to several men huddled up in the courtyard to begin unloading. Nick and I watched the ten or twelve men, all of whom looked poor.

"That looks like a fucking soup line," I said.

"It is," Nick said laughing. "They're buying us lunch. Listen, don't take David too seriously. His father's some billionaire oil guy. He makes a lotta stuff up. I gotta go get in the soup line."

I could see that Nick, even with all of his moron talk, was slowly being bitten by the movie bug. The same thing had happened to me. He'd received a good paycheck already, much more than he made doing odd jobs. He was a hard worker and was making himself available to everyone as a gopher, so much so that the art department crew learned his name and, when the other hungry locals were laid-off, Nick was kept on board. I noticed he didn't smoke dope with David and me at night and asked him why one afternoon.

"I swim, man. That's my drug. I swim every morning in the lake.

It's all about freedom and nature."

Sure enough, the next morning, I saw Nick out in the freezing cold lake. Snow was swirling in all directions in the granite bowl, falling into the clear blue lake, the sun rising over the icy water, illuminating every flake with a yellow glow, with a person swimming right through it. I thought I could see his point. . .

Production didn't think it was all about freedom, though. When they arrived in town, a nosy production secretary, seeing Nick swimming in the lake, something he'd done for years, called security and had him hauled out.

"He's gotta be crazy," she said. "He can't do that."

Nick wasn't angry and just said he'd swim somewhere else. It occurred to me that this was supposed to be a summer scene in the film (if the light snow melted off) and they would probably love to have a few swimmers in the background for effect. I told Nick about being an extra and that he might get stunt pay if he did it.

"What do I do?" he asked.

"There's extras casting right over there with wardrobe. Just go over there and ask if they need any swimmers."

"I don't know," Nick said. "Those guys in wardrobe, they looked like homosexuals."

"Jesus, Nick, they probably are and they're gonna want to put you in an old-fashioned bathing suit since this is a turn-of-the-century movie. If you can just get past that, you can make some good money."

" Alright. I just don't want them touching me, man."

" Whatever. . . "

In spite of his fears—or, I was starting to believe, hopes—of homosexual molestation, Nick was made an extra and, as I found out later, was kept on throughout the shoot in Mohonk, making hundreds of dollars jumping in the cold lake, something he did every day anyway.

With the arrival of the company, things had grown more hectic and there was not much time for recreation. One of the last nights I was there, Nick and David and I climbed up the Mohonk mountain. We kept getting lost following David, so Nick led us to a vertical crevice called the Lemon Squeeze, where you are wedged in by giant granite walls with no room to maneuver for a couple of hundred feet, climbing up on rock and flimsy wooden rungs. When we emerged at the top, it was truly amazing. A blue light from a large moon illuminated all of the rocks and boulders and cliffs, giving them an ancient cast, as though we had gone back in time on our ascent.

"This is great," I said and was thankful I hadn't gone to New York City with Brian and his friends, on a big trip he'd been talking about every day.

"It's nice," Nick said. "I stay out here in these mountains all the time. For weeks. You're completely free out here."

"It's complete freedom," David said. "There is energy up on this mountain. This is a special place. The native Americans came here. You can almost fly when you're up here."

He climbed up on a rock jutting out over a sheer, deadly drop and began to do a Tai-chi-like routine. "I have immense power on this mountain. I can feel it. I can fly." He started jumping straight up into the air, his arms out like a plane, coming very close to the edge, strong gusty winds pushing his small frame around, while Nick pointed out the lights of New York in the distance. David never did fly, or fall to his death, so we went back down the mountain, taking the easy way, a wide, soft path covered in pine needles.

Back at the lodge, Nick drove home to see his girlfriend in Poughkeepsie where he lived. David and I went to his room and did a few bong hits. I was surprised at how tiny the room was, maybe twelve by twelve with hardly any room for a bed. All of the help were housed in similar rooms in two dormitories. David had his cubicle crammed with books and tapes and recording equipment and computers. He mentioned that he was a musician, a guitarist, and I could see he spent a lot of time in there with his guitar. He played some of his tapes for me and again I was pleasantly surprised at how good they were. He'd made them himself, playing all the instruments, mixing his music with that of others and the disembodied voices of insane evangelists: a combination of gospel, Christian rock, rap music, and David's hypnotic guitar with titles like "Subservience to the Good That Should Rule Every Heart" , and "Safety is a Function of Speed."

We went back to the lodge and stopped for a moment in front of one of the constantly burning Mohonk fireplaces. David, looking about for eavesdroppers as he spoke, told me of his and Nick's plans.

"We're going to the islands. I have a friend there, he's very wealthy. He and his wife own several islands and they're going to let Nick and me and his girlfriend live there."

"What about your girlfriend?" I asked. I had seen David kissing an attractive young woman in one of their videos.

David bristled visibly, his steady calm finally broken. "She's out of the picture now. She would have gone with us."

"What happened?"

"She went to India to feed the poor people and decided to stay."

"Oh. Is that why you've gone insane?"

"I'd really rather not talk about it."

"Sorry."

He went back to the subject of the islands. "It's going to be wonderful there. I flew down there and visited a few years ago and it's all set up for our arrival. It's perfectly pure there. And there are several intelligent people among the ignorant natives."

"No homosexuals?"

"I asked a native once if they had any homosexuals. He said, 'Yes, one came to our village one day but we threw rocks at him and he went away.' You see, the few intelligent people there, they think in pages, do you know what I mean?"

"No, I don't."

"Well, some people, they think in words, like the movie people you work with and most people in the world. Others, like some of the scientists I've met here, they think in sentences. Beyond that, there are those who see the world in paragraphs, such as myself. But at the island, there are at least two people who think in pages, beyond your comprehension and mine. At least for now. . . "

"Sure, David." I changed the subject (with words) to the movies. I told David the film's budget and how much money would be passing through the hotel and his eyes lit up.

"I'm going to get some of that money," he said. "People always give me their money. It's amazing. Sometimes I don't even have to ask them."

He went on to tell me about other actors who had stayed there along with different writers, scientists, and political leaders. "The *Saturday Night Live* cast was here the other day. They were pigs, really. Incredibly rude and they had no respect for the mountain or the lake or the lodge, none of the history here. We hated them. Most actors are insane anyway."

"You think so?"

"I do, but I have to qualify that. They're insane in their normal lives and normal only when they're acting. You see, they need to act, they have to act. It's a function of their insanity."

"An outlet."

"Maybe, but I don't know if it's that conscious. I think they're just insane and their acting is a manifestation of their insanity. They have to do it."

"Why don't you try that theory out on a few of them when they get here. In fact, I just saw Mathew Broderick in the lobby on the way up."

"O.K.," David said seriously. "I will."

–20–

I wanted to stay up there on the mountain during the shoot until Christmas, rather than go back and slave twelve hours a day in the shitty Carolco studios in Wilmington. I blew it, though. Todd the standby painter needed help desperately and the designer wanted me to stay, but I messed up my simple reverse psychology with Brian Stultz and asked if I could stay one too many times. Though that had been the original plan, now that I'd snubbed him socially and he knew I wanted to stay, I could tell it was a wash. There were some local New York union guys picketing at the gate of the resort. Nothing was going to happen, but Brian used this excuse to slip me out, and replace me with a popular and talented New York scenic named John Ringbaum. Just before I left, I said good-bye to Nick and David who, standing together on the stairs, looked more than ever like a couple.

"Come see us in the islands," David said. "I'll send you a map."

"Yeah, man," Nick said. "It's nice down there."

"When are you going?" I asked.

David looked around for spies, as he always did whenever he spoke, and whispered, "Probably in the spring. Bill Clinton is coming here next month and we're going to help him out with a few things."

"Give him my regards," I said, and left.

The rickety American Eagle commuter plane ride back from our connection in Raleigh to Wilmington was terrible as we went through several giant thunderstorms. There was only one other passenger, a fellow painter, and the flight attendant. As the plane rocked all over the place, throwing us around the cabin, I looked at the other painter. On airplanes, I checked out my other passengers when I boarded and tried to discern whether or not they were marked for death in an airplane crash. This guy was definitely a future casualty, as was the flight attendant. Miraculously, we made it through the clouds and rain, fishtailed all over the runway, and came to a skidding stop, the still-scared flight attendant apologizing to us all the way across the tarmac.

I began working again in the Carolco studios on a gigantic set on stage 7 that was going to play as the interior of the Battlecreek Sanitarium, or the Mohonk Lodge. The set was supposed to be one of the very first American sanitariums, or a health club, built and run by Dr. Kellogg the same Battle Creek, Michigan doctor who'd started Kellogg's cereal. *The Road to Wellville* was based on his life. Anthony Hopkins was playing the doctor, who was something of a nut as well as a visionary. Based on the book by TC Boyle, the movie would accent some of the obviously anal doctor's stranger healing methods, such as fifteen-gallon yogurt enemas (all of his patients were enema-ed often) or running electrical currents across men's testicles, a treatment that actually killed those he tried it on. To give you an idea of his odd bowel movement obsession, one of the rooms inside the large set was a fecal collection room, full of, well, fecal matter. Someone told me that Alan Parker had been wanting to make this movie for a long time.

Far removed from that reality, I began to sand and putty holes, shellac woodwork, and marblelize miles of baseboard. The studios were even more unsafe than the last time I'd been there. There were still open, giant compressors operating, their belts and flywheels turning a foot away from you, no ventilation when we were spraying gallons and gallons of orange shellac while people choked and smoked cigarettes, several bucket lifts or condors, spewing exhaust and being steered with abandon by a group of insane, carny-worker riggers, who held heavy, metal, instant-death pipes precariously over our heads, dropping their tools from time to time while they screamed at each other and fought. I spoke with Jim Onate about the dangerous working conditions and he told me about a film he had just finished called *The Crow* where one night the crew watched the actor Brandon Lee get shot and killed. Jim introduced me to a young man who came by the studio to visit who had also worked on *The Crow*. The man had no face, no ears, nose, nothing, just a mass of scar tissue, two eyes, and a slit for a mouth. He had been operating a condor on the back lot and while in the bucket, extending the boom, he'd hit a power line above the set, a line that was too low, and electrocuted himself. A well-meaning carpenter, with a five-gallon bucket of water, in an attempt to put the fire out, for the man had instantly ignited, threw the water on him and it washed off his face. I spoke with the injured man briefly, who seemed remarkably well adjusted considering what had happened, and he said the case his lawyer was bringing was yet to be settled.

I also noticed that all of the African-Americans in the studio were still employed as low-paid clean-up guys, while only whites were carpenters, painters, and set dressers. This was no surprise, for I can count on one hand the number of African-Americans I've seen on movie crews over the years. Some in the Wilmington shop were more blatant with their racism. The out-of-town construction crew, Bill Bradford and company from Dallas, seemed like normal, professional guys, but some of the local rednecks were too much, leaving notes on scraps of wood they wanted to keep that read: Don't throw this away, nigger. I was forced to work with one of the redneck painters, one of the more obvious racists who carried a gun, knowing many on the clean-up crew wanted to kill him, an idiotic foreman named Alton Crow. Alton was always completely drunk and utterly stoned all day, so much so that he could barely stand up. Between his trying to order me around, which I put a stop to the first day, and an awful habit of crowing intermittently like a bird (Caw! Caw!) he would confide in me with his KKK stories, saying loudly for others to hear, "Round here the black boys stay away from the white boys if they know what's good for 'em." After only a few days, I was severely depressed with all of it.

One thing that was different this time in Wilmington was that Brian was losing some of his power. People were constantly badmouthing him, most all of his help did, even people on other movies filming there, specifically people on George Lucas's *Radioland Murders* . The carpenters especially had had it. They spoke of even killing Brian. On another film, the carpentry crew went so far as to rig a heavy board over a door Brian was expected to walk through so it would land on his head. His second, an unsuspecting Jim Onate, whom all the carpenters and coordinators liked since he was the one they really dealt with, caught the board on his head and went to the hospital for stitches. When Brian came back from New York, he aggravated the situation by moving the carpenters' work tables, setting up to paint purposefully in their areas, criticizing their work to superiors so that many of their projects had to be redone. When they complained, Brian gave his usual reply: "Bite me." Or a simple, "Fuck off," accompanied by a masturbatory gesture. One of the carpenter foreman with whom I worked, a good guy from Dallas named Tom MacDaniel, pulled me aside every other day and whispered, "Somebody's gotta do something about Brian. Someone has to kick his ass. He's gotten out of hand."

And Tom wasn't the only one who confided in me. Maybe it was the fact that Brian treated me, unlike most of his other employees, with some amount of respect, but I seemed to have been chosen as the guy to take care of Brian. I felt like Martin Sheen in *Apocalypse Now*. Six years had passed and I had been sent up the river to kill my own personal Colonel Kurtz. Every time I turned around, another painter or carpenter approached me. "He's gotten out of hand. . . We've got to do something. . . He's out there operating without any kind of restraint. . . Terminate his command. . . with extreme prejudice."

One of Brian's poor put-upon helpers, a hilarious young gangster from Brooklyn named Ray, told me how he'd handle it in his neighborhood. "We'd throw the little fuck out of a fucking window in a tall building, no questions asked. You know what I mean?" Sensing my lack of fear of Brian, Ray stuck to me like glue, telling me what he was going to do to his boss. "I'm gonna get that fuck an' kick him in the fuckin' nuts an' then start beatin' his fuckin' head in with a two-by-four. . . " on and on until Brian's voice rang out across the stage. "Ray! Get your fucking ass over here right now!"

Ray, who sounded like Rodney Dangerfield, would grudgingly go to his boss, assuring me before he left, "I swear to you, JR, I'm gonna do it. Today's the day."

I seriously thought about straightening Brian out, but the more I considered it, the more I realized how fairly he'd always treated me. He'd never raised his voice or said a cross word to me once. It was just understood. He worked me like a dog, but that's what I was paid for. My only complaint was his giving me shitty jobs when I wouldn't socialize with him. In order to get out of staining and puttying and into the easier, or at least more interesting, marblelizing, I'd been forced to go out with him and his wife, Kelly, once again, to the Wilmington sushi bar.

It was a vintage Brian night as he irritated the waitresses and people at tables around us. One of the restaurant's patrons was the actor Brian Benben from HBO's *Dream On*, who was acting in *Radioland Murders*. Once he spotted the actor, Stultz kept trying to get his attention to say hello when the man obviously had no idea who Brian was. Brian had also invited a few of his helpers, two young guys who told everyone they were a writing team trying to get into TV. One of them, Steve, the brains of the two, was a nice guy who hated Brian. The other kissed Brian's ass blatantly in the restaurant. Brian kept starting sentences with "Well, we're all writers here. . . " and "Being a writer myself. . . ," darting furtive, guilty looks at me, gauging how I felt, how drunk I was, and whether I would refute his writerly status. I felt it was all pretty sad and decided to say nothing to Brian on this trip. If his serfs in the Wilmington fiefdom wanted to overthrow him, they'd have to do it on their own.

I went to a theater one of those nights to see *Flesh and Bone*. I rarely went to movies anymore, but I had to see this one for one reason: I might be in it. Sitting in the theater, trying to stay awake through the dull film, I watched the screen intently. When I least expected it, I saw myself. Dennis Quaid's head filled the screen as he stood in a motel doorway, and far behind him, only a few inches tall and out of focus, a man in a cowboy hat walked past. That was it. Raised on movies all my life, I'd finally come full circle and was on the silver screen. Despite the small, almost invisible image of myself, I had a strange, almost happy feeling I couldn't explain. Only when I got back to my apartment that night did I understand what the feeling was: I was justified. In my little way, however briefly, I'd become permanent through film. I existed.

I could see I was getting drawn into the Wilmington world and would have to choose sides. Not having the energy to do so, I told Brian I was quitting and would leave at the Christmas break. He seemed unusually happy at my decision and said fine, no hard feelings. We were working up until Christmas Eve and Brian, in an expression of holiday good will, fired four people for being late to work— a few days before Christmas. When the shooting crew arrived, because Todd was wrapping things up in New York, Brian made me standby painter for the few days of shooting that remained before the break.

"You O.K. with that?" he asked me politely. "You O.K.?"

"That's fine with me," I said.

"You happy with everything?"

"Sure."

"Great," he said, and left for his vacation early, avoiding some of the fired painters who were now gunning for him. I haven't seen Brian since, but heard a small story about him, an incident that occurred after filming, one that seemed a just reward for his actions. Going back onto stage 7 for another film, Stultz was forced to move his shop into what was the carpenter's shop on *The Road to Wellville*. Inside the room, written countless times in letters sometimes a foot high, were the words "Brian Stultz sucks dicks." Brian got a can of black spray paint and, in what must have been a lonely moment, methodically blacked out his name again and again.

I gave Todd a call up at Mohonk one night and asked him how the shoot had gone, how Nick and David were.

"Well," he said, "David cornered Bridget Fonda and Mathew Broderick in a room and wouldn't stop talking to them, something about actors being insane. When he told Bridget that her father, Peter, had been killed by the CIA years ago, they called security on him. Nick did his swimming scene and everything was fine until he pissed off the shooting crew by faking a seizure after coming out of the lake. He was flopping all over the ground and everyone was going crazy and he stood up laughing. The stunt people were pissed."

"I guess he doesn't want to work on movies."

"No, he does. He's really taken with it. He keeps asking me to take him back down to Wilmington with me to work."

"Oh no. . . "

"He even said he'd work for Brian."

"That's too bad."

Just before filming on stage 7 began, I was standing there, covered in paint, touching up the exterior of Dr.Kellogg's office where several scenes would be shot. A man with closely-cropped white hair walked up to me.

"Excuse me," he said, "I'm Anthony Hopkins."

I put down my roller pole. He'd extended his hand, but I had paint all over mine. "That's O.K.," he said, and shook my hand. I told him it was nice to meet him and genuinely said I'd admired his work since *The Lion in Winter.*

"Well, thank you, thank you," he said, and actually blushed. "I just wanted to tell you how much I admire your work here. This set is absolutely marvelous. You men have done an exceptional job. Really."

I thanked him and we spoke for a few minutes about the Mohonk Lodge and the picture we were working on

"Well," he said, "this is a very odd film, don't you think?"

I'd been afraid to say so, but agreed. "It does seem to have an inordinate preoccupation with fecal matter."

"Yes, believe me, I know. Quite strange. Apparently, that's the way this fellow Kellogg was. A very odd man. This is probably one of the strangest pictures I've ever done. It's British though, you know," he added with a smile.

"I wonder how it will play in America. . . "

He furrowed his brow and shook his head. "I don't know, I don't know. . . "

He said good-bye then and walked off to compliment others. Though I professed not to be effected by celebrities, I felt a smile on my face and my work load lightened for at least fifteen minutes.

The scene that was being shot in Dr.Kellogg's office was this: Mathew Broderick, wearing a diaper, would come into the room, stand behind a partition, and give Kellogg a stool sample. Dr. Kellogg, Hopkins with funny glasses, a goatee, and buckteeth, would look at the stool sample and exclaim, "Awful! Just awful. Your stool is mushy, ill formed, and foul smelling."

"What should it look like?" a confused Broderick asks. "I mean, with all the yogurt enemas you keep giving me. . . "

"Young man!" Hopkins yells, "My stools are gigantic! Huge and solid! And they come out smelling no more than a hot biscuit!"

I heard those lines ,and variations thereof, for twelve hours. They are now solidly etched into my brain. I hung around the set, waiting for something to do, occasionally sneaking away to help a friend of mine, a scenic named Larry Shepard, with another section of the set, the dressing room. On one of these excursions, we were told by an a.d. to be quiet and to turn out the spotlights we were using to see on the as yet unlighted set.

"Wait," the a.d. said, listening on his headset. "Never mind. Just be quiet. The director is coming to look at the sauna set."

Larry and I went back to work as Alan Parker and another man came in to tour the set. One of our spotlights was directly in their path. I bent down to move it as they walked past me, my head just about level with Mr.Parker's large posterior.

"Oh, don't bother with the light," he said and farted audibly on my head.

He kept on walking and I straightened up, smelling something foul. I walked over to Larry.

"Hey."

"What?"

"The director just farted on my head."

Larry started to laugh. "You've hit the big time."

Maybe it was the content of the movie, but a similar incident occurred the next day. Somebody on set, Hopkins I guess, had a make-up man named Peter Frampton. Mr. Frampton seemed to think he was very funny and witty and flirted blatantly with any woman who happened to wander across the set. He spoke in a loud, I-want-everyone-to-hear-how-funny-I-am voice. The man had one slight problem, though, one that seemed like a hindrance when picking up women: he had uncontrollable flatulence. He was constantly burping and farting. Loudly. Every few minutes. Whenever he farted, he would walk a few feet away from the set and cough loudly as he let it rip. He also had a whoopie cushion he would use with abandon. None of my fellow crew members seemed to notice or care as he walked past with a loud "Braaat!" saying in a proper British accent, "I say, did someone step on a frog?"

I'm sorry if he had a gastrointestinal problem, but I tried to avoid Mr.Frampton as much as possible. Waiting for a scene where we would fly (move) several walls, I hid behind a clear screen, crouching down and waiting for a "Cut!" so I could go to work quickly. I heard something and looked up to see Mr.Frampton's posterior through the thin screen on the other side. Too late to run, he farted quite loudly in my face and I got angry. First Hutman, now Parker and this guy. Was this some new show business way of communicating? Perhaps it was something special I brought out in people? Or maybe they were just trying to get into the spirit of the movie. Either way, I was getting tired of it.

I stayed away from the set from then on, except when a commotion started one day because of the arrival of the actor and comedian Dana Carvey. Jim Onate and I walked over to watch the young actor do his scenes. Carvey, though, would not stop cutting up and he was making everyone on the set impatient.

"What is it with you Brits?" he asked. "Oh, I'm sorry, is that offensive? Is 'Brits' offensive? 'Limey' is out then I guess. How about 'Great Britain type English persons?' " He put his arm on Hopkins' shoulder. "How do you do?" he said, imitating Hopkins perfectly.

"I'm fine, how are you Dana?" Hopkins said playing along.

" 'I'm fine, how are you'—God, I love the way you people talk. It just makes you sound smart or uptight or something. . . "

Carvey moved to the flatulating makeup man, Peter Frampton, and mumbled something to him.

"What?" Mr.Frampton said, irritated.

"A sphincter says what," Carvey said quickly.

"What?" Mr. Frampton said again, obviously angry.

"A sphincter says what," Carvey said slowly. "It's a joke. Granted, a stupid joke. Get it?"

"No, I do not," Mr. Frampton said.

"Well, we made several million dollars off that stupid joke," Carvey said. "Can you believe it?" He went into a mock agent's voice. "Sixty million, Irving, worldwide—on juvenile crap like that!"

Carvey then broke into his patented George Bush imitation and even some of the stuffier members of the crew had to laugh. Carvey kept up his routine until the camera was ready, and he cranked out several scenes like a pro, following Parker's direction to the letter. I was having such a good time watching, I didn't realize my production designer was watching me. He was suddenly in my face.

"Excuse me, but don't you have something to do?"

Yes. Go home. "Yessir, I was just getting to it," I said and walked over to Jim Onate. "I'm going back to Texas."

"You're not going to finish out the day?"

"Will you cover for me?"

"Sure."

I thanked Jim and left him there, pensively awaiting Christmas and Brian's inevitable return.

–21–

Back home in Texas, I received a phone call from a designer named Howard Cummings in New York. He was coming to Austin to do a feature for Steven Soderbergh called *The Underneath*. Did I want to be his lead scenic? Tired and not thinking, I declined. But after a couple of weeks of no more paychecks coming in, I reconsidered and started making phone calls. John Burson called me and said he was the construction coordinator and that John Frick was interviewing with Howard at the Radisson that afternoon in Austin. I quickly called Howard at his hotel and he said he was looking at other people now. After a week of phone calls and pressure from Burson, Howard said I could be his second scenic working for his lead, a man from L.A. named Phil. I called Los Angeles and spoke to Phil on the phone. We got along and I was hired.

The show proved to be a great deal of work. We painted a fake plastic log cabin filled with fiberglass rock walls. Because it was a feature, we had more time to get the sets right. We produced some nice work that I could be proud of, although it bored me now to do it.

In the art department, I rarely saw my friend John Frick, who'd been hired as art director by Howard, with some misgivings, Phil told me. "He doesn't say anything and he doesn't inspire any confidence," Howard complained. He must have noticed John's disappearing act, too. He came up to me one day during the show.

"You've worked with John Frick before, haven't you?" he asked me.

"Yes, many times. When he was an art director and a designer."

"Well, what exactly does he do?"

Howard, like Hutman, was one of those constantly working designers, always around, tinkering with the set, making sure everything was perfect ahead of time, knowing what and how everyone on his crew was doing, and I admired him for that.

"Oh, different things. He's been doing all of your drawings, hasn't he?"

"No, not really. You say he's been a designer?"

"Well yeah, you saw his resume."

"I just don't see it," Howard said, sounding frustrated.

"He does a lot of good detail work," I said, trying to put a good spin on it. After all, Howard would leave town one day, and Frick would stay and I would have to work for him. I told Howard this so he would stop talking. I said Frick had always been this way and we knew how to operate around him on these small shows.

"I hear he's up for Aaron Spelling's *Texas* ," Howard said. "You'll probably be his scenic."

"I probably will."

"I don't know how you do it," Howard said and left, shaking his head.

There was certainly no lack of direction on *The Underneath.* The only problem was, it wasn't coming from Howard but from Elliot, the director of photography. The man had a reputation, in his mind at least, for genius, and he kept Howard jumping like a puppet throughout the shoot. I'd seen Soderbergh's most recent film, *King of the Hill*, which Elliot shot—"brilliantly" according to Howard and Phil. I enjoyed the film but saw nothing brilliant in the cinematography. Certainly not to warrant what Elliot was putting Howard through and, subsequently, Phil and me. Phil was at work almost every night until nine, producing sample board after sample board of colors that sometimes varied so little we could barely tell them apart. The theme here was blue and green, and before the film was over we had painted and glazed and washed every kind of blue and green there was for Elliot's approval. It got so ridiculous, they were bringing Phil and me in for hotshot runs to the set, just to put a little bit darker shade of green and blue glaze on a wall while the crew waited. I admired Elliot's having a theme, as it were, but it was bordering on pretension. It even became embarrassing when Soderbergh walked into one of the turquoise bedroom sets and exclaimed with dismay, "It looks like I'm shooting in a goddamn aquarium in here!"

Soderbergh, like Alan Parker, struck me as one of the few real movie directors I'd ever seen. He seemed to take his work, not himself, seriously. He definitely knew what he wanted and Phil and I took pains to deliver it. I spoke with the director one day at the Subway sandwich shop . He ate lunch there often and occasionally we bumped into him and talked a bit. In one conversation I mentioned a party I'd been invited to, but didn't attend, for the cast and crew of the movie *Dazed and Confused*. As it turned out, Soderbergh had gone to it. I told him the film had been ridiculous to work on and he rallied to Linklater's defense, saying he liked the film. He then mentioned a book he had with him called *A Confederacy of Dunces* . I'd heard he wanted to make a film of it, so I just quit talking, not wanting to mention, ever the spoilsport, that I hated the novel.

Because I was Phil's second, I didn't have to deal with Elliot, who was, in real life, a friend of Phil's, as was Elliot's wife, Susan. She had worked as a designer before, but on this film, she was hanging around the set with her small son, Paris, on her hip, trying desperately to throw around what weight you can as the wife of a d.p. Several times, she showed up to talk with Phil and disrupt our work, all the while saying twenty times, "I'm Elliot's wife, I'm the d.p.'s wife, Elliot, d.p., me, wife, etc. . . " She was also one of those people who think their child is the Son of God and want you to think so too. She stopped me working more than once, taking the wet paint brush out of my hand and giving it to her two-year-old to splash paint on the wall I was working on, all the while utterly ignoring me and the other painters. She went too far one day on a set we were working on in Travis Heights, making fun of our set decorator from Houston, a nice woman named Jenette. Mrs.D.P. walked into the house where we were painting and exclaimed, "Pretty!" in a silly, sing-song voice.

Her friend Phil, started to laugh. "I assume you're talking about Jenette."

She laughed. "Have you heard that woman? She sounds like a three year old. Pretty! That's so Pretty! I think that's her only judgment of the sets."

"Pretty!" Phil said, mimicking Jenette as well.

"Well, what do you expect?" Mrs.D.P. said, "She's from Texas.

That's what you're gonna get down here."

I stood up slowly from painting a baseboard. "Hey," I said, "there's some other people from Texas around here. . . "

Another painter from Austin chimed in. "We're not all idiots."

Mrs.D.P. turned red. "Oh, I'm just kidding, you know. I mean, I'm a Yankee. You know how we Yankees are. Just so. . . so. . . " She couldn't think of anything and gave up. She looked at Phil like, oh well, I offended your crew, but so what. They began to chat again and we went back to work.

The L.A. Thing was quite predominant on *The Underneath*. The L.A. Thing happened on most shows I was on, since the higher-ups were often from Los Angeles and made a point of telling you so. The L.A. Thing was the attitude that yeah, we're here in your state making a movie, but back in L.A., we do it this way, the real way. The L.A. Thing allowed transplanted Californians to put down everything and everybody in every state in the Union. I knew this because my friends who worked in other states saw the same thing. Nothing was as good as it was in L.A. This view could permeate a whole picture, down to my level, where I had to sit and listen to Phil tell me how in L.A. they have extra special putty that works better than the putty you get in Texas. . . I was getting tired of the magical movie people from L.A. putting us down on one hand, and then expecting us to kill ourselves for them, with the same old promise: we'll be back again next year to do another one and aren't you glad you work on a movie? I'd seen and heard enough lies and promises now to get sick of it and finally got a chance, at my level, to say my piece.

A young man who introduced himself as Frank to me and other men in the construction department, but as Francis to female crew members or anyone who seemed important, showed up on the cabin set one day looking for work. He lived in Los Angeles and had been bothering Phil for a job over the phone. He appeared in Texas one day, and Phil gave him some work as a day player. I had trouble figuring out just exactly what Francis did because his story changed every day, depending on who was doing the asking. One day he was a carpenter, the next day a writer, an actor, a construction coordinator, on and on. And, Francis, like some other ugly people I've known, thought he was a very handsome lothario and told me so often. Every day, I got a new, ridiculous story.

"Hey, JR, last night two beautiful topless dancers followed me out of the bar telling me how hot I was. They both wanted to fuck me." Or "Yeah, so I was just in this convenience store and this gorgeous woman, had to be a model, walks up and gives me a note with her fucking number on it, dude. She wants me. I might call her tonight. I've only been in town two days and I've got six women lined up. These Texas women are easy. . . ."

Using all the movie lingo at his command, Francis kept talking about his big show business connections, which pathetically turned out to be that he dated a young woman who was Henry Winkler's stepdaughter or something. He told me this secretively, as though he didn't like to say it. "I don't want to cash in on his stardom, you know. I'm an actor and I want to make it on my own."

He went on to tell everyone he saw about this small show biz connection, at least twice, to the point that a carpenter walked up to me and, pointing to Francis, asked me if it was true he was Henry Winkler's son. "Yeah, he is," I said, "but don't call him the Fonz whatever you do."

Francis was big on the L.A. Thing, constantly telling me how they made movies in L.A., how they constructed and painted their sets, the crux of each quality-control story being what a bigshot he was. One of the other painters, getting sick of it one day, asked me, "If he's such a bigshot, what's he doing a thousand miles from home working as a local for a hundred dollars a day?" One afternoon, having heard enough, I had to speak up. We were all painting the trim upstairs in the Travis Heights house when Francis began to go on about the poor quality of the carpentry. He criticized the fake wall they'd installed upstairs and some of the other sets. He then began to go on about the carpenters themselves, their lack of L.A. experience, their bad attitude. He finished up with a claim that he just might move to this state, set up shop as the primary construction coordinator, and show us how to build a movie set. I set down my paint brush to back him up.

"Listen, Francis——"

"Frank."

"Right. Let me tell you something. We've been doing just fine on our little movies here for several years now. If you think you can waltz in here and con us with that L.A. bullshit and move out the existing crews, your sadly mistaken. I know of three construction coordinators here in Austin, and about fifteen carpenters, all of whom have done

more movies than you. You'll have to go through every one of those
people to even get a job as a helper. We see guys like you on every
show and they go straight home. And when the fuck did California
become a haven for intellectuals and quality anyway?"

"If you don't like California—"

"Half my family is from California, all right? It doesn't matter
what state you're from anymore anyway. And besides, none of this shit
is rocket science."

Francis started to apologize. "Hey man, do I come off that way? I
don't mean to sound like a snob on anything. I mean, I'm really an
actor. That's what I really want to do."

I didn't care what he wanted to do. I just wanted him to shut up
while we worked. It was bad enough that I had to be there. . . Jenette,
our set decorator, walked upstairs then and I introduced her to our
actor/painter.

"This is Frank," I said.

"Francis," he interjected, and shook Jenette's hand.

"He's our new painter's helper," I said.

"I'm an actor," Francis said. "I go by Francis as an actor, Frank to
my friends. I thought it was a good idea. There aren't many Francises
who are actors."

"There's Francis the Talking Mule. . . " Jenette offered.

Just as *The Underneath* was finishing up, I heard John Frick had
landed the job as production designer on *Texas*. This would be the
biggest show he'd ever designed. When John Burson landed the job as
coordinator, I knew I had the job as lead scenic. The day before he was
to leave for Del Rio, Burson approached me in the production office
parking lot, a big smile on his face.

"I just talked to the u.p.m. on *Texas*. He's a real nice guy. His
name's JP. He gave me everything I asked for. Somehow he got the
idea we would work as locals with no per diem or anything. I said that's
bullshit, he'd never find a crew in Del Rio, and got us hotel and everything. You'll get a new rental truck and about this a week."

He showed me a piece of paper.

"That's the most I've ever made. That's damn good money, John."

"You gotta ask for a lot or they won't think you're any good."

"Exactly."

156

The Underneath wrapped and I said my good-byes to Phil and Howard. I'd enjoyed working with both of them. Though I'd never finished the script, I for once felt proud, if still bored, with the quality of the sets we'd done and even had hopes for the picture Soderbergh would produce. He seemed like an intelligent, talented person and with good acting from Peter Gallagher, it could be something. Sprinkle in some of Elliot's brilliance, and maybe it was art.

–22–

Aaron Spelling's *Texas* certainly wasn't art. I was forced to hit the ground running and put together a makeshift crew since we only had a week and a half of prep. In a desperate search for a decent second scenic and a standby painter, I called Brian out in North Carolina. He was working on another Hutman show. I got Jim Onate on the line, but Brian wouldn't come to the phone, professing to be too busy. I even called John Huke, the partially burned artist and friend of Rob "CIA" Janecka, forcing myself to be friendly to the sculptor extraordinaire. He was very evasive but gave me the name of Susie Milosavic, a scenic and sign painter from L.A. who had worked in Texas with him before. Huke, having hitched his wagon to the designer Peter Jamison, was touting himself as an art director now to what I'd heard were disastrous results. I know he called me twice in desperation on one of his first shows, offering me very good money to bail him out on a few sets for a forgettable piece of TV crap starring Dolly Parton. On the phone, he was acting even more superior than usual, talking about a new show he was doing, written by Austinites Bud Shrake and Gary Cartwright, and claiming that he was going to use Suzy for it. He suggested we share her and I said no way, I'd be in Del Rio with her for three months. Besides, I knew for a fact his show wasn't going to happen anytime soon—something he should have been able to figure out for himself. Eventually, he coughed up her number and I got off the phone, making sure to wipe off the receiver.

Suzy signed on from L.A. after telling me Huke had said he'd "have me for breakfast" if I chose to compete for her services with him ever again. I hired two of my regulars, Bill Lee and Robert "Hadji"

Trevino, set painters from San Antonio, and a guy named Greg Morgan in Dallas as my standby. Somebody had recommended him, somebody I'm still trying to find.

Once in Del Rio, ensconced at the lovely Motel 6, I made my deal final with the u.p.m., JP, and signed start papers. He mentioned that the local studio mechanic union rep, Ray Patterson, had been calling him saying I owed him union dues. I said Patterson had no real pull in this state, which was true, and left his office pissed. I'd joined the Austin local years before but immediately quit paying dues when I realized they'd never get me a job. In the parking lot, I ran into Patterson which came as no surprise and we got into a screaming match with him calling me a loose cannon.

"You guys haven't done shit for me," I yelled. "I know more about what movies are coming to town than you do! And don't you ever call a production manager about me again, Ray!"

"I know it's a fucked-up local!" Ray screamed, "That's why we need your help! You work all the time. We've got to have you as a good member, not running around on your own!"

"You just need my fucking money."

After we were through yelling, I did what I always did with these guys when they muscled in—that is, I gave in. I signed a piece of paper right there in the lot that said he and his union could have three percent of each one of my checks, promised to throw a few painters his way, and left, shaken down.

Suzy soon arrived in town in her, as she called it, "Sexy El Camino." I grew depressed when I saw Suzy, realizing she was possibly insane. A real parrot on her shoulder, spandex bicycle shorts, cowboy boots, and a shirt she would wear for a week at a time, she was a loud, obnoxious, alcoholic exhibitionist who mentioned her clitoris to me several times within five minutes. Her eccentricities would have been funny had she not been working for me. Like Jerry Palermo, she started drinking at eight in the morning, and continued on until her behavior reached a shrieking, shameful crescendo of madness. When I asked her not to drink, she was even worse, so we compromised on a couple of six packs a day—as long as she did her job and quit asking people to do things like suck her dick, as it were, and quit her habit of frequently breaking into tears. As others had said, she was at least good at her job and, thankfully, it turned out to be true. Her signs were done quickly, expertly, and on time. As long as she kept that up, she could drink kerosene for all I cared.

Greg Morgan, though, did terrible work and turned out to be a tiny little chauvinist pig. For someone of such small stature, he also thought he was a tough guy, something I'd like to take him up on if we ever meet again in the real world. In those first few days, he pissed off every last person in the art department. Construction crews as a rule have pretty foul mouths, but this guy went beyond the norm with his degrading talk of women, who, to him, were "cunts," "whores," etc. Suzy's language was as bad as the rest of ours, but when Greg started to comment on seeing women's "hairy bushes" and their "smelly pussies" at breakfast one day, I gave him a packet from the production office about sexual harassment to read. As soon as I left the shop, he made a big deal of throwing it in the trash in front of Suzy.

Greg was big on the L.A. Thing as well. Though he worked for me, he kept talking to me in a condescending way about real movies and how I should go to L.A. to work on one. He talked about how we Texans had attitudes and on and on, the same old shit. It turns out he was from L.A., in the scenic union there, and had come to Texas because, as he foolishly admitted, he thought we were stupid and would be easy pickin's. The last straw occurred one morning when Ronny Perkins and another carpenter, Rodney Brown, told me they'd almost killed Greg the night before in a local bar. These men had been on almost every movie I'd ever worked on and I counted on them. Ronny, a quite large but gentle person who had indeed had his share of nasty fights in the past, and remembered them fondly, seemed disturbed and embarrassed by the whole incident.

"JR, you know me," he said, "I don't look for trouble. But this guy was unbelievable. He ran down Texas for about an hour. Finally, Rodney and I had just had it. Rodney told him to go back to L.A. and I told him I was about to take him out to the parking lot."

"What did he say then ?"

Ronny laughed. "The little guy actually wanted to fight me."

"You're kidding."

"No, I'm serious. He said 'I been beatup by guys bigger than you!' I told him, son, I'm not just gonna beat you up, I'm gonna work you over. I'm gonna have a little fun with ya. I'm sorry, JR. The guy's an asshole."

"Yeah, there seems to be a consensus forming on that. I think he's outta here."

Ronny, a genuinely nice guy, looked worried. "Now, please don't fire him because of last night. I just wanted to tell you what happened."

I said O.K. and thanked him. I went and got Rodney's version, which was the same.

"That guy thinks he's just gonna waltz in here an' take us for a bunch of fools," he said. "He kept bragging about how he had your number and wasn't going to do any work on this show."

I thanked Rodney, found Greg, and asked him what had happened.

"Those two guys are assholes," he began.

"Hold on. Those guys are friends of mine and they're not assholes."

"They're lying to you, man."

"Why would they lie to me?"

"They just are, trust me. It's that bullshit Texas attitude you guys got. You have it, too."

He reached up and pushed my shoulder a little when he said it. The guy was unbelievable. I was twice his size, Ronny four times his size, and he wanted to fight us both. "You're the one who has the attitude problem," I countered. "And don't you fucking touch me again."

"See? See? There it is. It's because I'm from California."

"Man, I don't give a shit if you're from the moon. You can't keep acting this way and keep your job. I've worked with people from all over the world and that has nothing to do with it."

"Maybe you're threatened by my experience," he said. "All you guys stick together. You're ganging up on me. It's that cunt Suzy isn't it ? That bitch hates me. I'm so sick of fucking women thinking they can do a man's job that—"

"Hey Greg?"

"What?"

"You're fired. Pack your shit, put it in the back of my truck, and I'll take you to town right now."

"Why?"

I had to laugh. "Why? You don't know why? Look, just go get your tools. I'm sorry this isn't going to work out. Maybe in the future, on another show—"

"I don't fuckin' believe this shit!" he suddenly yelled. "J.R., don't you ever call me again for another show!"

I had to laugh again. "I don't think you have to worry about that."

He stormed off to get his things. Since we were on the Moody Ranch, fifteen miles from Del Rio, I would have to give him a ride. As we drove, he became more and more belligerent, screaming that he didn't work for me anymore and didn't have to eat my shit. I slammed on the brakes and threatened to throw his stubby ass out of the truck if he didn't shut up and leave him in the middle of the Texas desert he so despised. That clammed him up until Del Rio where I dropped him off, out of my life.

Aside from Suzy, now in turn, sexually harassing my mild-mannered, married painter, Bill Lee, my little crew was ready to go. But there was one problem: there were no sets built yet. I kept people busy with a little work here and there while we waited on the carpenters, who were waiting on instructions from John Frick and his art director, a young woman named Adelle Plauche. I'd met Adelle on *The Underneath* and hadn't liked her. She seemed blatantly ambitious and ignorant at the same time, a common movie-worker trait. She'd been a bit player on *The Underneath* working as a set designer and painter occasionally and was angry with my existence before I'd even met her, or so Phil had told me. He said she had thought she'd be the second scenic on that show and was pissed when I got the job, refusing to talk to him for days afterwards. I subsequently found out she was telling everyone she was the Austin lead scenic, even though she'd just moved to town and done one film there when I was in San Antonio on *Heaven and Hell*. As I considered myself the primary Central Texas scenic, I was irritated by this stranger with very little experience, and at best, mediocre painting abilities, as I'd seen on *The Underneath*, horning in on what I felt was my territory. She did have the talent of ingratiating herself with her superiors, more so than me now, which is really one of the most important talents you can have in the movie business. In a very smart move, Adelle had ingratiated herself to the malleable John Frick on *The Underneath* , and was suddenly his art director, a plum job she'd never done before, and filled a vacancy for another Austin art director. I'd seen the vacancy coming a couple of years before with the rise of Frick as a designer and tried to fill it myself, but John never took me seriously and kept me at bay with his worries of losing, as he put it, his best lead scenic. What was worse than all of this, though, was that this position now made Adelle one of my many bosses in the movie hierarchy. Now we had two neophytes at the helm of *Texas*, and after that first wasted week, I started to get worried.

Texas had a large number of sets spread out over a hundred-mile area. We needed every day we could get and they had thrown away over a week. Thanks to people like Ronny Perkins and Rodney Brown, operating almost completely on their own because of necessity, we finally got the primary Moody Ranch sets done, mainly the Stephen F. Austin cabin. The company was in the fake town and ready to shoot as we packed up. With television, you always have to stay as far ahead of the shooting crew as possible. Things move too quickly. John Burson, Rodney Brown, and myself could see the holocaust coming and pressed Frick to give us legitimate instructions, a direction, some plans, a set, something, but our designer either said nothing or was nowhere to be found. However, Frick and Adelle did show up the day before the company arrived and Adelle handed me a list of things to do. Not only had I already done everything on the list and more, I had questions for them about a new interior. They had no answers. I told Adelle her list was redundant and gave it back to her, an action she wouldn't let me forget.

We barely got out of the Moody Ranch in time and started working in Brackettville in Happy Shahan's Alamo Village. John was there that first day and decided I should paint more than half of the large Alamo and its walls for a smoky night shot of the Alamo assault, which would be intercut with Alamo battle footage from an educational production of the epic siege. His decision was overdoing it, but, thankful for direction, I said nothing and my crew and I got to work. Happy and one of his main lackeys, a man named Jerry, hovered around us making sure we didn't do any damage to the faux historical structure. Jerry was put on the payroll of most of the films that came to Alamo Village. He made a couple hundred a day walking around, watching us work, opening locked buildings, and serving as a go-between for the sometimes cantankerous Happy.

In the mind-numbing heat, we finished the Alamo and surrounding walls and moved a couple of hundred yards down to Alamo Village, which was going to play as several towns, each with several sets. My crew was killing itself now trying to get the many sets ready: churches, town streets, barns, buildings, general stores, capitols, you name it. Adelle and Frick, though, had disappeared again. Who knows where

Frick was, staring at a rock somewhere. Adelle, we knew, had decided to become the on-set art director, a new, unnecessary position, where she hung out for most of the rest of the show sucking up blatantly to the u.p.m. JP, and the director, her new friend, Rich. Mostly, she was busy taking credit for all of our work. I know this because I watched her standing in front of my now completed Alamo with JP's arm around her.

"The Alamo looks great, Adelle."

"Thanks, JP. It was a lot of work, but we got it done. Frankly, I'm just exhausted."

I was standing two feet away and couldn't believe it, thought about it, and could believe it. Adelle had not even seen the Alamo until that day. Not surprisingly, I also overheard and watched her slowly moving John Frick out of the picture. Whenever the carpenters or Burson begged her for the plans to the sets she should have been drawing, she would make Frick the bad guy, saying to them, "You know how slow John Frick is. I'm trying, guys. I just can't get him to draw anything or approve anything."

Rodney Brown, who'd built more buildings and houses than Adelle had ever seen, was so disgusted with her, when she brought him a set of unapproved plans for a building he'd already constructed and I'd already painted, he threw them on the ground and wiped his boots on them in front of her. I watched her stab Frick in the back with JP as well.

"Where's John Frick?" JP asked, standing before the Alamo. "I can never find him."

"Oh, you know John Frick," Adelle said. "Who knows where he is. I guess I'll have to figure this set out by myself. . . "

Even though I'd felt the same way, I certainly wouldn't rat to the u.p.m. about it. As I listened, JP turned and gave me a don't-you-have-something-to-do look and since I did, I walked off. I'd come up to talk to Adelle about a call I'd just received on my walkie to paint the top of the front roof of the Alamo. It shot next and she had no idea. Rather than interrupt their tête-a-ass, I grabbed a few painters and went to scale the walls.

We propped up a twenty-four-foot ladder against the Alamo wall and stormed it with our own supplies, running to paint it, for the company was thirty yards away, Santa Ana's men fully armed, coming our way. As we began to paint and darken the gravel roof to look like dirt and paint out the plywood bases of several cannons that the set dressers had placed up there, I heard the unmistakable shouting of Happy Shahan. Because the call to paint the roof of the Alamo had come out over the walkie, Happy and his foreman Jerry had heard. Jerry understood I was just following orders from the director, but Happy did not. Jerry came running up through the tall, wooden front gates, his belly flopping.

"JR! JR! Happy's coming! Get off the roof!"

"I gotta paint it, Jerry!"

Happy appeared in his cowboy boots and hat, a bandanna around his neck, walkie-talkie on his hip. He pointed to one of my painters, Robert Trevino. "Hey you! What's that Mexican's name? Hey Pancho! Hey Zapata! Git off that roof!" He pointed at me. "I guess some people ain't gonna be keepin' their promises. Those producers said nobody would be up on that damn roof. Somebody's buyin' me a new roof! Today! Now git offa there!"

The whole time he yelled we kept painting, trying to finish.

"That roof's gonna cave in, I tell ya! It's unsafe!" Happy yelled.

"Happy," I said, "I checked the supports underneath it and it's fine. Besides, there's a bunch of cannons up here."

Happy became unhappy, incensed really. "Goddammit, I'm not askin' ya, I'm tellin' ya! Now git off that goddamn roof!"

"O.K., I will, I promise. In just one second."

We kept painting furiously. What was with this guy? Did he think I was up on the Alamo because I wanted to be? Happy, an old man, and somewhat infirm due to a recent illness that caused him to limp, began to scale my ladder, coming straight for me. As he reached the top, his shiny new boots slipped on the stucco, forcing us to help him, saving him, I'm sure, from more than a broken hip and the company, I'm really sure, from a several-million-dollar lawsuit. No thank-you's from Happy though.

"Alright, alright! I got it, I got it." Once up on the roof, he walked around, looking at us as though he'd forgotten why he'd come up there.

"Happy," I said, "believe me. We'll be done in two minutes and be off of here."

"Those producers lied to me," Happy said. "They're buying me a new roof."

"Look," I said, "there's only three of us up here, four now counting you. If I was you, what I'd be worried about are those forty extras they're gonna plop up here to man these cannons. Hell, these cannons alone weigh more than us."

The old cowboy worked his way back onto the ladder, all of us holding our breath as he did. He stopped on his descent. "I like what you boys are doin' paintin' the Alamo. It looks good and you oughta paint the rest of it. But those people lied to me an' they're gonna pay for it."

I didn't know what to say except my standard Texas reply to my elders.

"Yes sir."

"Alright then," he said, and left us. We quickly finished and ran, like Davy Crockett, from the Alamo.

–23–

Frick, perhaps beginning to smell the smoke from the coming fire, hired yet another art director to design the sets Adelle wasn't doing, a young man named Jonathan Short. But Mr. Short was as inexperienced as Adelle and had her same superior I'm-above-the-workers attitude. This was a mistake, since the actual workers—with competent direction and planning—are what make the art director and designer look good. Between running around making pointless measurements and bumming joints off me every day, Short did manage to crank out a couple of drawings and a to-do list. He could never find Frick to get approval of his plans, though, and when he did find him, usually forty miles away from the set, Frick couldn't decide. Again, we were rudderless with only a scribbled, Xeroxed to-do list of things we didn't have time to do.

The situation had finally broken down to the point that the carpenter foremen, Rodney Brown and Ronny Perkins, and myself, were deciding which sets shot next, when they would be built, and what they would look like with Burson, our coordinator, busy shuttling to Del Rio making sure we had supplies and money to do it. Every once in a while, Burson and I would approach each other, running across the set, both of us saying the same thing: "What the fuck are we going to do?"

To give you an idea of the problem, I was standing on an exterior, plaza dance-floor set we were building and painting one afternoon. There was an actual plan for this set, but it had been overdone and was much too much set for a night shot and no time. Ronny Perkins was struggling to get several hundred plywood squares nailed down with four painters standing right on top of him. We were busy painting and glazing them to look like saltillo tile when I heard shouting and looked to see the gigantic-bellied director, Rich, sitting with our producer Howard. Rich, though he needed to exercise more, drove around every set in a golf cart with a large set of long-horns and the words "El Toro" on the front of it. He and Howard were sitting in it watching us work in the blazing sun. Oblivious to our being there, as though we couldn't hear or even understand his words, Rich continued to shout.

"Goddammit, Howard! What the hell are all these art department people still doing here?! I thought they were supposed to be out of here! This is bullshit! How can I shoot in this town with all these idiots running around running their saws and tools?"

Howard, not the real power center of this picture, mumbled that he'd try to move us along and talk to John Frick.

"Who?" Rich asked.

"Our production designer."

"Oh shit! I want them out of this town when we get down here tomorrow. I mean it!"

They pulled away, the golf cart straining to haul its cargo. I didn't have the heart, or courage, or authority, to tell our esteemed director that, not only would we not be gone the next day, we would be only minutes ahead of his shooting crew for the rest of this show, which had a script of over two-hundred pages, for over another month. Howard must have gotten the word to Frick because he started to show up on the set more. Much to our resentment and anger, though, he wouldn't arrive until six p.m., at the end of our working day, completely confused and ignorant of what we'd done that day or would do the next. He grew angry one evening and, with Adelle in tow, he approached me complaining.

"How come everybody leaves as soon as I get here? They just run off. . ."

"It's quitting time, John."

"Maybe we should all stay a little later," he said angrily.

"John, my crew is exhausted as it is. It's a hundred and ten degrees out here and we're working all day long."

I quickly changed the subject. Glad to finally see John, I could get some badly needed information. I began to rattle off important questions and received no answers, only silence. Instead, he and Adelle began to wander over to a finished set where the company was shooting, leaving me standing there foolishly. To top it off, Adelle turned and said, "Are you through talking with the designer? If so, he has some other things to do and. . . "

"You mean John Frick here? No, I'm not through, Adelle."

"I think you are. Perhaps you could talk to him later. He's busy and. . . "

Frick stood there, looking at the ground.

"I'll talk to John whenever I want to talk to John, Adelle. Right, John?"

Frick said nothing and looked up at the clouds, ignoring me.

"JR, don't you have something else to do?" Adelle said.

"What? I'm trying to do what I have to do right now."

"I'm sure you are," she said, patting me on the shoulder. "I know it's tough. I remember when I was a scenic artist, too."

She was now standing literally and figuratively between me and my old buddy John, and it was obvious she was his ally in incompetence. I was being told to run along. I shook my head.

"Never mind. When you get the time John, I have several questions."

"Right," Adelle said, "and you can talk to him later." With that, they wandered away.

I had begun to get some serious pressure from the set dressers as the company moved around the Village, hopping from set to set. One day, the shooting crew even moved me out of my paint shop to set up lights. Tom Christopher, a part-time actor who was trying to be a lead man for the set dressers and a towel boy for the director, had taken to throwing temper tantrums, storming up to me to demand when a set would be ready to dress and complaining he had no time, which was completely true. But neither did we. I could pressure the carpenters and laborers no more than I was already. I apologized to Tom after his first few tantrums, promising to give him the set as soon as I got it and painted it. After the third tantrum, on a hot afternoon, I threw one of my own, getting in his face and backing him up in front of his men. He came up to me at lunch apologizing. "You and I shouldn't fight," he said. Fine, whatever. You don't yell at me, I won't yell at you.

I almost felt sorry for Tom. Frick had abandoned him. His boss, our set decorator, was either absent or parked on set and very inexperienced, her only recent credit being the Kenny Rogers vehicle *Gambler*

5, which had just finished shooting in Alamo Village. The art department work on the country singing/rotisserie chicken magnate's classic was so abysmal that much of what we were doing was redoing their crappy sets. Perhaps sensing my growing surly manner, she avoided me after the first few weeks of the show.

In the midst of this utter chaos—with constant calls from the a.d.'s to "Hold the work!" which forced the carpenters to stop and start, with Tom breathing down my neck, the carpenters and painters so irritable we were greeting each other in the morning with "Where's John Frick?" instead of "Hello," the director Rich screaming at us to get out of town by sundown, Adelle sequestering Frick, John Burson's what-are-we-gonna-do look of dismay—it came down from JP and the producer we suddenly needed an interior cave set for Monday. And it was Wednesday. And I had two sets to finish that day, three the next, a few more for the weekend, and who knew what else for Monday. Things were looking grim.

It was the same day Cary White and Sully came to town scouting with Tommy Lee Jones and I agreed to stay on for *The Good Old Boys*. When I told Cary of our plight, he just shook his head, gave me a "Good Luck," and added that he didn't really see how we could do the cave. Before construction on the cave even began, Tom approached me, telling me, nicely this time that he had to have the cave by Saturday if it shot Monday. We negotiated and I promised he'd have it, at the very latest, by Sunday at noon. Burson made a good move and brought in a carpenter and sculptor, Jim Simard from Oregon, who had constructed caves before and with the help of a traveling spray foam man and his toxic mobile foam machine, we had a cave by Saturday afternoon, sort of. Jim did a decent job with saws and razor knives carving the rock interior, and when he and I felt he'd carved enough, my crew and I painted it. We all left exhausted Saturday. Suzy and I showed up on Sunday morning and aged it with several limestone colors in our spritzer bottles. It was noon and the set dressers were coming. Suzy and I stepped back, dripping with sweat and paint, to observe our work. Surprisingly, it looked good. Jim was impressed with how it had turned out as well. We packed up our tools and began to leave to enjoy our few hours of time off. Just then, John Frick showed up. Looking at the cave disapprovingly, he decided he wanted Jim to carve on it some more. All of us laughed, fully thinking he was joking.

"You're kidding, right?" I asked.

"I'm not joking," he said seriously.

I began to explain the process involved in painting the cave, something I should not have had to do, and told him what any designer knows:the cave had been painted with six different colors, including a base coat. It was a multiple-step, time-consuming process that involved each layer of paint drying in the humid heat. If Jim carved on it now, even if we could paint it, it wouldn't dry. We'd be there all night.

Frick grew angry. "I'm sick of hearing excuses. I thought we were all going to pitch in together and carve on this all day."

"Yesterday was the carving day, John," I said.

"Why didn't someone tell me?"

Because you weren't around, I wanted to say. Instead: "I don't know, John, I really don't know. But we're exhausted, and we're going home."

I left him there fuming, drove to Del Rio, showered, and fell asleep. Never mind a nice job or a thank-you for saving my friend's ass.

On Monday, I found Jim building a log and stick addition to the front of the cave, a new addition the director had ordered. I began to pitch in, all of us did, set dressers, carpenters, painters, trying to get it ready. Suzy, meanwhile, was cranking out sign after sign between beers and flashing her breasts and mooning the carpenters. Bill Lee and Robert Trevino were busy carving and painting and aging a wood and spray foam dome for the mission set, perched seventy feet in the air in a condor, having to stop between shots at the shouts of the a.d. At one point in the hectic morning, Adelle came in to tell me the ferry was being built and I needed to peel off a painter to go to Del Rio and paint two boards on its bottom before it went into the water.

"I can't let a painter off to go all the way to Del Rio to paint two boards, Adelle. We're very busy here."

"You have to, JR."

"There's no way. You should have told me two days ago."

"I'm telling you now," she said forcefully.

"I said I can't do it. Why don't you go do it?"

"What!?"

Suggesting manual labor and bucking her authority, I'd infuriated her. "You said you used to be a scenic. I'll give you the stuff and you can go do it."

I had her.

"But, but, I can't. . . "

"Why not?"

"Because I'm busy, JR. Now, I'm trying to work with you but you're not cooperating."

"What are you busy with?"

"I have things to do here."

Right. Like hang around craft service and watch the shoot. "Fine, let's ask John Frick what we should do." I'd seen him walk in behind her and quickly explained the situation to him.

"What do you have to do here?" John asked Adelle.

Caught, Adelle gave me a vicious look. "Well, I was going to check with you and see if you needed me and——"

Frick was in a pissed-off mood and it had miraculously made him decisive. "I don't need you here right now. You can go paint the bottom of the ferry."

Adelle stormed off for our paint shop. Frick kept looking at the cave and me disapprovingly and saying things like, "I really think it needed more carving" and "I just don't think it's done yet."

Almost immediately, JP, Rich, and Howard rushed into the set and pronounced the set ready and said they were coming to shoot. Howard and JP both made a point of telling me and the others that, considering the time constraints, the cave looked magnificent. Even the actress who was supposed to be living in it came in for a viewing and said she loved it.

I left, satisfied, to view the church dome to see if it was ready, after sending Robert and Bill off to paint several tin roofs to look like wood planks for a set that would shoot very soon. I ran into John Frick staring up at the dome on the church.

"Hey John."

"JR."

"Hey, they loved the cave. They got it dressed and Jim is adding some mud between the logs and Robert and I just finished hitting all the raw edges on the addition."

"Oh," he said, sounding depressed, staring at the dome. I looked up at it and was surprised at how good it looked. This was just hurry-it-up TV but they were getting a few good sets.

"The dome looks pretty good," I said. "That spray foam guy was handy."

Frick said nothing, rubbing his beard, looking up at the large church whose exterior walls we'd painted as well.

"I'm thinking. . . " Frick began.

Stop the presses.

"I'm thinking you should get up there and carve on that dome some more. It looks bumpy."

I was confused. "Bumpy?"

"Yes, bumpy, JR, that's what I said."

"John, it's seventy-five feet in the air. The shot is going through the front door with exterior banditos shooting and crap like that. No one's going to see the bumps. Besides, I have to get you over to the Washington-on-the-Brazos set for—"

"Well, shit! Fuck it then!" John yelled. He kicked at a rock and began to walk off.

I chased after him. "John, John. What's wrong?"

He whipped around. "I'll tell you what's wrong; I'm sick of the scenic department compromising my production design! That's what's wrong!"

I stood there with my mouth open. I'd climbed up many a rickety ladder on many tall buildings for this man. "Wait a second, you're mad at me?"

"You're goddamn right I'm mad at you!"

I leaned on a hitching post. "After all this shit, all these sets I've gotten ready for you, you're gonna take a shit on me? I'm the guy who gets in trouble?"

"Well JR, Adelle and I are tired of your operating on your own agenda and not listening to us."

"Not listening to you?" I became shrill. "What the *fuck* are you talking about?! The only thing I'm trying to do is finish these goddamn sets! I've done enough shows to know that if they're not painted, no matter what reason, I'm gonna take the fucking heat for this shit!"

"It's the cave, JR. I really thought we were all going to carve on it on Sunday. You went against me on that. I'm sick of all the bad attitudes around here and nobody listening to me or Adelle. You should have carved more on the cave."

"John, John, John, forget the goddamn cave. The producers, directors, everybody just saw it. They love it."

"Goddammit, I know that, but I didn't think it was finished."

"We were tired John. We've been under a lot of pressure and Jesus Christ, it looked good."

Frick didn't seem to hear anything I'd said. "And now this dome thing. . . "

I walked away then, my ears burning, my teeth grinding, my ulcer reacting, completely overwhelmed by stress. I walked down to the Alamo, climbed up on the roof and smoked a joint (sorry, Happy), trying to relax. People fought with each other constantly on movies, I reminded myself. I thought about what had just happened and knew it wasn't John Frick's fault anyway. It was mine. Every designer had a different approach, and it was up to the scenic and the rest of the art department to conform and adapt to his method and opinions. When Frick had worked for Cary, I'd never taken him seriously, usually ignoring his often inane requests and going with Cary's decisions. I couldn't ignore John anymore. He was the same person, only now a designer. I was the one who had changed. He had every right in the world to make me stay until midnight on a Sunday painting on a finished set, as long as he thought it wasn't finished; he and every designer I'd ever worked for had the right and often used it. The movie hierarchy had to be obeyed simply because everyone did fight. With all the different personalities coming together on a movie, only each person staying in his place and doing his little job and following his superiors over the hill could make it happen. And my job that moment was to obey my designer, no matter what. Either that or quit, leave the circus, and go home. The show would definitely go on without me. I took one last hit off the joint and walked back down to Alamo Village. I ran into Frick on the exterior porch of the cabin Stephen F.Austin would die in. We sat down on a bench, both of us smiling now, making small talk, avoiding the subject of the upcoming sets.

–24–

Within the next few days, our work finished at Alamo Village, my crew and I made a mad dash for the next set, which was the Quimper's Ferry crossing on the beautiful Devil's River. The location, a rough hour's drive from Del Rio, was an amazingly clear, Caribbean blue river of rapids and deep blue pools set between high limestone bluffs arising out of nowhere in the desert above Lake Amistad. The carpenters had one day to build two ferry landings (docks), and set up the cable and winches that would pull the ferry across the hundred-yard stretch of rapids in the river. We had a day to paint the docks and ferry and the exterior of the cave house set, an unpainted monstrosity of spray foam yet to be assembled. Needless to say, we were hurried, but it was fun diving in the cool river, swimming back and forth with supplies on our mission to finish.

We were so rushed, in fact, that when the shooting crew arrived, pointing their cameras in our direction in no uncertain terms, we were still jumping in and out of the river trying to age the new wood of the docks and the cave exterior while the carpenters frantically untangled winches and cables trying to get the ferry to work. Amidst all of this confusion, I noticed Adelle wandering around, trying to find something to do. What she chose, sadly, was to grab a hatchet and take a few weak chops at the posts on the dock. They had been painted with three different colors of latex washes to make them look old. Her few chops exposed large, obvious chunks of new raw wood, something unacceptable on any set. I walked over to her amid the shouts of the shooting crew and our own.

"Adelle, what are you doing?"

She turned to me and began to scream. "JR, I think these posts need more distressing and I'm doing it, so just leave me alone!"

"You're messing them up, Adelle. Besides, the shooting crew is here. We have to get out of here."

"Listen to me, I'm the art director and the set's not finished until I say it's finished!"

"Fine, that's fine. If we have to do it then, let's do it right. If you want the posts distressed, I'll grab a few carpenters, a couple of chain-saws, and we'll have it done in five minutes and it won't look like this stuff you're doing."

She wasn't listening. "Goddamnit, I'm the art director and you have to do what I tell you!" She was shouting so loudly I could see her tonsils.

I started to get pissed. "Look, I'm not disagreeing with you, Adelle, just let us handle it and——"

"Just shut up, JR! Just shut up and get to work! Now!"

"Listen goddammit, you don't tell me to fucking shut up!"

"Why not? You tell me what to do! You made me paint the bottom of the ferry! Now get to work!"

"Just get out of here!"

"I'm telling John Frick!"

"I don't give a shit who you tell," I said and turned to Rodney Brown who was laughing and enjoying it all. I asked him to distress the posts and grabbed Robert Trevino, a couple of Hudsons, and started mixing two new latex washes. An a.d. ran up when the chainsaws began to roar.

"What the hell are you doing?" she asked me.

"Following orders."

"I thought you were through with this set. We're ready to shoot."

"Give us four more minutes," I said and got to work.

We ran around, jumping in and out of the river, trying not to get any paint in it. John Frick showed up on the set for the first time and Adelle ran up to him. I could see her gesturing wildly in my direction. By the time they reached me, I could also see and hear John waving her off saying, "We'll talk about it later, Adelle."

Finished with the posts, I sent my painters over to the exterior cave and plunged back into the river to help Burson, diving down to the bottom beneath the rapids to untangle the cables. Once the line was ready, he and the carpenters shipped out while my crew and I put the finishing washes on the cave to tie it in with the existing surrounding limestone with camera asking us to move out of the way the whole time. Not thirty seconds before the first rolling was called, we packed up our supplies and tools and, in a caravan of dust, got out of there.

We had one main set left for *Texas*—a hacienda exterior with a wrought-iron entryway gate and some corrals. The main action would occur in the corrals, and initially they had called for just one wall, a simple facade, for the hacienda and a tack room. But somewhere in there, since the scout, Frick and Adelle had exploded the set into a quite large two-story stucco building with a giant stucco entryway gate, a long retaining wall, the corrals, and a mobile tack house. It shot in four days and nothing had been built. The set was on Pinto Creek on Moody's Ranch and would incorporate several log cabins we'd built and painted for *Lonesome Dove*. Several of those cabins would have to be painted and the logs rechinked as they were to play as the town of Goliad. All in all, it was daunting. We should have had ten days, not four, for a set like that.

That first morning, as we waited on the beleaguered carpenters to build the giant hacienda, all the while shaking their heads, we started on the Goliad buildings. Adelle drove up in her little car and ran up to me where I was painting—you know, working.

"Good morning, Adelle."

"So, are you going to let me do my job today?" she asked me.

"No one's trying to stop you from doing your job, O.K.? Now, we have a huge amount of work to do here, so I really don't have time for any more of this bullshit."

"Right, right, sure, JR. Everything's aggression with you, isn't it? You're always using passive aggression with me, aren't you?"

"What the hell are you talking about?"

"See, see, there's that aggressive behavior again."

As she spoke, I was trying to show two of my painters the finish I wanted them to do.

"So," Adelle demanded loudly, "I want to know right now: are you going to let me do my job or not? Are you?"

"Fine," I said. "Do your job. Here are the sets. There are the plans. Tell me something to do. Go for it, as they say. In the meantime, I've got to start somewhere because I have so much goddamn work to do."

The whole time I spoke, she nodded her head in mock approval saying, "Sure, sure, right. I can hear that aggression in your voice. There it is again."

I sighed. "Adelle, can't you see I'm painting right now? What are *you* doing?"

"Trying to do my job! You won't let me!"

"Jesus Christ, you don't even know what you're job is!"

John Frick drove up then and Adelle ran toward him. "We're gonna settle this once and for all !" she screamed.

I followed her over to John Frick, who began to actually back up, then walk quickly toward the river with an I-don't-want-to-deal-with-this look on his face. I didn't want to deal with it, either, but I had to be there to plead my case. Adelle started in on me, going on and on about how I hadn't listened to her on the Devil's River set, how I had given her her painting list back on the Stephen F. Austin set, how I had made her paint two boards on the ferry. Fully expecting John to set her straight and side with me, I was shocked when he didn't.

"JR," he began solemnly, "as you know, being an art director is a tough position. It was hard for me when I was the one trying to get people to listen to me. I know you once expressed an interest in being an art director too, so you should understand Adelle's frustration. Now, this construction department seems to have a real macho, sexist, bad attitude, and frankly, I always thought you were above that."

"Oh, O.K., you're saying I'm being sexist now? That's a serious charge. That's what you're saying? Because I disagreed with Adelle about some paint on some posts on a stupid set that was about to shoot?"

"No, I'm just saying that I thought you were above this."

"You're compromising John Frick's vision by not listening to me," Adelle said.

"Look," I said, "all I give a damn about is finishing the painting on these sets before they shoot. I have no problem talking about the paint on these sets. I would talk about it with you all day. I swear to you, that is all I give a damn about out here. And I certainly don't want to compromise John Frick's *vision* of *Texas* ," I said, sarcastically accenting the telltale word. "Let's just talk about the sets and nothing else and I bet we'll get along fine."

"I don't want it to be like that," Frick said somberly. "I want us all to be friends, too."

I had a vision just then of Buck Henry in *Catch-22* talking to Yossarian, asking the unthinkable. "We want you to like us. That's all. Like us." Adelle and I stared at each other, no friendliness in our future.

"All I want to know," Adelle said, pushing up her horn-rimmed glasses, "is that you, JR, are going to do what I tell you to do."

"O.K., sure."

She and John looked at me.

"Well," Adelle said, "are you?"

I sighed once more. "Of course, Adelle. I'll do what you say."

She smiled. "Good."

With that, we walked to the set and looked at the plans. Adelle did not say or contribute one word. John had little concern with my concern over the set's size. I took great pains to emphasize that I wasn't trying to compromise his blurred vision, but we had time constraints and. . . As usual, Frick was preoccupied with the tiny, insignificant details, not the big picture. All he could talk about were the fake plywood saltillo tiles he wanted on the porch and balcony. He'd liked them so much on the plaza set, he wanted them all over this one. The only time concession I could get was that I wouldn't have to paint individual squares of plywood on the balcony floor; could I instead, he wondered, just paint on lines to look like tile up there? I tried to explain that it was actually easier to paint nailed down squares and began to feel my anger coming on that I was wasting time talking about this. I tried to bring up the fake stucco, that I would use Structolite, and what about the corrals, the log cabins, the entryway and gate, if we——. He didn't want to hear it. He just wanted to talk about those tiles. Adelle wandered off and John promised to get back to me on those upstairs tiles no one would ever see in a millennium. Soon he left the set, as did Adelle, and that was it. Those were my instructions, basically a lecture to obey Adelle, who had nothing to say except, "Obey me."

I didn't see Frick again until the night before the set shot. Adelle wandered around, lost, every day, picking flowers or something, giving me no input, no advice, instructions, nothing. Even when I tried to include her and explain what I was doing to make her at least feel like she was giving input, she blew me off with a patronizing, go away, "That's nice, JR. You have lots of little painting tricks, don't you?"

For those four days, the carpenters and the painters and the laborers busted our collective asses. All of us were ragged and on the edge, snapping at each other. My painters,Bill and Robert, were beaten, defeated. Suzy was fried by sun and alcohol, spending more time upending beer bottles in her sexy El Camino than painting on the set, entertaining the laborers from Ciudad Acuna with her sexual exploits, telling them of the "Suzy sandwich" two wranglers had made the night before. To make things worse, it began to rain sporadically, not a condition conducive to stucco drying. We managed to move over a ton of Structolite, though, from powder in bags to fake stucco troweled on the walls and then aged it all, including the large corral and, of course, the ever important plywood tile on the bottom of the porch. And, at some point in there, I received an urgent and, to Frick, helpful message that I did not have to paint faux tile on the balcony, the last concern, next to a shark attack, I had.

We got lucky with the rain showers and finished the set, but it was very close. The stucco was still wet in parts and a hard rain could have washed some of it off. The carpenters and I were still trying to frantically finish the entryway and gate that last morning. There was a late call and we had thirty minutes before the company arrived. The Teamsters had already pulled up their trucks and the caterers were serving breakfast. I was aging the stucco entryway as Bill Lee was painting the iron gates while I screamed at Suzy to get to work and repaint a door on the nearby Goliad set because her first pass looked ridiculous.

"It's just TV!" she screamed back at me.

"I know it's just TV but it looks like shit! Now take sixty seconds out of your life and repaint that fucking door!"

John Frick drove up and wandered over. Adelle came up with him and expressed her concerns about the downstairs plywood saltillo tile.

"It looks dirty," she said. "I think you should clean it more."

"O.K., Adelle, I promise I'll get to it as soon as I finish this entryway and gate. We're talking about fifteen minutes here."

"JR, I want this done."

"I said O.K., Adelle, but you have to understand, that's a floor that will read just fine as it is on film if it has to. This is the front gate that everyone will definitely see. I have to prioritize and finish it first. I don't just want to, I *have* to."

She walked away angry and came back with John Frick. I heard zero, nothing, nada about the giant set we had just finished with little or no guidance or support. No, I heard about the tile.

"JR, Adelle has some concerns about the tile being too dirty and dusty," he began.

"Yes, John, I know. I told her I'd do it in fifteen minutes. I promise."

Why the fuck was I begging these people just to let me do my job? Didn't they understand I wasn't painting the gate for a religious experience, but because it shot in minutes? And wasn't it their job to prioritize the set, hell, any of the sets, in the first place?

John Frick cleared his throat. "I have concerns about the tile, too, JR, and we want you to clean it now."

"O.K., O.K., we'll clean the tile." I sent Bill over to sweep any dirt off the tile porch and then to mop it. When he was through, he came back to help me. Adelle came running up.

"It's still too dirty," she said. "You need to scrub it."

"O.K., alright." I called Suzy over from her breakfast to finish aging the stucco. I grabbed several rags and a Hudson sprayer filled with water, wet down the floor, got down on my hands and knees, and scrubbed it. As I neared the end of the tile, I felt someone watching me. I looked up and saw Adelle smiling, the happiest I'd ever seen her.

"It still looks dirty," she said. "Do it again."

I turned around and began to scrub it all once more, even though it looked fine before any of this, and she walked off saying nothing. When I was through, I went back to the gate to finish. Frick walked up.

"Did you scrub the floor?"

"Yes, John, I did. It looks good."

"Let's take a look at it."

We walked over to the porch floor, recessed under the balcony. John stared and stared, finally muttering, "I don't know. . . "

" Please, John. It looks much cleaner. Don't we want some dirt on it? It's outside, next to a corral, there's dust everywhere, it's an old hacienda. . . "

"I guess so, JR. . . " he said reluctantly, as if I were trying to put one over on him. "Well, I have to leave and go to Brackettville. I have a speeding ticket I'm going to contest."

Most designers wait for the set to "open" for the company, checking for last-minute changes. John's relationship with the director had deteriorated to the point that Rich rarely spoke to him, even going out of his way to aggravate his designer. John jumped in his truck and quickly left the set as the director walked up to see the grand hacienda for the first time. Several of us who had built and painted it stood there proudly and physically spent. Rich walked up with Howard our producer, J.P. and several others.

"Jesus Christ," the director said in disgust, "this looks like a cheap California condo. It's way too big. Shit. Oh well. I'll shoot around it." He waddled over to eat breakfast, leaving us standing there.

Howard walked up to me. "Good job, JR. It looks nice, but. . . how come it's so big? On the scout, Rich said he just wanted a wall and the corral and a much smaller gate and entryway."

"I don't know,Howard."

JP made a point of thanking the exhausted construction crew for pulling the set out, adding, only half-jokingly, that he was signing everyone's paychecks that week except for John Frick's.

Feeling for my old friend, I thought it was a good thing he'd left. The company had arrived in force by then. Tired of running into us and our messes on every set of the movie, they were rude and pushy, hustling us out of there. We gathered our things and slinked away, doing as told.

–25–

I was forced to leave *Texas* three days early in order to work on *The Good Old Boys*. Though everyone knew I was doing this, and all the sets were essentially finished and three painters were staying on, I sensed there were a few hard feelings with Frick. For one thing, we stopped talking to one another. He and Adelle, inseparable now, huddled together talking in the art department and abruptly grew silent whenever I walked into the office. I didn't care. I was leaving. I figured they were mainly pissed because I was going onto another movie and they weren't. Adelle, in fact, had tried desperately to get on *The Good Old Boys*. Not understanding how things worked on movies yet, her pleas, maneuverings, and other efforts were all futile since the people doing the hiring were my friends. A few well-placed words to Sully squashed any hopes she might have had, giving me some petty satisfaction.

Again, we hit the ground running. Cary and Sully had taken care of all the planning and creative decisions, so all that was left was for Ed Vega and me and the other two painter's helpers to do the work in the one-hundred-and-ten-degree heat. As the summer wore on, the heat factor increased, forcing us to pace our work accordingly to avoid heat stroke, a very real threat that can sneak up on you when you're standing up on a three-story building, balanced on a twelve-inch board on pump jacks with nothing below you at five in the afternoon at one-hun-dred-and-fifteen-degrees after a ten hour day at the end of a fourteen or twenty-one day work stretch. After days like that, my co-workers and I spent the warm evenings guzzling beer around the Remington Hotel pool or had dinner and drank down at the Cripple Creek restaurant where everyone from *The Good Old Boys* usually ate.

The only other decent place to eat in town, was the Thai Restaurant. I was down there one evening and bumped into Cary and Sully having dinner. The subject of the trials of *Texas* came up, and I complained bitterly of John Frick's performance. Both men immediately took up for their old art director.

"I've had tons of screaming fights with John Frick," Sully said, "It doesn't mean anything, JR."

Cary chimed in. "JR, do you know how much prep time I had for this movie?"

"How much?"

"Five weeks. John Frick only had a week."

"No, he had two weeks."

"Either way, it was a short prep and I think that was part of the problem."

"Yeah, Cary, it was one of many problems. Many."

Cary and Sully kept trying to lighten it all up and put a happy, oh-well spin on it, but I wasn't budging. "Gosh," Cary finally said, "between you and Vega I'm gonna have to start calling you guys the cynic department instead of the scenic department."

I had to smile. "That's probably appropriate."

I fell into a routine: work, dope, beer, dope, dinner, dope, beer, sleep. The next day, start all over again. I was down at the Cripple Creek one evening toward the end of the show. I had the script for *The Good Old Boys* with me that Jones had written. I'd started reading it weeks before, but it was so silly and boring I could never get through it. Ed and I had talked about it and decided it was more simplistic and clichéd than anything else. The Cynic Department. I walked into the Cripple Creek, enjoying the cool air conditioning, my face deep red from four months in Del Rio, Texas. I was determined to finish the script over a good prime rib dinner. Seated near the front door, I saw the construction coordinator, Dave Wilt, sitting with our young art department coordinator and a man in a cowboy hat who I thought was my friend Rodney Brown. I walked over to say hello and maybe join them since there were several empty chairs.

"Hey Dave."

"Hey, JR, how's it goin'?"

I held up the script. "Thought I'd read this thing while I eat dinner." I was a millisecond away from saying something rude about the script, like I hoped it wouldn't put me off my meal, when Dave, sensing this I'm sure, spoke up quickly.

"What are you trying to do, suck up to the director?" he said, laughing. "He's sitting right there." He pointed to the man in the cowboy hat.

"Huh?" I looked and saw it was Jones sitting there. Feeling caught, I jumped visibly in surprise.

"Huh?" Jones said, mimicking me and acting startled as I had.

"Oh, I didn't know you were here," I said, smiling now.

The actor looked away and said nothing, ignoring me. I had just been ready to sit down, my hand on a chair. It was an awkward moment, for me at least.

"So. . . " I said to Dave, "how's it going?"

Dave kept nervously looking at Jones, who obviously didn't want me joining their party.

"O.K.," Dave said. Dave kept giving me a get-out-of-here look, but it had been a particularly hard day and I wanted to let my taciturn director know it.

"It sure was a hot son-of-a-bitch today," I said, looking at Jones, who still wouldn't look at me.

Dave began to look very nervous now.

"Well," I said holding up the script, "I guess I'll go sit in my corner and read this."

"Yeah, why don't you do that," Dave said, relieved I was leaving.

As I walked off, I heard their conversation resume. As it turned out, my prime rib au jus with horseradish was excellent. I finished the whole script and didn't get sick once.

The last sets we were working on were several exterior street scenes and some interiors in Alamo Village. Happy had his cowboy minions performing four irritating gunfight shows a day, allowing us to hear the town's mock sheriff scream "I'm the toughest man in town !" and shriek through the rest of his routine all day, firing off blanks before groups of overweight tourists ranging from three to five people, if he had an audience at all. We worked hard, long days that week, the whole art department a solid functioning unit with our leaders, Cary and Sully, out there with us almost every day, pitching in with everything from carpentry to set dressing to painting signs. On the last day we were to be in town, with the company arriving the next morning, our efforts reached a hurried pitch. Around five o'clock on that Friday, with almost everything done, I walked down the street and found Cary surveying his western town, a stack of old western posters in his hand he'd been gluing up all over town.

"JR buddy," he began, "you look like you've had it."

"I'm afraid I have, Cary. I'm going home."

"I want to thank you for staying on," he said. "I know *Texas* was tough and so was this. You came through like a champ."

"Thanks, Cary." We shook hands and said our good-byes.

I went to find Ed Vega, crouched over probably the millionth sign he'd painted in his career, and said so long. I packed up my tools and ladders in my blue pickup loaded down now like something out of *The Beverly Hillbillies* . I filled the leaky engine with oil and began to limp home in the old Ford.

–26–

If this were a movie, I suppose it would have ended on *The Good Old Boys*. But this is not a movie, and as soon as I got home, I was persuaded to take another show at the request of the construction coordinator John Burson, a show that, in actuality, is more indicative of my meager movie career. It was a horribly cheap movie of the week for CBS entitled *The Devil's Bed*, starring Richard Roundtree, Piper Laurie, Nicolette Sheridan, and Joe Lando. I told Burson I was really through with all of it this time, but he lured me to the small town where it would film, Elgin, Texas, with promises of very little set construction and painting.

As I found out, there was indeed very little to do on *The Devil's Bed*. Our designer was a nice elderly man named Tracy Bousman, who had done over sixty-five movies of the week. He had a pretty home in Sedona, Arizona, another real movie job waiting, and wasn't too concerned with this one. Adelle had somehow managed to squeeze in there as the art director and, as Burson later told me, had done everything in her power, short of telling Mr. Bousman I was a serial killer, to keep me off the picture, still not understanding the friends-in-power theory, and ignoring the fact that I had done more work as a local than she had. I not only got on the picture but stayed on long after she'd been laid off. Adelle seemed much less forbidding now, just another carny worker trying to get ahead like the rest of us. On *Texas* it was probably her coming between John Frick and me that had bothered me more than anything else. We pretended to get along and avoided each other. Because it was much harder for her as an art director to hang out on the set doing nothing on such a small show, our cutthroat u.p.m. not only axed her, but after a few days, banished our production designer as well. The u.p.m. was forced to reluctantly keep us on as a skeleton construction and paint crew, and we managed to stay or look busy with a few little projects each day.

I bumped into the stars of the show occasionally in small-town, dirt-poor, Elgin. The actor Joe Lando from *Dr.Quinn, Medicine Woman* hung around talking to me, bugging me, really, while I painted several obligatory Styrofoam tombstones. I thought he was an extra and said little. I didn't recognize Richard Roundtree, either. A very nice man, he came up to me, a cigar in his mouth, and we chatted while I did some painting on an exterior insurance office.

"Aging it down, huh?" he asked.

"Yeah, making it look old. Are you one of the extras?" I asked, trying to be nice.

He stiffened. "Principal," he mumbled gruffly.

"What?"

"I'm one of the principals."

I remembered then seeing his name on the call sheet. "Oh, you're Richard Roundtree," I said. "I'm a fan of your work." It was my standard actor greeting. All I'd ever seen of his was the movie *Shaft* in a drive-in when I was a kid. The man smiled now, pleased.

"What do you think of Elgin?" I asked.

He looked around and shrugged, as if to say, "not much." He looked bored watching me paint, so I pointed out a used-book, record, and video store on the corner across the street. He walked to the store, went inside, and came back across the street thirty minutes later with a shopping bag full of merchandise to show me.

"Look at this," he said, and held up an old collection of Sammy Davis Jr.'s greatest hits.

"Does it have 'The Candy Man?'"

"Yeah," he said happily, "and it only cost a dollar. I'm going back in there."

He went back to shopping and I went back to painting. As for the main star, like Joe Lando, I didn't know who she was, or, rather, that she was somebody. The actress Nicolette Sheridan walked into the construction department one day while I was talking to one of the carpenters.

"Do you guys know where I can get a Coke?" she asked. "Last

night was just. . . " she put a hand to her head, indicating a hangover. "I've got to have a Coke with some caffeine—now."

"There's some in that ice chest," I said pointing.

She turned around and bent over the chest and pulled out a soda. We went back to talking as Ms. Sheridan drained half of her coke, then let out a long, very loud and powerful, burp. We looked at her, surprised, and she belched again loudly.

"That's much better," she said. "Thanks guys," and walked back to the set, another brush with greatness.

Due to my usual ineptitude with finances, I was broke again and in debt on *The Devil's Bed*, every paycheck I would collect already spent. To make things worse, my old Ford finally died one day, throwing a rod on the streets of Elgin. I put a sign on it, reading "$200" and it sold in five minutes at Elgin prices. Working as a local, two hours from home, I was in big trouble for a place to stay until I imposed on a man named Damon and his wife Terry, who owned the used-book and video store Roundtree had loved. Damon, a house painter like me, who wanted to get into the movie business, had worked as an intern for me for a few days and offered his house as a place to stay. This was very kind, but after a week, we were getting on each other's nerves. Damon and Terry were alcoholics who mainly sat on their couch drinking beer and watching videos until one or both passed out. His wife Terry became more belligerent with each beer—which I bought for her, up to a case a day—yelling at me by nine o'clock about her miserable past, letting me know clearly she didn't want me around. After one drunken night, fortunately at the end of the show, with her screaming about her husband picking up "stray fuckin' people like they was stray fuckin' dogs" and how she was "fuckin' sick of it," and with Damon dressed like a drunken monk, telling me he thought he was the Son of God and meaning it, the smell of their dog's shit on the floor wafting through my nostrils, I had had it.

I was walking to work now, from their house, through Elgin, to the art department, in the hot September humidity, to go do a job I didn't want, to make money I had already spent. Fortunately, filming was soon over. One Saturday, my other truck out of the shop, I loaded up all my tools and ladders and unceremoniously went home.

Within a month, I was back in Austin on a TV show, a Hallmark special on American pioneers entitled *A Lantern in Her Hand*, a two-

189

hour piece of sentimental, watered-down, historical claptrap with no stars to speak of unless you count one of the *Facts of Life* girls—which one, I couldn't tell you. John Burson and the company, desperate for a scenic, lured me out with a deal memo for more money than I'd ever made, warning me, though, that there would be some serious work involved, and indeed there was. With no prep time, I hired up to eight scenics and proceeded to kill my crew with work, painting Willieville for the umpteenth time and many other pioneer-like sets. The movie was such a horribly disorganized and embarrassing experience I would have to write another book to go into the messy details. Suffice it to say, John Frick and Adelle Plauche, both openly disdainful of me now, were at the art department helm, and the show turned out much like Spelling's *Texas*, only condensed and intensified into six weeks of hell. By filming's end, it was obvious Frick and I would never work together again, since I told him as such in a heated argument. This meant John Burson and I were through as well, since he counted on Frick's design jobs often. I figured it was just as well. Frick was bringing on so many incompetent people who were in line to kiss his ass, or just listen to him, it was starting to look like a new crew to me anyway. I took my toys and went home.

–27–

After this last television debacle, I turned off the answering machine and severed all ties with most everyone I knew in the movie business. I had started up my unemployment benefits to tide me over until I entered the real world again when I received a phone call, several phone calls actually, from one John Balling, who needed me to be his foreman on the new sequel to *Ace Ventura, Pet Detective*, to be called *Ace Ventura Goes to Africa*, or, according to the last rewrite of the self-proclaimed, highly confidential script I read, *Ace Ventura:When Nature Calls*, starring Jim Carrey. A third of the film would be shot in Texas on a large ranch, John Balling told me, outside of San Antonio. The rest of the filming would be done in South Carolina. Even if Carrey, more often than not in his films, seemed to be acting like an idiot, I was curious to see what the filming on this forty-million-dollar picture would be like.

Though John promised me autonomy and the great outdoors working on the ranch location, I found the first couple of weeks involved much slave labor at the dungeon of a warehouse where we'd filmed *Eight Seconds* and *Heaven and Hell* in San Antonio. The construction coordinator for the film was a short, red-faced, hungover and screaming hardass from Florida named Harold Collins. He had brought in a group of six men, half of whom were inexperienced, as foremen to lord over the locals from Houston and Austin. He called his crew "Harold's Naildrivers." For the most part, these guys stood around and watched the Texans do all the work while they smoked cigars and practiced genuflecting before Harold's most probably withered and white posterior. This supplicant behavior was one of the many things Harold required from his "naildrivers." Harold, an incredibly uptight ex-cop, who screamed at grown men for being one minute late at the beginning of a fourteen-hour day in the sun, told his carpenters how to wind up hoses, how to hold a nail gun, a saw, a hammer, everything. He had a long list of written rules his carpenters had to obey, reflecting a hatred of long hair and a bias against the drinking of hard liquor or any drug use. He promised all of us he would turn in his own mother if he caught her smoking dope. Of course, most all of his "naildrivers" were complete dope fiends, and when they weren't watching us work, smoking cheap cigars, or guzzling beer and liquor, they were literally and irritatingly begging us for dope, inhaling and sucking down even the tiniest roaches we produced. Fortunately, seeing that I had short hair and was nothing but business, and, I assumed, not knowing I was smoking dope every day under his nose in order to make the work tolerable and half-ass interesting, Harold left me alone and, away from the sets, was actually cordial to me at times. Knowing that he needed me, the cordiality was necessary.

After two weeks in the warehouse, I was soon ready to quit. The sets we were constructing to be moved to the ranch location were in a large stage area surrounded by an upper level of balconies and windows occupied by the production offices and the art department's upper echelon. Our distant designer, Stephen Lineweaver, and his art director, an often rude snob named Christopher Nowak, would occasionally appear on the upper level and watch as Jim Kanan, my old friend from Houston and I worked on the sets. They never deigned to speak to us underlings or learn our names, even though both of us did a large portion of the scenic work in Texas. To make us feel even smaller, the production manager, a heartless representative of the financial dark side, one Andy La Marca, like Big Brother, would look down on us from his office window to make sure we were working. One afternoon, seeing Jim and me laughing and talking as we were working with hatchets and hammers distressing a Styrofoam African hut, Mr. La Marca felt he wasn't getting his full money's worth and immediately sent word down to Harold Collins and John Balling that he didn't want us talking or laughing anymore while we worked. With great difficulty, I swallowed my comments and went back to work, thoroughly discouraged that I was apparently still in elementary school.

I realized that afternoon, though he was a nice guy, the head scenic,

John Balling, was playing good cop to Harold's bad; somehow, even with apologies, he was always executing the madman's orders, knowing which side his Harold was buttered on since both men had done many films together over the years. Even more of a cynic than me, Balling and I traded movie-job horror stories, many of his easily topping mine, especially his most recent experiences on the film *The Specialist*, starring Sylvester Stallone and Sharon Stone. "Sly" had John Balling painting expensive faux finishes throughout the megastar's mansion in Florida as well as the sets for the picture, a home which Balling described as incredibly gaudy with nude statues Stallone had commissioned of himself situated around its grounds. When Balling finished the work on the actor's home and tried to go back to his real job, the sets for the film, the actor kept calling him back to the home for more free touchups and odds and ends to the point that Balling said, no more, I have to, you know, get the movie ready. Stallone became angry then and promptly cut Balling's credit from the picture. "He likes to destroy people," Balling said. "He's done it to others. He likes to draw you in, be real nice to you, and then destroy you."

I couldn't get over the statues. Weren't the movies enough? "He has statues of himself?"

"Oh yeah. With all these big muscles and everything. The guy's really into his muscles."

"I noticed that."

Just when I'd reached my breaking point of being watched from above twelve hours a day in the Pit, I was sent to the ranch location with Jim Kanan and a trailer of tools, where I basically became the lead scenic, without the perks and pay, for the rest of the filming in Texas. John Balling showed up a couple of times; once to videotape the sets and weeks later to buy us lunch and say good-bye.

The biggest irony of *Ace Ventura II* quickly became apparent in that this supposedly pro-animal film, which includes numerous scenes featuring Carrey's asinine indignance over the mistreatment of animals, was being filmed in large part on the 777 Ranch, wild game and canned hunting outfit. This 15,000-acre spread forty minutes west of San Antonio near the small town of Hondo is run by a character made for films himself, one Slim Crapps, or Mr. C., as those of us on the crew were instructed to call him. Slim, a dashing figure, well over six feet tall with long white hair, a white beard, and a propensity for wearing safari outfits, began his career building carports with a welding machine out of the back of his pickup in San Antonio years ago. He is now a powerful, modern Texas rancher and businessman dabbling in massive construction projects and serving up the plump bodies of exotic, and somewhat tame, animals to be blown away by other rich, and not so rich, businessmen. In a similarity no one from production seemed to notice, or care about, the extremely obvious bad guy from the script, Vincent Cadby, the Console General of the fictional Bonai Province, is also a powerful, wealthy landowner who cares little for the lives of African animals. There is even a scene where Ace, the animal lover, finds himself in Cadby's animal trophy room and almost faints at the number of heads on the wall. Of course, Slim has a room just like this in his main lodge and supplied many of the actual animal heads for the scene. It was hard to move through the art department warehouse without seeing the heads of a number of animals: zebras, exotic deer and rams, stuffed lions, and even a bodiless giraffe. Unlike Slim, though, Cadby doesn't instruct all the armed guards at his many compound gates to shoot any stray dog, cat, or coyote on sight. After all, this is a kid's movie and in America, at least according to the movie, all dogs, stray or not, go to heaven.

As I found out, at the minimal cost of two hundred dollars a day, blood-hungry men who don't have the time to, well, actually stalk a deer or wild boar, or wait all day to catch a fish, come to the 777 to hunt or fish in Slim's many overstocked lakes, or large ponds rather, and then throw back all they catch, although Slim himself is allowed to keep the profits from those clients he's reeled in financially. Before and during the filming, many of us on the crew stayed at one of his bunkhouses on Sugar Lake, which is nothing other than a large fish tank, equipped with an aerator to oxygenate the water crowded with fish fed from the docks. As Slim says in his brochure, "Everything needs water and you will see lots of it on the 777 Ranch," much of which is supplied by the pure and somewhat protected drinking water source for all of San Antonio, and many other Central Texas cities, towns, and farms, the Edwards Aquifer. Slim taps directly into the aquifer, from which he gleefully pumps thousands of gallons of scarce Texas water with abandon, filling all of his lakes to the brim and even creating artificial creeks for his fisherman's, and the company's, amusement.

For additional fees, up to $12,000, one can kill, at fairly close range, some of Slim's ostensibly wild game, such as the vicious zebra (prices vary), the lithe buffalo (over $3,000), a number of exotic goats and sheep, native whitetail and exotic deer, elk, javelina, and the Scimitar Horned Oryx, the last animal being so unflappable that the second unit tried everything but dynamite in a futile attempt to get a herd of the animals to run, or just get out of the way finally, in what was to be a typical sweeping vista shot of running African animals. All of the admittedly beautiful animals are fed every day from white feed trucks, getting fat, until a businessman, I mean a sportsman, is led out in a white jeep to shoot a particular animal, which is fenced inside holding areas of the ranch with names like Muy Grande and Turkey Creek. I even saw what looked like a bunker one day hidden in the ground not ten feet from a feed bin, most probably for the more elderly and near-sighted sportsmen. And, as a reward I suppose, for his asinine behavior, our construction coordinator, Harold, was even given a free shot by Slim at one of several majestic axis deer that had earlier roamed playfully through one of our sets until Harold blew it away. As they do for any guest, Slim's on-site taxidermy staff promptly cut off the animal's head, skinned and gutted the body, and sent the whole package to the short white hunter in Florida.

The Deuce Production Company, at the behest of Morgan Creek and our designer, Stephen "On-set" Lineweaver, at no small cost, built three large sets on Slim's ranch for this sequel. Two of the sets were villages, the Wachati village, which is populated by peaceful vegetarians, their huts made of leaves and twigs and fake bougainvillaea, and the Wachootoo, or meat eaters', village, their huts made of Styrofoam mud and sticks, their village strewn with real animal bones, severed legs, heads, and skins, and sundry parts hanging malodorously from the trees, much of the carnage provided courtesy of Slim. The last of the large sets was a giant entryway gate a la *Jurassic Park* with a Styrofoam rhino head at its center. This gate would lead the movie's many extras into the fictional Quinnland Safari Park, where Ace would have many adventures in his search for the missing giant white bat, which the evil Cadby has stolen in an effort to provoke a war between the two African tribes so he can steal their precious supply of bat guano. If this sounds suspiciously like the plot of every *Scooby Doo* episode ever made, it's because it is.

When I had time, I spoke with some of the animal handlers on *Pet*

Detective II and observed the many animals they had on hand to make Texas look like Africa, namely, several giraffes, lions, monkeys, mandrills, zebras,and a couple of wrinkled, mostly manacled elephants, all of which seemed to perpetuate the movie-as-carny notion even further. Though the animal handlers seemed to love and care for their livelihood, myself, I couldn't help but feel pity for these animals so far from the plains where they normally roam freely, being kept in small cages and pens. Again, though they seemed to be treated as well as possible, I saw one giraffe that had somehow escaped and run through several barbed wire fences, its legs, chest, and neck cut to pieces. Though the wounds were still open, it would surely be used for filming. All the giraffes were carted around in an obviously uncomfortable trailer, their long necks bent severely, back and forth to the set, subject to the worries of the u.p.m and a.d.'s over the weather and exterior shots. The giraffes fared better than Slim's animals though. Crippled or injured animals there are usually shot by a guest (at a discount?). I was stopped on my way to one of the sets one day, when the roads were blocked off so a crippled deer I'd watched hobbling for days could be run through an area to be shot, making something of a sport out of it, I suppose.

Several trained monkeys played as Ace's sidekick in the movie. The animals were forced to do a number of humiliating and ridiculous, mimicking scenes alongside Carrey, including being tied to a raft and going over a waterfall. Carrey had to do the gags as well, but Carrey was making thousands and millions of dollars for his efforts and wasn't forced to wear a diaper between scenes. Actually, he was wearing a diaper-like loincloth between takes one day, so maybe they were both being ridiculed.

A diaper metaphor may be appropriate here, for Carrey was something of a baby on this film. Exactly how many thousands of dollars the millionaire actor was making on the show was the subject of many rumors, with figures running from five to ten million. Carrey was definitely said to be unhappy about having to do the sequel, having agreed to it before the phenomenal success of the first *Pet Detective* and *The Mask*. Some said he'd turned down a fourteen-million-dollar show in order to resurrect Mr. Ventura. Either way, Carrey had probably licked enough boots in his time and was ready to have his own spit-shined. Personal information about the star was so sought after during filming, and Carrey was so paranoid about it, that special memos were issued at the beginning of the show warning that none of us on the crew were to talk with the press, especially the show *Hard Copy*, which had been trying to find anything on Carrey. It was a reasonable request, but the dramatics involved in the handling and transportation of the actor bordered on the ridiculous. I was staying in one of the lodge bunkhouses on Sugar Lake the night the transportation captain, Larry Alexander, and his non-barking dog, Zero, brought in "the package" as Carrey was being appropriately called. No one was on the ranch save those of us on the crew and a few guests; and yet, there was a heightened, super-secret tension to his arrival, as though Boris Yeltsin were being hustled in. Mainly, it was the children of Hondo who wanted to see Carrey most, or even knew who he was. I knew from eating lunch in Hondo every day that the town's younger citizenry were desperate for a glimpse of the man but, as I didn't have the heart to tell them, had no chance of doing so. Larry, standing on the porch with us, was clearly perturbed with all he was having to go through to make Carrey happy and get him ensconced at one of Slim's private residences on the ranch. "Poor Mr. Pet Detective," Larry mimicked in a whiny voice. "He's all alone up there in Slim's screw shack with nobody to talk to. He's gotta have somebody with him every two seconds. Well, shit!" He jumped back in his truck, with Zero in tow, to go placate "the package."

Later, I spoke with one of Slim's friendlier gate guards and he too complained of the arrival of "the package" at Slim's house, a house which the pet detective apparently had no qualms staying in, even going out of his way to ask for a tour of the Rancho de Muerte upon his arrival. The guard also mentioned that the pet detective had seen a wasp one morning and, having been scared to death by the tiny insect, had sent out an all-points bulletin for wasp traps and wasp spray. One of the ranch hands was dispatched to the store to procure several wasp traps, which were promptly hung all over Carrey's lodgings, most probably attracting all the wasps of South Texas then. The guard also told me, in a moment I'm sure *Hard Copy* would have salivated over, of a midnight visit of an attractive masseuse from San Antonio. He'd been forced to pull over the woman's driver when he tried to run the gate in an attempt to deliver the package to the package, priority mail, as it were.

Though most of us in the art department were unceremoniously and without notice booted from our rooms when production arrived, our luggage placed outside and our beds removed from the buildings to make room for more important people, Carrey's lodgings, apparently, were something of a problem as well. In keeping with the movie-star credo of having as many ostentatious residences as possible, Carrey, when not in Slim's house, had a giant, super R.V. travel trailer called the Grand Teton that came with a fold-out living room for when he was on set. This wasn't good enough, though, and halfway through shooting, a gigantic superbus, a roaming home on wheels that would make Willie Nelson envious, was brought in that cost of over $700,000. Meanwhile, our u.p.m., Andy La Marca, was busy screwing all of us Texas locals out of gas for our vehicles, our tools, our time, our labor, our lodgings, our meals, telling our union shop steward that we could go fuck ourselves when he brought up the matter of honoring the local union contract that *someone* from Deuce Productions had signed.

His star having risen possibly to its apex, there was no doubt as to who was really in charge of the production. Carrey was in almost every scene in this juvenile movie, which opens with the comic genius yodeling out of his asshole off a mountaintop. In the course of the script, he proceeds to be in humorous contact with a variety of animals, including being swallowed by and cut out of a crocodile, as well as climbing naked out of a $200,000 mechanical rhino's butt. He imitates Abe Lincoln, pulls a kernel of corn out of a tall native's rectum, is chased by angry natives a number of times, and, in one my favorite scenes, he gets sodomized by a gorilla—twice. I watched Carrey one hot day during a particularly stupid scene, earning his money. The gag was this: Carrey would be pulled behind a jeep, parasailing, while he whips out a telescope and spies on some bad guys in the safari park. Special effects, at a great cost to the company, had planted two gigantic cranes in the middle of one of Slim's pastures and an intricate network of cables and pulleys to shoot this tiny little scene. Everything that could go wrong did; the jeep wouldn't run, the sail didn't work, and the scene ended up taking two days to shoot. Carrey, apparently known for his nervousness at doing his own stunts, was strapped into a massive harness, even though he was being pulled only fifteen or twenty feet into the air. Before action was called on the first take, he yelled out, "Excuse me, but if I shit my pants you guys can cut that out in post-production, right!?" The third time the jeep's engine cut out, I almost felt sorry for the actor as he hung there in the air, swinging in the heat, in his harness and ropes, in his ridiculous outfit, calling out in a whiny voice, "It's the jeep damnit! Somebody's gotta fix the goddamn jeep!"

For the most part, the consensus on the crew seemed to be that Carrey was a nice, normal guy, even shy at times, and except for the sporadic bursts of idiotic behavior, I mean acting, he was just doing his well-paid job. However, he didn't have to be too nice of a guy anymore. Not long after the actor abruptly booted one of his female co-stars, when the film's director, Tom DeCerchio, kept asking him for too many takes, Carrey retreated to his trailer one very expensive day and wouldn't come out until the director was gone. Tom, new and inexperienced when it came to feature films, was taking too long to shoot the picture, and he and his a.d. team seemed to have no regard for the schedule. There were several stories of disorganization, including accusations that the directorial team was spending more time at breakfast with the caterers than setting up the day's first shot. Others said it was Carrey himself, with his excessive clowning before, during, and after takes, and not Tom who was responsible for the schedule overruns. Several straight takes were done and then usually a couple of takes where Carrey would go berserk, on his own. While the unpredictable spring weather probably had more to do with the delays than anything else, one of the final straws for the director was a rude memo banning all children and visitors from the set. Though the director caught the heat for the memo, it was Carrey supposedly who had given the order after having seen one of the shooting crew's children on set and, pissed off, had demanded no more visitors. Tom apologized to the crew the next day, but damage had been done, especially since rumors had already been floating around the set that Tom didn't know what he was doing. As usual, it doesn't take long for the hatchet to fall in the film business.

When Carrey retreated to his trailer, Tom was asked to stay one more day and finish the week's filming. Carrey then flew to L.A. Tom was promptly put on a plane back to who knows where and everyone got a day off. When the crew returned the next week, to no one's surprise, one of the star's best friends, Steve Oedekerk, who had written the film's stellar script (and put his name on it in broad daylight) was in the director's seat of this multimillion-dollar production. Having recently seen an excerpt of an early film Carrey and Steve had made that was beyond stupid, I had to admit he seemed to be the man for the job, having also penned such scenes in the script when Carrey, dressed as

Abe Lincoln, utters, "Why there was a time when a booger from my nose could put you on easy street!" or "I could purchase a year supply of corn meal, just for letting someone sniff my stool!" William Goldman, watch out.

The whole a.d. team was then sacked as well, and Steve brought in a group he'd worked with before and made a point of introducing everyone to the new crew. When he got to one of the new producers who'd come along for the ride, a grip raised his hand and asked "Who's he replacing?" Everyone had a good laugh, except, of course, those Carrey had occupationally beheaded.

Being a local boy, and having been caught and corralled by Slim Crapps more than once into doing work for him and his ranch rather than working on the sets, I spoke often with Slim and his sidekick, Thumper, the ranch liaison, a manic young country boy whose only claim to fame was a seven-year stint as a prison guard sadly cut short by Thumper's slapping a handcuffed prisoner. I observed firsthand the phenomenon that happens so often when a movie comes to my state. The filming slowly worked its way into both men's lives, and though they had been wary before the company's arrival (Thumper had worried to me one afternoon, "They ain't gonna have any faggots with them movie people, are they? I mean, we already ran all the faggots out of Texas"), by the time filming was over the company had Slim in yet another safari outfit, this time a Quinnland's Safari Park uniform and driving a safari park jeep as an extra, giant elephants were climbing in and out of Sugar Lake probably crunching a slew of well-caught bass with each step, and young Thumper, wearing a headset and working with the shooting crew, was ready to quit the ranch job he so loved and follow the company to South Carolina for the rest of the shoot. Knowing the fickle business of working on a movie crew, I wanted to warn Thumper not to quit his day job just yet, that production might not be so kind to him in South Carolina when they didn't still need him as a location cushion to Slim, that they could still pull the plug on this film, any film, before it was all over.

No plugs were pulled, though, and the rest of the filming in Texas was uneventful, for me at least. The company would go on to screw the locals in South Carolina where a mad rush was on to construct the remaining sets. I'd been asked to go with the art department but declined, having had enough of traveling with the circus. As the show wound down, I found myself one night, after a drunken barbecue at Sugar Lake, sitting on the asphalt in the bunkhouse parking lot with Zero, the transportation captain's dog. Larry had become quite a fixture on the set as he caught six-foot rattlesnakes out of the brush and put on live snake shows for the crew. He came up to me one day on the Wachati set with a gigantic rattler he said he'd just pumped two nine-millimeter bullets into and was keeping in an ice chest in the back of his truck. He held the snake by the tail, playing with it, and as it was still striking wildly, I told Larry he must have missed. He asked me to find a piece of rope then. I found a small section of twine and Larry grabbed the giant rattler by the head, looped the twine around its neck, and quickly strangled the snake to put it, as he said, out of its misery. Later, with one of the Scimitar Horned Oryxs downed in the road, with Thumper accusing production of running over it, Larry pumped three slugs into the head of the wounded beast and it still wouldn't die. A vet arrived and, shooting the animal in the heart, killed it, after pointing out that the animal had been gored by another oryx and not hit by one of Larry's fellow Teamsters.

Sitting with Zero that night on the asphalt, I had mixed feelings about it all. Though I liked the dog's owner, a man I hardly knew, Larry was a little too trigger-happy for me and a bad shot to boot. He had given me free gas from the company fuel truck , something the u.p.m. would have never done, and for that I was in his debt. Tequila having made me inquisitive, I asked Zero, who was obviously Larry's best friend, why Larry was killing snakes, why Slim and the 777 were raising innocent animals for men to slaughter and call it sport, why Jim Carrey and Company were spending forty million dollars to create a couple of hours of escapism for American children on a Sunday, making fun of two warring tribes in Africa, the Wachootoos and Wachatis, whose names are so similar to one another, much like two other happy-go-lucky African tribes, the Hutus and the Tutsis, whose children are busy getting hacked to death with machetes while most of ours munch popcorn, gazing at the antics of an unsedated Jerry Lewis.

I realized that night I had an almost intangible, bitter feeling in my chest. Trying to figure out what it was, I decided, rather than heartburn or anything else, it was a sense of betrayal. Not by any person. Not by anyone I knew, except maybe myself. As a child, I had spent many an hour in front of the television set, watching movie after movie. When I was old enough, I went to the theaters, almost lived in them, seeing up to three movies a day, much preferring the cool air of the dark theater and the places it took me over my real life at home. As an adult, I'd done the same, seeing movie after movie, everything that was released. I had worshipped movies. But now, after seven years of working on them, I was saddened at the reality behind them, from the stars on down. I'd thought I was a struggling writer, removed from the petty bickering, absurdities, and vanities of the movie crew, but now I knew I'd become a part of it as well. I could see that this business was a business and it was all about money and power, permeating down to me, and it had become my life.

I wondered then, out loud, to a now perplexed Zero, wasn't what we were producing and recording on film ultimately false, even if it was a purported representation of reality? Wasn't the real movie on the set? Wasn't that life, not the pretense of life, in front of the camera? Films could never wholly duplicate reality, I said, but then again, why should they? Wasn't reality horrible? It was the headless, bloated torsos floating down and choking the rivers of Rwanda, or the nightly rape and death report on your local news stations. Wasn't that the reason we made movies in the first place, to escape all of those dead bodies bothering us on television every night? If so, then now I had no escape. No movie I'd seen of late could completely take me away. I thought of Scott Greene, my electrician friend on *Flesh and Bone*, telling me one night in West Texas, as we both anesthetized ourselves with a bottle of cough syrup, "I keep taking all these drugs," he said, "all my life, I've taken everything. But when it comes right down to it, and I've taken so much I can't even see, or I don't know what I'm seeing, when I think I'm completely and totally gone, I hear this little voice inside that sounds just like me. And it says, 'I'm still here, man. I'm still here.'"

There would be no more Gregory Pecks for me to look up to, no more Lawrence of Arabias to emulate, which was just as well. After all, I was a grown-up now, all of thirty-two years old. There was a phrase in the movie business: you were either above the line or below the line, that demarcation being where the real money and power started and stopped. I was through being below the line. I'd have to design my own life if I didn't want others to do it for me. I was sick of living in other people's scripts anyway, tired of wasting my precious finite time waiting for something to happen, not listening to what the old man at the hot springs had said about each of my days being a life. Did I really want my one day, my one life, to be painting a Styrofoam tombstone for *The Devil's Bed* ?

Zero, a quiet dog, of course said nothing.

J.R. Helton lives on a ranch in Texas with his wife Tracy where they run the Southern Animal Rescue Association, a no-kill sanctuary for dogs and cats.